The Trouble With Monkshood

THE **TROUBLE** WITH **MONKSHOOD**

BY
JOYCE IGO

XULON ELITE

Xulon Press Elite
2301 Lucien Way #415
Maitland, FL 32751
407.339.4217
www.xulonpress.com

Paperback ISBN-13: 978-1-66286-541-1
Hard Cover ISBN-13: 978-1-66286-542-8
Ebook ISBN-13: 978-1-66286-543-5

ABOUT THE BOOK

Wedding bells mix with murder in this third adventure of Jo Elliott and her gospel music-singing family. Jo is now engaged to the charming sheriff deputy, Brad Edwards, whom she met during the Harold Ashton murder in "The Shadow of a Man."

In "The Trouble with Monkshood," Jo and her family scramble to prepare a new home for the happy couple in the middle of the murder of a loved family country doctor. Intertwined with his death are old mysteries that directly involve the Edwards family. Hidden treasures and old sins will be disclosed along with the revelations that tie the doctor's murder with past family secrets.

Can Jo and her family unmask the truth before the murderer strikes again, and can they discover his identity before it is too late for members of her own family?

Follow Jo and her family as they find the answers to old and new mysteries.

Author Joyce Igo has been a traveling gospel singer for over thirty years and uses her knowledge of that lifestyle to create another thrilling novel in the series.

As you read "The Trouble with Monkshood," you will be inspired by the knowledge that God has a plan for your life and challenged to grab the opportunities God gives.

TABLE OF CONTENTS

CHAPTER ONE

I stared out the car window at the rapidly passing scenery along the roadway. There had been little to see. The landscape had remained unchanged for the last hour. It was a blur of green shades with a few dwellings scattered across the hilly terrain. The sky overhead was a cloudless blue, so I couldn't even pretend to see pictures in the clouds. Lately, we had followed the bends of a river alternating with the shiny gleam of railroad track rails curving and straightening with the lay of the land.

I wasn't bored. After all, I was traveling with my future husband, and to be jaded this early in our relationship would have signaled future trouble already.

I turned to my companion with a question. "Brad, where exactly is your Aunt Lillian's house? There hasn't been anything but woods for miles and very few houses."

"We are almost to Willis." My fiancé assured me. "That's the closest little town to my aunt. It was a thriving community at one time, but the kids who grew up here in the last several years moved away as adults. It still does have a grocery store and a post office." He grinned at me. "So we won't starve, and we can get our mail. Oh, and I think they have a volunteer fire department if the house catches fire."

I grinned back. "How far away are these retirement apartments that your aunt is moving to?"

"Twenty-five to thirty miles. They're in Morrisville. My friend, Jason Pierce, is the sheriff of the county. I've already talked to him about transferring over here. I gather they've had some turnover. It's not the best time to be in law enforcement. On the positive side, I'll get a raise because of my experience." His forehead wrinkled into a half frown. "That is if you like the house. It all depends on you."

"And this house is your family home?"

"On the Edwards side. My great-great-grandfather, Albert Edwards, bought the property before the Civil War and built a stone house there. Albert was killed in that War and passed it on to his son, William, who was father to the man who built the present house, Ernest Edwards, my grandfather. Great-grandfather William was forty-six when Ernest was born. He married later in life. His wife was only twenty-one years old, but from what I've heard, it was a happy marriage. My grandfather, Ernest Edwards, was a different story. He married a girl named Rose-my grandmother. They didn't have a good relationship."

"I imagine it's more about the people and their temperament than the age," I commented, reminded again about my being older than this man I had promised to marry. I hoped he didn't believe I was desperate for a husband or, even worse, assumed that I had agreed to marry him out of gratitude because he had saved my life. I pushed that thought from my mind. I didn't need to go there. "So, how many children did your grandparents have?"

"They had my father, Eugene, and three girls. They named the girls all after flowers-Lily, Violet, and Rosemary. Of course, Rosemary is an herb if you want to argue the point."

"But I thought your aunt's name was Lillian," I objected. "And I wouldn't think of arguing the point."

Brad laughed. "It was Lily until she turned twenty-one, and then she went to court and changed it to Lillian. She hated Lily."

"What did her parents say about that?" I wondered aloud.

"Well, her father was dead by then, and her mother said she didn't blame her. My dad seldom talked about his father. He was fond of his mother and sister, Lillian, but everybody got a funny look when Grandpa Ernest's name came up."

"What kind of a look?"

"Disgusted. My grandfather died right after the baby daughter, Rosemary, fell down the stairs and broke her neck. She was only four, and Grandma Rose was devastated. She was pregnant again and lost the baby over it. The baby was far enough along that they knew it was a boy. I gather that Grandpa Ernest was pretty hateful about the whole thing. He didn't have a lot of empathy for my grandmother. At any rate, he had a heart attack and died shortly after that."

"That's awful!" I said, slightly startled by the story. A child is such a part of one. I couldn't imagine losing two children close together. One would have been horrible enough. I couldn't envision losing any children at all. It would be an appalling heartbreak.

"From what Dad said, it was a tough time for the family," Brad responded.

"So, has your Aunt Lillian ever been married," I asked, curious about this family I was joining.

Brad shook his head. "No. She's eighty-two and had plenty of chances, but she was never interested."

"So that takes care of Lillian, and your dad and mom got killed in an auto accident. So Rosemary died young. What happened to the other girl, Violet?"

He shrugged. "Nobody knows. Aunt Lillian says she hasn't heard from her. When Aunt Violet turned twenty-one, she left home with one of the local guys and never returned."

I frowned. "Did no one even try to find the poor girl?" Privately, I might have run away too if no one was more interested in me than that.

Brad was turning onto another highway. "My grandmother contacted the family of the man she ran off with, but they didn't have any information either. Apparently, Violet didn't stay with the guy she left with. They did find that out. You have to remember we didn't have all the technology we have today back then. If you wanted to disappear, you could. I don't think things were too good at home when her father lived. She has never tried to reach out to anybody in the family. Aunt Lillian searched for her when Grandma Rose passed, but she just hit a dead end. I always suspected she changed her name and moved where nobody knew her. It's what I would do if I wanted to disappear."

"Have you tried to find her?" I questioned, thinking that the police had more access to information than regular citizens.

He shrugged again. "I looked into it briefly when Grandma Rose died, but nothing came up. She doesn't have a police record, not that I could find."

"So you could have cousins somewhere and not even know it," I mused.

"I guess so. If Aunt Violet is still living, it will be up to her to contact the family. With all the current interest in genealogy, someone may hunt us up someday. Aunt Lillian and I are the only two I know about left in the Edwards family."

I reached out and covered his hand with mine. "I'm glad you're still here, Honey."

He squeezed my hand. "Me, too."

"So, how often do you come and see your Aunt Lillian?"

He didn't release my hand. "I see my aunt as often as I can. I used to come here on summer vacations. Grandma Rose was alive then. She only died five years ago when she was ninety-six, and she was still as sharp as they come. Grandma was active up until the end. She loved gardening. So does Aunt Lillian. You'll see. It's a beautiful place."

"What did your grandmother die from?" I asked curiously.

Brad's face tightened. "It was a terrible accident. She fell down the main stairs of the house. She was too old to be climbing those steps. Lillian kept her off them if she caught her, but my grandmother had a mind of her own, and if she wanted to do something, no one could ever stop her."

"She died just like her little girl!" I exclaimed, thinking there was a lot of tragedy in this family's story.

"Doc Masters came right over. He's Aunt Lillian's next-door neighbor. Grandma died holding his hand. He said she made some comment about dying as her baby did." He looked at me. "You'll have to ask Aunt Lillian what she said. I've forgotten."

I continued with a query. "So you know some of the people around Willis?"

"Oh, yeah. I made friends during summer vacations. We had the run of the house. Aunt Lillian worked at a bank, and Grandma Rose thought kids ought to be kids and have fun. She had a mischievous sense of humor sometimes. All of us loved her. It's a big house, and we could play hide and seek on a rainy day. We'd play cops and robbers, race up and down the stairs, and tear through the house. She never minded."

"Lillian lived with her mother?" It was a question.

"She did. My dad and mother had their own place, and Dad thought since Aunt Lillian was willing to take care of his mother, she ought to have the family home. The oldest son has always got the family home, but Dad never liked the place. He thought it was too big and cost too much in upkeep."

"Now, you *do* have me worried. Are we going to be able to afford it?" That had been the problem with most of the places we had looked at in the last six months. We either didn't like them, the location was different from what we wanted, or the price was too exorbitant. Some of the more affordable ones needed so many repairs we neither had the time nor the finances to fix them.

Brad laughed. "I think you are going to love it. My aunt is giving us a huge break. Aunt Lillian wants it to belong to someone in the family. Of course, she could leave it to whoever she wanted. Grandma Rose left it to her."

A fresh thought occurred to me. "I hope your Aunt doesn't change her mind when she meets me."

Brad grinned at me. "You'll get along fine with my Aunt Lillian. She's happy I've found somebody. Neither she nor my grandmother liked Audrey."

I didn't respond. I didn't particularly like Brad's first wife either, who had died a few years ago. I hadn't known her, had only met her briefly, but she wasn't the type of woman I admired. Her lack of caring for anyone besides herself had not impressed me.

I returned to looking out of the car window. The woods were clearing and opening up to a row of buildings on each side of the road. All were either boarded up or obviously closed. A hanging sign moved gently in the breeze, advertising a once-operating restaurant. The bare store windows showed no merchandise, just quiet reminders of an earlier era.

There was one traffic light, and it was red. Brad eased the car to a stop while I took in my surroundings. A brick church with a tall white steeple stood majestically on the corner.

"It looks dead," I said, speaking about the town.

Brad laughed again. "There's still a little life." He gestured towards the church. "That's Willis Community Church, where all my family attended. Aunt Lillian still goes there, I believe. I know the Pastor, Don Franks. He's an older guy-good man."

We passed the grocery store and the post office. Then I noticed the bank.

"You forgot to tell me they had a bank," I teased.

"So I did. That's the bank where Aunt Lillian worked. She retired from there."

The town was already behind us, and we were back to passing trees.

"Aunt Lillian's house is two miles out of town. She has two neighbors. One is beside her, and the other is about a mile down the road, and it's a campground." Brad turned on his signal to turn right onto a narrow paved country road.

In a few minutes, Brad pulled up beside a large three-story house with a stately turret. It was magnificent.

I got out of the car, slowly taking in the white home with its black shutters that gleamed in the sunshine. I caught my breath as I surveyed the wrap-around porch, the turret that stood proudly out from the top of the house, and the beautifully carved wood that made up the porch columns. How did Brad know I loved old houses? I turned to see him resting his arms on the top of the car and grinning at me.

"You've been talking to my daughter, Alaina," I accused him. "She told you how much I love these old houses."

"Guilty as charged." He came around the vehicle and slipped his arm around my shoulders casually. "I thought of this place as soon as Alaina mentioned it. What do you think?"

"I think it's beautiful, but Brad, I don't see how we will afford to buy it. I've saved some money, but not nearly enough to purchase this." I could feel my forehead wrinkle into a frown.

"Well, I need to talk to you about that, but I wanted to wait until you saw this place first. I've found someone who wants to buy my house in Alcott. It's got a lot of property, so I am getting top dollar. Not that there is anything wrong with the house. Harold Ashton kept it up, but I don't want us starting our married life in a home that has

JOYCE IGO

bad memories for both of us. And I am selling the trees on it before I let it go. It has some good timber growing on it. As I said, Aunt Lillian never married, and she's made wise investments over the years. We'll be getting this for far less than it is worth, but I'm the last of the Edwards, and she thinks it should go to me. She would outright give it to me if I let her, but I can't allow her to do that."

I felt slightly dazed by it all. "Do you think Aunt Lillian will approve of me, or she's going to say I robbed the cradle?" I asked, looking up at my younger fiancé.

I loved the lines at the corners of his gray eyes when he laughed or grinned.

His sandy sideburns were graying, giving him a distinguished look and an air of authority. Of course, he was a cop. I could stand to lose a pound or two, but I still had a decent figure. I thought I still looked good with my shoulder-length dark brunette hair. My eyes were green, and my peaches and cream skin saved me from looking as old as I was. According to my grandson, Joseph, I didn't look or act my age. I had that going for me.

He hugged me to him. "I asked you to marry me; you didn't ask me to marry you. Don't forget that. Aunt Lillian is different, but I think you two will get along. You'll have her eating out of your hand just like you did with Maude Ashton."

I laughed, remembering the little woman I had met when I first met Brad.

We walked up to the porch, and the front door opened to a tall woman, slender with short snow-white hair, dressed in gray slacks and a white dressy blouse with a string of pearls around her neck. She acknowledged Brad, and those fine gray eyes swept over me.

Brad propelled me forward, his hand resting on my shoulder. "Aunt Lillian, this is Jo Elliott, and for some strange reason, she has agreed to marry me."

I stuck out my hand, and she took it solemnly.

"It's nice to meet you, Jo. Brad has told me all about you. I understand you are a traveling gospel singer. That must be interesting work." She stood aside so we could enter the house.

"Yes," I explained. "I sing with my grandson and his wife, Joseph and Ashley Cochran. We get to do what we love, so we're blessed."

Inside the house, I stared around as my eyes adjusted to the light. A beautiful carved wooden staircase wound up to the second floor. The floors were made of hardwood-the real thing, not laminated. Thank goodness no one had covered up that fabulous wood with carpet.

"This is gorgeous. I don't know how you can stand to give it up." I said with appreciation.

Lillian smiled faintly. "Well, it's staying in the family, making it easier." She paused. "Anyway, everything comes to an end -sooner or later." She walked out of the foyer and into the living room as she spoke.

The entry had a wide carved wood console table with a large mirror erected above it. A coat tree, also in wood, stood in the corner. The living room was charming, with large windows draped with sheer curtains. A fireplace with a lovely carved wooden mantel stood at one end from the ceiling to the floor with lilies and palm trees etched in the wood. Brad's Aunt Lillian was watching me.

"It's mahogany." She told me. "My great-grandfather made it. He was a carpenter and stone mason. This mantel came from the original house that Albert Edwards built here."

"He must have been talented." I could tell that pleased her. "That mantel is wonderful."

"Let me show you the house," she said. "And then we can sit down and talk."

I followed her into a formal dining room. The china cabinet covered one wall, also built of mahogany. Dishes filled it, many of which looked to me to be antiques. The wooden pedestal dining room table could seat at least eight people.

Next to the dining room was the kitchen. It had been modernized and had plenty of windows, cabinets, and light. It was a warm early June day, and the windows were open. The white curtains stirred slightly with the breeze.

"There's a bedroom and bath on the first floor and what I call my office and library. The bedroom was Mother's until she passed. Right now, I'm using the room." She looked at me. "Arthritis, you know. Too much lifting and lugging when I was younger."

"I can always use an office for my music ministry," I told her.

Lillian's bedroom was neat and filled with antique furniture. The bathroom was modern, with a shower and tub, and tastefully furnished.

Brad's aunt moved towards the stairs, and I followed close behind her. On the walls along the stairs were large portraits.

She stopped moving and gestured toward the pictures. "This is my father, Brad's grandfather, Ernest Edwards. And this is his wife, Rose, my mother. I never knew my grandfather, William. He died before I was born, but I was close to my grandmother. Her name was Christine. Here are their pictures too." She continued up the steps. "And here are the first Edwards who bought the property, Albert Edwards, and his wife, Rachel. Grandfather Albert bought the place before the Civil War. That's how far back it goes."

I studied the portraits with interest. The ones of Brad's grandparents and great-grandparents were in black and white in old-fashioned oval frames with concave glass. Ernest Edwards looked arrogant. I decided I would not have liked him. William and Albert Edwards appeared very solemn, as people always did in old-time photographs. I wondered, briefly, why people back then never smiled. I guessed there was no one there to say, "Cheese."

Brad spoke from behind me. "Grandfather Ernest was a bit of a tyrant from what I remember hearing my dad say."

"Yes, well, I was just little when he died. My mother never said much about him at all. It was like, 'he's gone, let's forget about him.'" Aunt Lillian shook her head and moved on up the staircase.

"Didn't you think that was kind of strange?" I asked curiously.

"You had to know my mother. She wasn't much of one to live in the past." Lillian stopped at the landing and laid her hand on the next portrait, one of the early colored photos. "These two are Brad's parents, Eugene and Phyllis Edwards."

I examined the photos of Brad's parents carefully. There were two pictures professionally done. The photographer's name was in the corner of both views. Brad resembled his dad in his build and gray eyes, but he had his mother's smile and hair color.

We had reached the second floor. It had four bedrooms and a bath. I was pleased to see the tub in the bathroom was claw-foot. At some point, someone had installed a large shower. I was thankful for that. As much as I loved to relax in a luxuriant bubble bath, I seldom had the time. There was a small staircase at the end of the hall.

"That goes up inside the turret and three other bedrooms," Lillian explained. "You will have to forgive me, but it's a little steep for me these days. The rooms are furnished, but haven't been used in years."

"Could I see them, and especially the turret?" I asked.

Brad went with me. The bedrooms had a dusty, unused feeling. But it was the turret that fascinated me. Inside the rounded room, large windows encircled the tower. There were no draperies or blinds.

I walked towards the windows and stared over a vast backyard that looked like a paradise. The front of the house was adjacent to the road and was more formal with neatly sheared evergreens, but the back was engrossed in color. Red, pink, yellow, and peach roses were blooming. I recognized several peonies with their large pink, white, and red flowers. Clematis vines went up a trellis. Stalks of yellow, pink, red, and blue lupines and blue delphiniums graced the beds. There was color in every direction.

I had always thought I would like to garden, especially the flowers, so I had poured over enough gardening catalogs to recognize some common perennials. Someone had expertly created a paradise. It didn't appear that cost had ever been a factor. It was simply a Garden of Eden. The turret itself was empty. There was a sense of peace about it somehow.

I turned to Brad. "It is wonderful. I love it."

He wrapped his arms around me, and we stood drinking in the beauty outside the windows. I could see the side of the house next door across the yard. It sat farther back from the road.

"Who lives there?" I asked.

"It's Arthur Master's place. He's the retired doctor I told you about. He's ninety-six years old and doesn't look or act it. His dad was a doctor too. His dad was half in love with my Grandma Rose, but she never thought about marrying again after her husband died."

Aunt Lillian was waiting on us when we came back down the stairwell. "Well, what did you think?" she asked me.

Impulsively, I reached out and hugged her. She stiffened a bit in surprise. "It's beautiful," I told her. "I will never be able to keep it up so well."

"It was my mother's garden." She started down the stairs, and we followed behind her. "There is a vegetable garden on the side of the house, but the backyard was her domain. The turret was hers too. That's where she used to raise her plants. Then she would sit in her rocking chair and watch everything grow. Gardening was her passion."

Sitting in the living room with glasses of iced tea, we discussed the house's price and the upkeep cost, like taxes and electric bills. I had never dreamed of being able to live in such a beautiful home. Lillian wanted us to keep the furniture if we wanted it. It was primarily antique. There was no doubt it belonged with this house. Most of the furnishings would be too large for her much smaller apartment.

"I'm glad you appreciate old houses like this one," she said to me. "It would have been hard to give it up to someone who could have cared less." She smiled suddenly,

16

and I could see Brad in her face. "Would you like to go out in the backyard and get a closer view of the garden?"

The small back porch was screened in and cluttered with garden tools and baskets. Gloves and boots lay on a work table.

We followed Lillian down the steps. I was sure much thought had gone into laying out this garden.

I breathed in the beauty and the fragrance of the roses. Oaks and maples raised their stately heads in parts of the yard, and shade-loving plants graced the ground around their bases. The deciduous trees mixed with blue and green spruce.

"Some of these plants are really old," Lillian shared.

I would never remember them all, I thought to myself. It was overwhelming.

"This pink peony was put here when they built the house. They planted some of the spring flowering shrubs back then too. Some plants are short-lived, and others last for years. Just like people, I guess." She continued to stroll along, naming different species.

Once, she stopped and asked. "How did you and Brad meet?"

"Didn't I tell you, Aunt Lillian?" Brad answered for me. "It was during a murder case; you remember when Harold Ashton got killed."

"Oh, yes, you may have told me, but I forgot for the moment." She looked at me. "I think you were involved with another case recently, weren't you?"

I shivered. The terror of that case was too fresh to have passed yet. "I could have got myself killed in that one. Brad and my grandson probably saved my life and a couple of others too."

Brad's cell phone rang, and he pulled the phone from his pocket. "I've got to take this one." He strolled back across the yard, leaving me with his Aunt Lillian. She was thoughtful.

"You are older than Brad, aren't you?" she asked unexpectedly.

"Yes," I replied honestly. "Does that bother you?"

"Not particularly," she responded. "It's not my business. I want Brad to be happy. He hasn't always had an easy life. I guess you know that."

I nodded. "I know that. I did have a good marriage, and I promise you, I will do everything I can to make this one good. You have to be happy with yourself to make someone else happy. You can't count on other people to make you content."

"True." She stopped beside a plant that was not blooming yet but looked healthy and had grown to a sizeable tall clump. "This is an old plant too. It's a perennial, which means it comes back every year. My mother planted it years ago. It's called Monkshood. Have you ever heard of it?"

I shook my head. "I've never had time to garden much. I used to plan flower beds that never got planted. My daughter and I put out a small vegetable garden, just tomatoes, cucumbers, and a few squashes. We buy annual flowers in the spring-like impatiens, salvias, and marigolds. I've never gardened on this scale."

"Well, Monkshood has a beautiful flower. It comes in blues, bi-colors, and whites. Occasionally, you can find a yellow or rose color. They're not as pretty. The blue is my favorite. It looks like a hood of a monk-hence its name, but it's a deadly poison plant. I was warned as a child to stay away from the Monkshood."

"I'm surprised your parents had it in the yard with children in the house," I commented.

"Well, my mother had four children, but I don't think they would have dared to touch it. She put the fear of God in us to leave it alone. They say back in the Middle Age; it was outlawed in Europe because wives were poisoning their husbands with it."

I grinned. "I'll keep that in mind."

Lillian laughed. "You have a sense of humor. I like that." She sobered. "Jo, Brad tells me you're getting married in August. It's June now. It will probably take that long to go through everything in this house. The bedrooms upstairs on the second floor have been catch-all rooms for everything imaginable."

"Why did your father build such a big house?" I questioned curiously. "If he only had four children, I wouldn't have thought he would need so much room."

Lillian grimaced. "Well, when my father and his father, William, built the house, my father expected to have a large family. I think he wanted a large family. I'm not sure how Mother felt about that, but it ended up that it didn't matter since Father died soon after Mother lost the last baby."

"I guess when there have been several generations living in a house, a person ends up with a lot of stuff," I said

"And it's not just my life in this house. It's my parents' and grandparents' things too. There are pictures, letters, and scrapbooks. I've never taken the trouble to go through all of it. When I worked at the bank, I didn't have the time, and since I've retired, I threw my energies into the garden and church activities. I know you work, but could we finish everything in time for your wedding? I want to move into my new place by then. That's my plan, anyway."

"I don't see why not," I replied. "Joseph and Ashley could help, I would think, and Alaina, my daughter, could probably manage some days off from work. We'll get it done, Lillian. Brad has to clear his place too."

"I'm taking some of his furniture off his hands. Audrey had good taste. I'll give her that." Lillian got a look on her face, and I ascertained that she had not been fond of Brad's dead first wife.

"I didn't get the feeling too many people liked poor Audrey," I commented.

"That's putting it mildly," Lillian responded. "Of course, she didn't like any of us either." She made a motion with her hand. "That's old news. Nothing to worry about now."

I wondered if she had a bit of her mother in her. It seemed she was not one to live in the past either.

Brad was walking toward us. "That was Jason Pierce. I've got the job in the sheriff's department if I want it." He looked intently at me. "It's up to you, Jo. It's your call. Do you think you could stand to live here, or do you need more time to think about it?"

I put my arm through his. "It's wonderful, Brad. If you think we can swing it, I already love the idea of coming home to this place."

Brad and his Aunt Lillian exchanged glances, and she nodded as though satisfied about something.

CHAPTER TWO

We walked back to the front of the house and passed the vegetable garden. Everything looked to be growing.

Lillian absently pulled up a weed beside the path. "The garden's looking well. We won't starve this summer."

"So Dr. Masters is our only neighbor?" I asked.

Lillian nodded. "Yes, he's been here longer than me. My father and grandfather built his house too. Both of them were stone masons and carpenters. He's older than me, but we've been friends for years. He and my mother were good friends too. He was a great doctor but never seemed to get close to anybody except my family. He always said it didn't pay when your patients could die on you. He figured it was best to keep your distance. I don't know whether Brad told you about when my mother fell down the steps. She lived a few minutes. Doc came right over and was holding her hand when she passed. His father was here when my father died, and my little sister died too. The Masters have always been part of our family. Doc is a bit eccentric, I suppose."

"In what way?" I asked curiously.

"He's not someone you need to avoid," Lillian assured me. "He's just different. Never married and keeps to himself." She gave a half laugh. "Sounds a lot like me, doesn't he?"

"You could have married if you had wanted to, Aunt Lillian," Brad spoke up. "You just never were interested."

"I think it's my mother's fault. She never liked a boy I brought to the house. She kept saying none of them were good enough for me." She grimaced. "I guess I believed her." She stepped up on the front porch. "Let's eat. I fixed lunch."

Lunch consisted of baked beans and pork barbecue, which Lillian had kept hot on a warming tray. She brought a bowl of potato salad from the refrigerator and refilled our iced tea glasses.

Lillian looked at me. "Do you like to cook?"

"Yes, I enjoy cooking."

"Good, then you can cook this summer. I hate to cook. Today was a special occasion, so I made myself." She laughed softly. "Half of the time, I forget to eat. I snack a lot. I'm too busy with the garden. I cook a big pot of soup in the winter, which lasts me several days."

"So, have you worked out how to get everything sorted through before the wedding?" Brad asked.

I answered him. "I think so. We're probably going to need your help. I'll be gone on weekends, but Alaina might be willing to come over and help if she could stay the night. It's a good two hours from her house to here."

"That's fine," Lillian assured me. "I look forward to meeting your daughter and family."

"I must go through a couple of weeks of orientation," Brad explained to his aunt. "I've got to clear my house in Alcott; then I'm selling it. I'm letting my apartment in Alcott go. One of the guys I worked with in the sheriff's department over there wants it. My boss now, Sheriff Jason Pierce, is an old friend of mine. He and his wife have a large house near Morrisville with an extra bedroom. He's invited me to stay with them until Jo, and I get married. I can come over on weekends when you're gone, Jo, and do what needs doing here whenever I'm not working. It will be easier to stay with Jason than drive into work daily while I learn the ropes of this new job."

I watched him as he got up from the table and helped himself to more barbecue. I hadn't had to say a word. Brad knew I would have reservations about our staying in this house simultaneously, even with his aunt with us. Keeping a good reputation in ministry sometimes gets complicated. We had already had the conversation about not sleeping together before marriage.

Brad was putting away the barbeque. "This is good, Aunt Lillian," he commented.

"It ought to be. I bought it at the barbeque place over in Morrisville." A grin eased her features.

We laughed.

"That's the Morrisville Aunt Lillian will be moving to and where I will be working," Brad informed me. "It's the county seat and about thirty miles from here. It has more than one grocery store. It's a nice-sized town."

I helped Lillian with the dishes and then went back outside. I wanted to take pictures with my phone to show Alaina and the kids what the place looked like.

I stared up at the turret on the side of the house. It had a good view of the backyard and down the road. I might bring my rocker from Alaina's home and put it in the turret. It could be my quiet place.

I moved around a wisteria vine wrapped around a large wooden trellis filled with hanging purple blooms and nearly ran into the man on the other side. He was short and stocky-elderly with a gray plaid newsboy hat. We startled each other.

I recovered the fastest. "I'm sorry. Have I rambled off of Lillian's property?" I asked.

He shook his head. "No, I'm the one trespassing. Lillian told me her nephew and his future wife were coming today. I wanted to see what the woman who had snagged old Brad looked like." He was managing to look sheepish.

"You're looking at her," I responded and stuck out a hand. "I'm Jo Elliott, soon to be Jo Edwards."

He took my hand and stood there staring at me. "Well! Well! Pleased to meet you, Madam."

He released my hand, and I said. "Call me Jo. Everybody does."

"Jo." He said it like he was tasting the name. "Nice name," he commented. "Is it short for Josephine or Joanne, if you don't mind my asking?"

"Josephine," I admitted ruefully. "My daughter calls me Josephine when she's trying to exasperate me. I can't say I've ever been thrilled with the name. I like Jo better."

He beamed at me. "Miss Jo, it will be then," he promised.

I smiled gratefully. "And so, who are you? You must be a near neighbor. Would you be Dr. Arthur Masters?"

His face lightened. "So Lillian told you about me?"

"She told me you were the only other neighbor. It was just a lucky guess." I responded with a half laugh.

"Well, to tell you the truth, I usually don't take much interest in what goes on around here. Some fellow put an RV park in about a mile down the road, and all kinds of strangers come walking and biking past here."

Doctor Masters removed his hat to reveal a balding head and then replaced it. He shook his head. "Times have changed, of course. I remember when Lillian's mother, Rose, was living here. I knew her father, too, the old rascal. You won't believe this, but I'm nearly ninety-seven years old. I still live by myself, do my own cooking, and put out a garden every year. I can doctor myself, so I stay away from these modern doctors. My father was an old country doctor. He always said the good Lord made all kinds of suitable plants to heal people. He wasn't one for handing out pills right and left. He said good common sense and eating right were better for you than taking all these chemicals in pill form. Said you'd cut your life short. I thought he was crazy when I was young. Fresh out of medical school, and knew it all. I found out he knew what he was talking about. He lived to nearly a hundred. Never sick, he wasn't."

"How did he die?" I asked curiously.

"Got shot deer hunting one autumn. Some young idiot who should have never had a gun took him for a deer. They said it was an accident, and nobody was charged. I don't go hunting. I doctor myself and no hunting. Maybe I'll live longer than my father."

He grinned and peered at me as if he could barely see me, so I guessed he didn't go to the eye doctor either.

I was still drinking in the beauty of the yard. From somewhere, I could hear a stream of water.

"Is there a fountain here? I can hear water."

"The Cherokee River runs at the back of the property," the elderly man confided.

He was moving around some more shrubbery, and I could see where the land sloped down into a river. It appeared to be about seventy feet across.

The river was moving leisurely downstream. From the clear view of the river bed through the water, I could see it was rocky. A couple of substantial weeping willows stood stately along its banks, and the ends of the branches were dipping into the flowing water. It was a tranquil noise and peaceful scene.

"I love the sound of water running!" I exclaimed, "And look, there's a gazebo here too."

The gazebo perched on the grassy knoll right above the river. It was white with a black shingled roof and a rooster weather vane swirling gently at the top. Flower baskets filled with pink, white, and lilac petunia blooms hung around the perimeter. I was finding it all overwhelming. Everything I had ever wanted, I was being offered. It was hard for me to grasp it all.

"Yeah, Lillian's father built it. He did all that fancy woodwork. He was a good carpenter, even if he was a royal pain in the rear the rest of the time." Dr. Masters glanced sideways at me to see my reaction to his words.

"He sounds like he was quite a character."

"I had the misfortunate of meeting the old goat. Ernest Edwards died of a heart attack while I was away at medical school. My dad was the doctor who pronounced him dead. Dad was out on a call, and it took him a while to get back here, and by the time he did, Ernest was dead. Dad didn't have any use for him, even if he were his patient. He thought a lot of his wife. She was a good woman. She's the one who started this garden." He gestured around with his arm.

I heard movement and turned to see Brad walking toward us.

"Hello, Doc, I see you've met my fiancé." Brad was sticking out his hand, his other hand on the older man's shoulder.

"Yes, I have. I walked down, hoping to get a look at Miss Jo." The older man seemed pleased to see Brad. "You did all right, Son, I tell you."

Brad laughed and winked at me. "I think so. We're going to be your neighbors this fall."

"That will be good," Dr. Masters said. "Nice to think more Edwards' are going to live here. Of course, I'll miss Lillian. She and I go way back."

"She'll miss you too," Brad assured him.

"I look out for her. Always have. My dad told me to. I looked out after her mother, Rose too. She and I both liked to garden, and we swapped plants occasionally. Lillian and I have kept up the tradition."

"I may need your help on all these gardens," I told him. "I don't know what half of these plants are."

The elderly man beamed. "I'll be happy to help you, little lady. I think it's fair to say I know what every flower is over here. I probably gave Lillian half of them. You'll catch on."

"I'm going to take you up on that offer," I returned. "I want to keep it up. It's so beautiful."

He peered at me. "Did Lillian show you the Monkshood plant?"

I nodded. "Yes, she said it was poisonous."

He cackled. "It is. Pretty flowers. I used to tease Lillian and tell her that's why she couldn't find a husband. When they found out she grew Monkshood, it scared them off."

"Well, Doc, you never found a wife either," Brad came back at him.

The other man laughed again. "Didn't want one. The only girl I ever wanted didn't want me. So that was that. I've got to get back over to the house. I've got my gardening to do." He shuffled off as quickly as he had come.

I grabbed Brad's arm. "Did he have a crush on your Aunt Lillian?"

He grinned. "Yes, he always has, but it never got him anywhere. They've stayed friends. He's quite a character. He liked you, I could tell. I guess he'll be watching after you now."

The sun went down when we pulled away from the Edwards family home. Lillian hugged me. We exchanged phone numbers so we could plan my coming to work on the house.

"I take it there are a lot of old photos and letters. That kind of thing to go through," I shared with Brad. "It will give me a chance to learn more about your family. It should be interesting."

"Don't find any skeletons in any closets. There's no basement here, but now that I think about it, there was a cellar under a building out back. It was where they smoked their meat. They called it a smokehouse. They tore it down years ago, and the cellar's been covered with cement. There was a cistern out back too. I have no idea if it still exists or not."

I had stiffened slightly at the mention of a cellar. "I'm glad the cellar is gone, or I'd have to leave that for somebody else to go through." I heard myself mutter.

Brad reached for my hand. "Sorry I mentioned it. My fault; but you did like the house, didn't you?"

I smiled at him and pushed the cellar to the back of my mind. "I love it! It's just that I need a break from mysteries for a while."

"Well, I only know about one mystery connected to the house, and that is what happened to the gold and silver my great-great-grandfather Albert Edwards was supposed to have hidden during the Civil War," Brad told me. "This was ground zero, and the Union and the Confederates raided around here. Albert didn't want either side to get what he had worked for, so he hid it. He wasn't sure which side would win, so he had greenbacks and confederate money hidden along with silver and gold coins. No one seems to know whether he buried it or what. It's never been found. Not that anyone knows, anyway. I used to try to find it when I spent summers here. I never did. I think it is just a story someone came up with."

"Who told you the story?" I questioned.

"Grandma Rose told me one summer, so my friends and I nearly tore up the place searching for it. We were even digging in the yard. Grandma stopped us when we got too close to the Monkshood plant. That's how I knew it was poisonous. My usually calm grandmother threw a fit over that. She chased us all out of the yard and told us to play in the river. We decided to go swimming rather than searching for buried treasure."

"So you don't think it's a true story?"

He shrugged. "Who knows? These tales get passed down from one generation to the next. Just don't mention it to Doc. He believes it and gets quite worked up talking about it."

I laughed. "Doc's an interesting man. He looks at things differently than most of the doctors I know. He thinks treating people with natural products is more effective than all these manufactured pills."

"He's an old-time doctor, just like his father was. He was still making house calls when all the other doctors had stopped doing that."

I leaned back comfortably in the car seat. "Well, I love the house, and if I run across any treasure, you'll be the first one I tell." For a brief moment, I thought of the cellar again. I shivered involuntarily.

Brad looked at me. "You're not cold, are you?"

I shook my head. "No, just thinking of that cellar. Sorry. Finding buried treasure would be an improvement over finding dead bodies on church pews, cellars, and RV bays."

"Thankfully, that is in the past," Brad said. "Now, we're concentrating on getting our new home ready."

I smiled up at him. If only my life would go according to plan!

CHAPTER THREE

Alaina, Joseph, and Ashley were thrilled with the pictures I brought back on my phone. They adored the house and grounds, exclaiming over the hugeness and grandeur of it all.

Alaina hugged me and commented. "Mom, I can't think of anyone that deserves a beautiful home like this more than you."

I wasn't sure about deserving it, but I did love it.

Brad was in orientation in Morrisville at the sheriff's department, and Joseph and Ashley had come with me to Lillian's house to help organize and go through the things she wanted to keep, give away or discard. Joseph and Ashley had been through the entire house and grounds before I could get them settled down to work. I didn't blame them. The home and property had so many nooks and corners that it would take months to explore them all.

Lillian was going through her bedroom, and I finally got the kids involved in helping her to go through the big closet in her room. I heard laughter coming from there and surmised they were all getting along well. Joseph had never had any trouble communicating with anyone. He could charm them into liking him if he wanted to. Ashley was quieter, but I had no doubt Lillian would manage to bring her out of her shell if she wished. I had already figured out that Lillian very seldom pushed. If Ashley didn't want to be included in the conversation, Lillian would probably leave her out of it. Joseph could talk enough for both of them. I heard him asking Lillian questions about different items, and Lillian seemed to be enjoying giving him the history of everything.

I ran my hand over my forehead. I was hot and sweaty. It must be in the nineties, I thought. Air conditioning was the one thing my perfect home did not include. Most of the time, there was a good breeze coming off the river, but today the air was still- heavy.

I decided to take a break and get myself a glass of iced tea. I discovered that Lillian kept the iced tea pitcher filled regularly.

I casually glanced out the kitchen window as I filled my glass with the brown liquid. Someone was crossing the yard near where the ground began to slope towards the river. I just saw a glimpse of the person, but I thought it was a man. I went down the back porch steps, glass in hand, and casually strolled across the backyard. There wasn't any breeze, only heat and no cloud in the blue sky. Butterflies were flittering through some flowers, and I could hear the sounds of birds chirping from some of the trees.

As I moved towards the water, I noticed several people in brightly colored tubes drifting lazily down the river. They were yelling cheerfully at one another, and when one saw me, they waved. I waved back and grinned. They looked like they were enjoying themselves. I wondered if they came from the RV Park down the road.

I was startled when I realized I wasn't alone. It was Doc. He perched on a large rock on the shoreline under one of the weeping willows. He grinned at me when he realized I had seen him. He pointed to the stone with the cane he carried.

"Have a seat, little lady, and watch the traffic on the river."

I smiled and walked over to sit beside him on the flat-topped rock.

"I was in the garden this morning, and then it got too hot for me," he informed me. "I decided I'd rest down here and cool off." He gestured with his cane down the river. "Since that campground went in, there's always people tubing or walking along the river this time of year. It was more peaceful last year before they reopened that confounded place."

"Who opened it back up?" I asked.

"Some Whitlock fellow. He lived here years ago. I delivered the boy." He peered at me. "Of course, I delivered most folks around here his age."

"Have you met him?" I queried.

He came close to snorting. "I met him. He was walking along the river one morning when I was down here. He caught me when I sat down on this rock and talked my ear off. He and Brad used to play together when Brad came to see his grandmother in the summer." He gave me a sheepish look. "There isn't anything wrong with the boy. He seems like a nice young man. It's just me. Since I retired, I have objected to being surrounded by people and all their problems. I got enough of it when I practiced. I don't like people much anymore. I asked him why he wanted to come back here, and he said he always remembered living here and wanted to return. Surprised he remembers much about it. He was only eight or nine when his parents moved away." He slapped his thigh. "I forgot to ask him about his parents, whether they were still living. My memory is not as good as it used to be." He glanced at me again. "I was walking out around my garden in the backyard a while ago and heard voices. My hearing's not bad for my age. I thought I'd better find out who was out here. It was just the folks from the campground, but I've got to keep an eye on Brad's bride." He grinned at me.

I grinned back. "I'm fine. I got hot in the house and went downstairs for some iced tea." I glanced at the glass in my hand. "I guess the ice has all melted."

I took a sip. It was still cool. "I thought I saw somebody moving out this way and decided to come and look."

"You are likely to see people along the bank or in the river," Doc told me. "Don't know where they've come from or who they are. I hope that Whitlock fellow doesn't get some serial killer in his campground. We might wake up one morning to find we've all been murdered in our beds."

"I guess we'll have to make sure we keep our doors and windows locked," I said brightly.

"And a gun handy or a rolling pin," The doctor suggested.

"I don't know if many people use a rolling pin anymore," I said.

"Probably not. Everybody eats all this fast food, or they heat it in the microwave. I won't have a microwave. It makes people lazy. I don't like lazy people. Never have." He put his thumbs behind the suspenders of his overalls. "Too many lazy people around nowadays. Want something for nothing."

"I'll have to tell Brad about Mr. Whitlock. What is his first name?"

"John. Johnny, they called him. Johnny Whitlock." The older man tapped his cane on the sand. "I wouldn't have known him if he hadn't told me who he was. He does have his dad's laugh, and I thought I could see his mother around his chin and lips. He was a child when he moved away, so naturally, he looks differently as a full-grown man. I remember the family well. Good people."

"Brad talks like he had a good time visiting here as a child," I informed the doctor.

"He did. All of the kids liked to play here. Brad's grandmother, Rose, was always so happy to see him; she loved having a house full of kids. She said children always made any sacrifice worth it. She loved Brad's dad and Lillian. She loved Violet, too, of course. It hurt her that she never heard from her once she left here. With the Whitlock boy and Brad moving back, I half expect Violet to show up any minute. I hope she does it before I pass. I'd like to see the old girl before I die. I imagined she turned into quite a character." There was a decided twinkle in his blue eyes as he struggled unsteadily to his feet. "I've got to get out of this heat, little lady. I will have to wait until this evening when it cools down to do any more work in the garden."

"I'm sorry I kept you," I apologized. "I need to get back to work too."

I strolled back towards the house. I was feeling less excited and more overwhelmed by the day. There was just so much stuff to go through. Lillian was typical of her generation and saved absolutely everything. I had been going through magazines and newspapers all morning. The day was hot, and I was hot, and not all from the temperature. It didn't help my disposition for Lillian to tell me that some old magazines and newspapers might be worth some money to collectors. I wanted to tell her I didn't care and start a bonfire which would have just made it hotter.

I had opened all the screened windows I could get open, but I was still sweltering. I imagined Joseph and Ashley were overly warm also. They were helping Lillian to go through correspondence. She had kept every birthday card and every letter she had ever received. I thanked God for the email when Joseph and Ashley shared with me how Lillian had given them the history of every card and note. At this rate, we were never going to get done in time for my August wedding. December was more likely.

The dust from old papers and magazines was starting to get to me, so I stayed outside to enjoy what little breeze was available.

I walked past the shade garden whose spreading shrub branches covered several different colored leaves of hosta, bleeding hearts, coral bells, and other shade-loving plants. I particularly liked the coral bells, under oak and maple trees, with their different leaf colors-gold, purple, red, and striped. They should be pretty all season, I thought. Out of the corner of my eye, I spotted the Monkshood. The weeds were getting out of hand in that flower bed. I made a mental note to come out one evening after it cooled down and weed some. I hoped I could work out some of the mental stress "this going through stuff" was creating.

When I opened the back door, Joseph heard me and yelled for me to come to Aunt Lillian's room. I went down the hall to find complete chaos in the large bedroom. The bedspread was concealed by every type of card known to man and letters-some typed, some handwritten. Lillian was in a straight-back chair, and my grandson and his wife were sitting cross-legged on the floor sorting all the mail.

Joseph looked up when I entered. "Aunt Lillian has come up with a perfect idea," he explained. "At least, I think so." He seemed uncertain.

I was hesitant too, but I managed to appear interested. So many things seemed like excellent ideas to Joseph that I was reluctant to agree.

"What kind of idea?"

Lillian answered for him. "As hot as it's been, we might need a break. Joseph tells me you don't leave until Saturday for the weekend. It would be nice to arrange a cookout for some folks around here for Friday evening. I want to invite some friends from church, and we could ask the campground owner since Brad and Johnny used to play together when he came here in the summers. I've only seen him once or twice. Of course, he has been busy getting the campground ready for the season. Brad probably has some friends at work he may want to invite. Of course, Alaina is welcome if she's free. I have yet to have the pleasure of meeting her. I'll get the hamburgers and hot dogs with all the trimmings, and everyone can bring a covered dish. What do you think?"

"Sounds nice," I said. "Do you think people would come?"

Lillian's hand rose and fell on her lap. "Of course, they'd come. Everyone will want to meet my nephew and his bride. We haven't had anything like this in a long time. It will be like the good old days when people often got together." She looked at Joseph and Ashley. "And don't let me forget to mention it to Doc. He would be so hurt if I forgot to invite him. He's around so much, I think of him as part of the family and assume he knows he can always come, but he's old school and likes to be asked."

"Do you think your Mom could get away early from work to get here?" Ashley asked Joseph shyly.

"I'll text her right now and see," Joseph said, picking up his cell phone.

"I'd better call Brad and make sure he's not working Friday evening," I commented. "I'll tell him to invite anyone he wants."

Lillian pulled herself to her feet. "I'll get on the phone with a few people at church. Most of them are older, but they'll be happy to get out for an evening." She regarded the chaos on the bed and floor wistfully. "My entire life is wrapped up right here. It doesn't seem possible I am eighty-two, but when I look in the mirror, I can see all the changes." She moved slowly from the room.

Joseph looked at me. "Mom just texted back. She's taking a vacation day. I think she's eager to see the house. It's different seeing it in person than seeing it on the phone."

"True." I pushed some letters back and sank down on the edge of the bed. "Joseph, do you think we can take care of Aunt Lillian's stuff before August? It's June now."

His forehead wrinkled into a frown. "I think so, Mamaw. Don't worry. We're all pitching in to help. Aunt Lillian slows down progress because she has to tell you about everybody who ever sent her anything in the mail. But she enjoys it so much; you feel bad about rushing her."

I grimaced. "I know. Oh, well, it is what it is, as Alaina says."

Friday dawned with a clear sky. It was a perfect day. Rain was not in the forecast, and the temperature had decreased enough from the rain the day before to make it more pleasant outside. Brad was off work, and he and some of his fellow officers had gone to Lillian's church and borrowed chairs and tables.

The gardens were beautiful, and the yard was neatly mowed and trimmed. Brad had come in early to cut the grass, and Joseph had done the weed-eating. Lillian's riding mower had a grass catcher, so at least we wouldn't be tracking dry grass all over the house. The flower beds still needed some weeding, but it would just have to wait.

By five o'clock, visitors started arriving. We planned to eat at six. Brad had two grills going, and the aroma of hamburgers and hot dogs were spreading across the yard. I made some deviled eggs and potato salad, and Alaina contributed a German chocolate cake. Ashley was helping Joseph with the tables and chairs. Lillian was in her element. Some of her friends came early carrying all sorts of delicious-looking dishes. I hoped Aunt Lillian wouldn't make a habit of cookouts and dinner parties, or I would have to go on a diet!

At six, everything was in full swing. Aunt Lillian stood and welcomed everyone and introduced Brad and me, Joseph and Ashley, and my daughter, Alaina. I was used to standing in front of strangers since I had been a gospel singer for the last twenty years, but it was slightly scary to be on exhibit as Brad Edwards' fiancé. I felt a bit like a schoolgirl. Everyone was very cordial and friendly.

As I stood beside my intended, I looked out over the tables and noticed who all were there. Brad had invited a couple of guys from work with their wives. They were younger but seemed nice. I particularly liked the sheriff, Brad's boss, Jason Pierce, and his wife, Julie. I thought I could be friends with her. Johnny Whitlock from the campground came. He had someone taking over the office for him as campers and RVs lined up to check-in. Brad was happy to see his old school friend but admitted to me that he would have never recognized him.

"The smile is the same," he confided. "But he's changed a lot in looks. He still seems to have his mischievous sense of humor. He used to get all the rest of us in trouble a lot."

I imagined that was easy to do with that group of boys.

I enjoyed Lillian's church friends. I had already surmised Brad planned on attending her home church when we were not on the road, or he couldn't go with me and was free on Sundays. There were three couples present, counting the pastor and his wife and some single older women. The latter cloistered around Lillian and kept everything moving smoothly.

Brad pointedly introduced me to the Pastor and his wife, Don and Elsie Franks.

She was a silver-haired woman, somewhat overweight for her short stature. She had that peaches and cream look   .

that made an older woman appear younger. She had an infectious laugh, and I could hear her laughing throughout the evening. She seemed to enjoy life, although her husband was more somber. He wore a short sleeve blue shirt decorated with his white minister's collar. There was no doubt he was a pastor. He had an aura of authority, which probably stood him in good stead in pastoring the church. Brad told me he had been there for thirty years, and knew everything about everybody since he had dedicated their babies, married their youth, and buried their aged. According to Lillian, he was also closed-lipped about his parishioners, which the younger people appreciated. Still, he irritated some of the older ones who had nothing better to do than investigate all wrongdoing or suspected wrongdoing.

It was a fine evening for the cookout. There were around thirty people there. I heard voices coming from the river, so I imagined swimming and tubing were going on.

Doc was there, but I was not too fond of his color. He was sitting at our table in his overalls and short sleeve blue shirt. It wasn't very humid, but I saw him take his handkerchief out of his back pocket several times and wipe his face and forehead with it. He looked a bit ashen.

I leaned forward to speak to him. "Doc, are you all right? You don't look like you feel well."

Lillian heard me and turned to gaze with concern at her old friend. "Arthur, you are looking a little green."

He forced a weak smile. "I'll be all right. Just a little indigestion. Maybe I need a doctor." He slapped his hand to his forehead. "Oh, I forgot, I am a doctor." He grinned sheepishly. "I'll be okay. Don't worry about me. I'm not going anywhere. I always say, 'I'm too good for the devil and too bad for God, so I'll just have to stay.'" He took another spoonful of potato salad as he spoke. "I don't know who made the potato salad in that blue bowl, but it sure is good."

"That's Jo's, Doc," Lillian informed him. "She's a good cook. She's kept me fed while we go through all my stuff."

He peered at me. "Good thing you like to cook. Cook and garden. As I remember it, Brad liked to eat. His grandmother, Rose, liked to cook too. I couldn't keep up with her."

"I got the green thumb from her, but the cooking passed me by," Lillian admitted. "Nobody's ever asked me to make one of my special dishes or for one of my recipes."

Brad grinned at me. "Jo's good at anything she sets her head to do. At least I haven't found anything she can't do."

"I can't swim," I volunteered. "But I have to admit that river looks inviting."

Joseph spoke up. "I tried to teach her. She said she could drown well. I didn't want that, so I told her to stay out of the water."

"Her driving leaves a lot to be desired, too," Alaina added to everybody's laughter.

"I drive just fine," I said defensively. "It's everybody else that needs practice."

After the meal, people started mingling, and groups sat in shady spots all over the lawn, conversing. I looked around for Doc and saw him talking to Lillian before he shuffled across the yard toward his house.

I intercepted him before he crossed the property line. "You okay, Doc?"

"This heat the last few days has got to me, Miss Jo. I'll be all right. I thought I'd go home and lay under the shade trees in the hammock. I haven't been sleeping too well. Probably just tired." He reached out and patted my cheek. "You're a good girl. I'm glad Brad found you. You're a welcome asset to our little community here. You've got a nice family too. Lillian is so happy to have all of you in her life. It's good you and Brad are going to be close to her. She doesn't have anyone else, and I think she is worried about what will happen if she gets where she can't take care of herself."

"Brad and I will be here for her," I promised.

"I get it," the old man said. "I will be ninety-seven on my birthday if I live. I haven't got anybody either. All I've ever had since Dad died was Rose and Lillian. Now Rose is gone." He shook his head in sorrowful remembrance. "Everything changes all the time. Folks that are here today are gone tomorrow."

I touched his shoulder. "Doc, I'm certain Brad and I will keep an eye on you. I can tell he thinks a lot of you, and I already like you."

I watched his lower lip tremble, and he struggled to get his emotions under control. "Do you care if I hug you, Miss Jo? That's the nicest thing anyone has said to me for a long time."

I reached out with both arms, and we hugged one another. I thought I saw Doc wipe a tear from his blue eyes. I wasn't sure. Then, without another word, he turned and moved towards his house and his hammock.

Everyone had left by eight-thirty, and dusk was creeping over the yard. Brad and I were relaxing on the front porch watching the lightning bugs flash their lights across the front of the house and listening to the night sounds of the insects. Joseph and Ashley were watching TV in what Lillian called the den. Alaina and Lillian were in the kitchen. Lillian was making a list of everyone who had attended her cookout and sharing vivid detail about each of them. I sighed contentedly, kicking my shoes off, stretched my legs, and wiggled my toes.

Brad looked at me searchingly. "Happy, Jo?"

I nodded. "Very." I had met so many people I hoped I could remember them all. "I liked your old friend, Johnny. He seems like a lot of fun. I think he could easily be the life of the party from his looks."

Brad was sitting in the swing beside me, and he put his hands behind his head, and I could tell he was reminiscing.

"Johnny was always a lot of fun. He says he's never been married, and he's in between girlfriends right now. I think he enjoys the single life myself." He looked at me in the dusk. "Want to walk over and check on Doc before it gets too dark?"

"Lets," I said. "I didn't like the doctor's color this afternoon. I think he's been getting out in the heat too much."

We walked hand in hand across the darkening yard. All the trees and shrubs cast dark shadows around us. I caught the scent of an old-time shrub rose as we strolled.

I saw Doc lying in the olive green hammock in the gathering shadows. It was tied between two spruce trees and looked cozy. He was lying on a pillow with his arms folded across his chest. I grinned. I hated to wake him.

He didn't move when I slipped up beside him. I touched his arm lightly. "Doc," I said gently. "Are you feeling any better? It's Jo Elliott."

There was no response, and I shook his arm harder. "Doc, are you all right?"

I felt rather than saw Brad come up beside me. "Is he okay?" he asked with concern in his voice.

I frowned and shook him gently again. "I can't seem to get him awake."

Brad leaned over and put his finger on the side of his neck. Now he was frowning. He placed his hand on Doc's chest and then looked at me. "He's not breathing, Jo." He was surveying the scene with a professional eye.

I put my hand on Doc's wrist but could not detect a pulse. His hand was cold to the touch. Tears rose in my green eyes. "Oh, Brad, poor old Doc."

Brad was dialing 9-1-1 and speaking rapidly into the phone. I put my hand over Doc's hands and felt tears rolling down my cheeks.

Brad stepped to my side and put his arms around me. I buried my dark head into his shoulder and let the tears spill freely.

"He's dead, isn't he?"

Brad nodded against my hair. "I'm sorry, Jo. He was a fine man. I'm glad you got to meet him. He was always good to me when I came here as a boy. His death is going to upset Aunt Lillian. He was her right hand."

I raised my head to look into Brad's face. "At least it's a natural death." I rubbed the tears from my eyes. "I don't think I could take another murder."

Brad's hand caressed my back soothingly. "No, no, probably had a heart attack or stroke. He's nearly ninety-seven, and it has been roasting the last few days. He always plants a garden, whether he can or not." He took my hand. "We'll have to go tell the others." He studied my face. "Are you all right?"

I nodded and squeezed his hand. "I've got to stay strong for Aunt Lillian."

He kissed me on the forehead, and we started across the yard to the house.

We walked inside the back door. Lillian and Alaina were still sitting at the kitchen table.

Aunt Lillian looked up. "Where have you two been?"

"We were checking on Doc," I told her.

"Was Doc doing okay?" she asked Brad.

Brad sat down across from her and took her hands in his. "Aunt Lillian, you've got to prepare yourself for a shock. I am so sorry, but Doc is no longer with us."

Her thin face began to pucker, but she quickly controlled herself. Her grip tightened on Brad's hands, and her lips quivered. She was staring at the table, but I doubted she saw it.

Aunt Lillian looked across at Brad. "Take me to him." It was a command.

Brad glanced at me doubtfully. "Are you sure that's a good idea? It's dark out there."

She released his hands and struggled to get up. "Arthur is my oldest friend. He's family to me. I want to tell him goodbye in my own way, not in front of a crowd of people."

Brad and Alaina helped her the older woman to her feet, and I opened the storm door while the three of them went gingerly down the steps. Brad had turned on the light on his cell phone to guide the way.

I went to the den to inform Joseph and Ashley. "Brad called 9-1-1, so the ambulance should be here shortly, but it's too late. He's gone. He died in his hammock. Brad thinks it was probably a heart attack or a stroke."

Joseph and Ashley exchanged glances. "This is going to be a shock," Joseph commented. "Everybody around here knew Doc. The way they talked about him at the cookout today, I felt nobody ever expected him to die. He was one of those people you imagine will be here forever, even when you know that's impossible."

In a few minutes, we all were standing around the hammock. Lillian was standing beside him, smoothing his thinning hair back with her hand, whispering to him. Her back was straight, and I didn't see any tears. She would cry in her own time by herself, I surmised.

I heard the ambulance's siren coming down the road, and Joseph and Ashley went out front to lead them back to where Doc lay. Watching them cover him and hide him from view inside the black bag was hard.

I leaned into Brad, who stood beside me with his arm around my shoulders, and he hugged me closer to him. I felt his strength and was thankful for it. We stood in a row solemnly watching our old friend carried across the yard into the waiting ambulance.

Brad went to Doc's house and locked it. The rest of us waited on him. None of us spoke as we walked back into our place.

Lillian went out on the front porch and stared into the darkness for a long time. Joseph and Ashley, and Alaina slipped off to bed. Brad waited with me for Aunt Lillian to return inside, and he and I conversed softly together in the kitchen. When she came in, she went to her room and closed the door without speaking to us. It was like the house itself felt the solitude of someone passing.

It was the next day that Brad called me. We were already on the road going to our Saturday night concert. He seemed upset, and I understood why when he told me what was happening.

"The coroner isn't satisfied with Doc's death," Brad told me. "Doc hadn't been to a doctor in years. They're going to hold off the funeral for a few days and do an autopsy. I don't think they expect to find anything, but unless he checked it himself, no one knows whether he had any history of high blood pressure, which could have caused a stroke or heart disease. It's just precautionary. Jason says this coroner never likes to sign his name to anything unless he's sure. He's the kind that all the paperwork has to be done exactly right, and every t crossed and I dotted."

"Oh, well," I said. "I'm sure it will be fine. Doc was nearly ninety-seven."

But I was wrong. On Tuesday, I got a call from Brad while he was at work. It was early morning, and I started to weed in the shade garden, working towards the Monkshood plant. I sat on the ground with my small spading fork, vigorously digging out the entrenched weeds.

I answered Brad on the second ring.

"Are you sitting down?" he asked.

"I'm sitting on the ground, weeding one of the flower beds. I think I saw your aunt in the vegetable garden, but

I've been so engrossed in this that I wonder if she's still outside or not. What's up?"

"I don't know how to tell you this except to blurt it out. We got the post-mortem report here today on Doc."

"Oh, good. What did it show? Were we right, and it was either a heart attack or a stroke?"

"Well, you're not going to like this any better than I do, but he says from his exam, Doc didn't die of natural causes. Without going into vivid details, apparently, somebody suffocated him."

I could feel the strength ebbing out of me and the color draining from my face. "Suffocated? Oh, Brad, no, no!" My mind refused to accept that Doc's death could be anything but an older man dying of old age.

"I know, Honey. Jason is making this a priority. We're getting a warrant to search his place. I'm curious about that pillow under his head, so I am coming to get it so we can examine it."

"But who would want to hurt that sweet old man?" I demanded.

"I don't know that either, but I am going to find out sooner or later," he replied.

Another thought occurred to me. "But Brad, there were at least thirty people here Friday evening, plus the campground was full. We could be talking about a hundred people or more. We're all suspects."

"I know, Jo, but only one of us killed Doc. I just wanted you to know that it is no longer a natural death-it is murder."

CHAPTER FOUR

I heard the phone click and sat back on my heels, trying to take in this new set of events. My mind felt muddled. Who in the world would want to kill that elderly doctor? I pictured the entire crowd who had gathered here at the cookout. They had all known Doc and, as far as I could tell, had liked and respected him. None of them were strangers. Doc had been part of most of their lives at one time or the other. Of course, there was always the campground. Who knew where the folks who camped there came from? They could be anybody from anywhere. But why would a perfect stranger want to do in an elderly family doctor? I shook my head in exasperation.

I continued digging out the weeds until I heard the cars go by out front. I walked over to the edge of the property and watched Brad and another officer follow Sheriff Jason Pierce up on the front steps of the stone house next door. I heard the door open as the police officers entered the house. I couldn't go over there now that it was an official crime scene. I sighed. Just what I needed, I thought, another murder. They seemed to be following me around.

"What are the police doing at Doc's house?"

I hadn't noticed Lillian come out the back door and to where I was standing until I heard her voice. I turned and looked into her troubled features. It seemed to me the lines on her face were more finely etched since Doc had died. I hated to add to this lovely woman's grief.

I forced the words out. "Oh, Aunt Lillian, Brad called me a few minutes ago and said the autopsy showed that Doc had been murdered-smothered-in fact."

I watched the faint color on her face fade away. She swayed a little on her feet, and I put my arm around her to steady her.

She was forcing herself to regain control. "Why did they need an autopsy anyway?"

I was choosing my words carefully. "The coroner refused to sign the death certificate because Doc didn't have a family doctor."

"He didn't think he needed one since he could doctor himself," Lillian was sure about that. She was silent for a moment, then, "But who in the world would want to kill Doc? Are they sure?"

"The coroner is," I told her.

"But that means it could have been one of us at the cookout!" She covered her face with her hands. "No, no, I refuse to believe that. No one here would be guilty of such a thing."

"It's not just the ones who were here," I said. "There was a campground down the river full of people on Friday night, and we don't know a thing about them."

Her hands slipped from her face, and she stared at me. "Doc mentioned to me on several occasions since they reopened that RV Park that we'd probably all be murdered in our beds some night by some serial killer from the campground."

I grimaced. "Doc told me the same thing. Well, it is true. We don't know any of them except Johnny Whitlock."

Lillian dismissed that idea out of hand. "Johnny wouldn't hurt a flea. I knew his parents and that boy when he was a youngster. Mother used to feed him about every day in the summer when Brad was here. He was always running in and out of this house. I enjoyed talking to him the other evening. He was a naughty child but a very nice young man. Very polite."

I glanced back at the doctor's house just in time to see Brad step out on the porch. This time he noticed his Aunt Lillian and I standing in our yard and strode our way.

Lillian's voice sounded pleading when she asked. "It's true? You believe Doc was murdered?" I could tell she wished so much Brad would deny it.

Brad put his hands on her shoulders and met her gaze squarely. "It's true, Aunt Lillian. I am so sorry. I know how much you thought of him." He touched her cheek gently. "I promise you; we will leave no stone unturned until we find out who did this. This one is personal."

She reached up and held onto his arms with both hands. "You all can't let me down on this, Brad. I have to know. It's important to me."

"The sheriff and all of us are working on it. We'll find out." Brad turned to me as he dropped his hands from Lillian's thin shoulders. "I'll let you know as soon as I know." He touched my hand, turned, and walked away.

"Just get some answers," I called after him.

Something like pride was on Lillian's face as she watched her nephew purposefully cross the yard and meet up with the other cops in front of Doc's house.

I took Lillian's arm. "Come on. We need a glass of iced tea."

A faint smile touched her lips. "I used to think tea drinking was a cure-all, but this is such a shock." Her steps slowed, and I matched my pace to hers. "This reminds me of when my little sister, Rosemary, fell down the steps and broke her neck. Of course, the police weren't involved, but I was only five and playing in my room. I remember hearing all the commotion and Mother screaming. I came out of my bedroom, and my little sister lay at the bottom of the staircase. At the time, I didn't understand what was happening. Mother was kneeling beside Rosemary, and then she picked her up in her arms and rocked her back and forth, crying the entire time. It seemed so strange. She was lying limply in Mother's arms-not moving. Dad was upstairs, too, because I seem to remember him coming out on the landing. He cursed and swore at Mother and stomped down the stairs. I ran into my room, crawled into bed, and covered my head with my fingers stuck in my ears so I couldn't hear the shouting between my parents. Sometime later, Mother came upstairs and laid down beside me. She held me tightly, and I clutched her like I would never let go. I felt her tears falling on my face, and I asked her, 'Mommy, why are you crying?' She said, 'it was because my little sister had gone to Heaven and hadn't even gotten to say goodbye." She sighed and looked at me. "I don't know why this made me think of that, but it did. I never talk about it. I'm not sure why I did now." She forced a smile. "I saw you were weeding in the garden. If you help me get down and back up, I'll come and help you. I can't get my mind on going through stuff in the house."

I put my arm around her frail shoulders. "Are you sure you're able to weed?"

"I can sit down on the ground with your help. I've got a piece of plastic on the back porch I sit on. Getting back up is the biggest problem." She gave a tiny laugh. "It's dreadful getting older. It's okay in some ways. What used to worry you no longer seems important. Material things don't mean as much, but pictures, letters, cards, and people you love all become a more significant part of your life. You've made your friends, and if you're blessed, you've got family who loves you. The people who don't like you don't bother you. You're not out to impress anyone. You've lived your life, had your successes, and made your mistakes. Age has its compensations." She searched my face. "You're easy to talk to, Jo. I don't usually open up this much to anyone. I think I'd better be quiet and get busy and weed or you'll get my entire life story out of me."

I laughed. "Maybe we can change the subject to what all these plants are and how I'm supposed to take care of them. Doc was going to help me…." I stopped. "I'm sorry, Lillian. I'm going to miss him."

We reached the back porch, and Lillian went inside for her blue plastic sheet. "If I quit talking about those who've passed at my age, I will soon run out of people to talk about. I'm glad you got to meet Doc. I could have married him if I had wanted to. He asked me, but I laughed and told him I liked him better as a friend. His father wanted to marry my mother after my father died, but my mother said once was enough. My parents didn't have a happy marriage. They fought a lot. Brad's dad, Eugene, got away as soon as he could. He usually didn't bring Phyllis with him when he came to visit. I would have liked to have known her better. As for my other sister, Violet ran away as soon as she was twenty-one. Dad was long gone then, but she told me the place depressed her, and she just wanted to escape. She did a good job of it. She's never been back. I don't think she married the guy she ran off with. We do know from his family that they didn't stay together. I've tried to find her by his last name on the internet, but nothing has ever come up. Mother and I talked about hiring a private detective to track her down, but we decided to leave it alone. If she didn't want us to know where she was, that was her choice. I don't know if we did the right thing or not. I don't even know whether she is still living or not."

"That's why it was important for me to like the house, wasn't it?" I asked, my hand pausing its digging with the spading fork. "You wanted to be sure Brad's future wife would appreciate the family home."

She regarded me solemnly. "I wanted to ensure you were a woman who would stay the course and not run off when things got tough. I would have never offered Brad the place when he married Audrey. He fell head over heels in love with her, but Mother and I both could tell she wasn't a keeper. Mother tried to talk to him, but he wouldn't listen. I didn't try. When people have made up their minds, there is no use talking to them. I knew he would find out for himself. When he told me about you, I decided to defer judgment until I met you."

"So, do you approve?" I asked, still not going back to the weeding.

"Very much. Brad says you both will look after the house and me, and that's all I can ask for." She took her spading fork and began digging vigorously around one of the hostas.

I smiled to myself and went back to work. We were silent for a few minutes until my spade hit something. At first, I thought it was a rock. I stopped digging and smoothed the dirt back with my hands until it revealed part of a light green-colored glass.

"I think I've hit something here," I pronounced.

Lillian looked at where I was pointing. She frowned. "That's strange. It looks like a Mason glass jar. Here, let me help you. You're getting close to that Monkshood roots. We'll have to be careful."

Between us, we removed more dirt, and slowly a half-gallon green Mason jar was exposed in the soil. Gingerly, I lifted the glass from the ground and brushed the earth off it. It appeared to be full of papers. The lid was covered with some brown substance and was hard. I handed the jar to Lillian.

Lillian was frowning. "Somebody went to a lot of trouble. That's sealing wax over the lid. Mother used that to seal the bottle when she canned homemade catsup."

I was surveying the mess we had made in the flower bed. "Do you think we should check and see if there are any more?"

"Go ahead, but keep your gloves on. We're getting close to the Monkshood roots, which are poisonous."

I carefully dug around near where we had discovered the first jar. In another moment, I heard another clink.

"I think there's something else here," I announced.

It was another jar, the same as the first-a half-gallon green Mason jar. I brushed off the dirt and realized that it, too, was filled with paper.

I checked around to be sure there were no more jars, then swept the soil back into the holes we had made. I got to my feet and pulled Lillian up beside me.

"Let's take these up to the house," she suggested. "I hope I don't have to break them. They're very old, but I want to see what these papers are inside the jars."

"Do you think they could be your mother's?" I asked tentatively.

"Possibly. I'll know when I see the handwriting. Whatever made Mother bury them in the garden is beyond me."

She picked up a small hammer on the back porch table and began chipping away the sealing wax. Underneath the wax was an old zinc lid. She handed me the jar. "My arthritis probably won't let me get that off. We may have to use the hammer on that too."

I hammered gently around the lid, putting indentations in the metal. I didn't want to break the glass.

Finally, I could twist the zinc cap off the first jar. I picked up the second one to work on it. Lillian eagerly took out the papers, straightened them, and studied them closely.

"This is Mother's handwriting. It looks to be a gardening journal. This page says, *'today, I planted peas.'*" She pressed the papers to her chest. "Oh, what a wonderful surprise, and to think we found them before I moved. It is such a God-sighting, Jo. That's what I call God's little surprises and treasures that He gives to us."

I smiled at her excitement and handed her the other opened jar. "It should give you a lot of pleasure reading something your mother wrote."

She frowned as she took the glass. "I don't know that I have time to read them right now." She looked back down at the paper and the faded ink. "Oh, dear! Right after the peas, she says,

'Ernest says it's too early, but what does he know? He'd let us all starve because he's mad I lost this last baby-a boy.'

She looked up, concerned. "I'm not sure I want to know what's in these. Do you think she wanted anyone to read them? It's sort of like reading someone's diary."

"I don't think she would have gone to all the trouble of making sure they would survive by burying them if she didn't want someone to find them," I said, sounding practical.

Lillian was thoughtful. "Mother could be secretive, and I always knew there were things she wouldn't tell me about. I can remember Mother and Father arguing all the time. I don't know, Jo. I feel very vulnerable right now with losing Doc. I tell you what. You read them first, and if you don't think they'll upset me, I'll read them later. How's that?" She slipped the paper back into the jar and handed them both to me.

Now I was frowning. "Are you sure you want a stranger reading this? Especially if you think there might be something you wouldn't want anyone else to know."

She drew herself to her full height, forcing me to look at her. "Are you marrying my nephew, or aren't you?"

"I am marrying your nephew," I said meekly.

"Then whatever you find will be your right to know too." She pushed the green glasses at me. "Take them. If you marry into this family, you may as well know the worst." She stalked off into the house, leaving me with my mouth open and two half-gallon Mason jars in my hands.

Thoughtfully, I carried the jars inside the house. Lillian was nowhere in sight. When I looked out the side window, I saw her in the vegetable garden with a hoe in her hands.

I climbed the stairs to the second floor and then up the narrow steps to the turret. I placed the jars in one of the corners and stared out the window towards Doc's house. The police cruiser was still sitting out front, and when I opened the windows, I could hear the faint sound of voices.

I stood there thinking about Doc and the papers that sat silently in the jars. How long ago had Rose Edwards buried them, and why? Who buried garden journals in the ground? I stared at the jars. Subconsciously, Lillian seemed to know there was a possibility that her mother had written much more than just gardening advice. I wondered if she were right. She had appeared to be almost afraid of what she would discover in those papers. Lillian had opened up a lot today. I suspected she would regret that and close down on me. Brad's aunt wasn't one to share her deepest thoughts. Doc was probably the only one she had come close to, allowing him to know her dreams and fears. I thought she had lived a lifetime keeping everyone at arm's length. Now that she was older, all she had was Brad and me. The other person she had depended upon had been savagely murdered!

CHAPTER FIVE

Just as I thought, Lillian was quiet at supper time. She would answer questions in short sentences, but she never volunteered any conversation. When we finished, I suggested she leave the dishes to me, and she left the room quietly. I heard her bedroom door close behind her.

Brad still needed to call me, but I wasn't expecting him to call early. Sometimes he came for supper, but I didn't expect him tonight. He had been busy today. I sat on the front porch awhile, and when darkness fell, I started up the grand staircase.

I turned halfway up and tried to picture the scene Lillian had described the day her little sister died. It must have been a horrible shock to a five-year-old little girl. I sensed she was seeing it all over again in her mind's eyes when she recalled it.

When I reached the landing, the front door opened, and to my surprise, it was Brad. He looked up at me and gave me a tired smile. I came back down the stairs, and he folded me in his arms, resting his chin on the top of my brunette hair.

"Tough day, huh?" I asked.

"Yeah, tough! Where's Aunt Lillian?"

"She's already in her room," I answered. I looked up at Brad. "Want some supper? Have you eaten?"

"I had a sandwich a couple of hours ago."

"There's some food left over. It won't take me but a minute to warm it up." I slipped from his arms, and he followed me into the kitchen.

I watched him eat and waited on him to tell me about his day. He pushed the plate back and took a long iced tea drink before he began.

"Nothing showed up in Doc's house to help us. He'd been looking at some of his and his dad's old medical files. There's a mountain of them, and we will have to go through them individually. He saved all kinds of useless stuff-old newspapers and magazines. His age group does not throw out anything. They remember what it was like to live hard and want to be prepared if it happens again." He swept a weary hand through his sandy hair. "There were no threatening letters. He didn't have an answering machine or computer. There's not much to go on at the house. We'll have to go through it inch by inch anyway."

"So, were there other fingerprints on the hammock or footprints on the ground?" I questioned cautiously.

"There were too many fingerprints. We weren't the only ones who went over and checked on Doc that Friday afternoon. He had everyone concerned about him."

He looked at me. "Can you tell me where everyone was every minute of the afternoon?"

"No, of course not. It was a cookout-a get together. I wasn't looking at anyone with suspicion. People entered the house; they walked down to the gazebo and the river. I can't say where anyone was all the time."

"That's the whole problem." He took another drink of iced tea and leaned back in his chair. "I talked to Johnny Whitlock today. He was upset. He couldn't get it into his head that it could be true. He's making sure everyone in the campground knows what is going on so they can get in touch with the sheriff's department if anyone sees or hears anything. It will be difficult if no one admits to seeing or hearing anything. I'll have to start again in the morning. A trail gets cold in a hurry."

My eyes narrowed. "You do think you can find out who did this, don't you?"

"We're going to give it our best shot. Murders don't happen around here every day. Some of the guys at work had heard about the case in Hoover, so they think I know all about solving crimes like this."

"I hate that we found the body," I said ruefully. "It's getting to be a habit."

Brad grinned. "Maybe that's why you're marrying a cop. You're attracted to crime."

"Now, you sound like my family accusing me of reading all those mysteries, so now I want the real thing."

"Life happens, Jo. We don't always get to say in what direction it takes us."

"True. I had something interesting happen today."

He leaned forward again. "Yeah?"

"Yeah. I was weeding near the Monkshood, and your Aunt Lillian was helping me. I managed to dig up two light green half-gallon Mason jars. They're sealed with wax and filled with papers stuffed inside them."

"Did you open the jars?"

"We did. It was something like a gardening journal. It was your grandmother's."

He stared at me. "Really?"

"Really. The jars are in the turret if you want to see them."

"How come you have them and not Aunt Lillian? She was very close to Grandma Rose."

"She opened up to me a lot today, and by this evening, she had regretted it. She barely spoke at supper. Losing Doc is taking its toll on her."

"She always has kept most things inside. Grandma Rose did, too, if you want my opinion. I don't think that would upset Aunt Lillian if it's just gardening journals."

"That's just it. Your grandmother made little comments. She mentioned sowing the peas and that your grandfather thought it was too early, and then she said something about him not knowing anything about it; he wouldn't care if they starved. There was something else about her losing the last baby, apparently, a boy, and her husband was mad about it. It sounded like she thought he believed it was her fault. Anyway, Lillian got upset and decided maybe it would be better if she didn't read it and gave it to me."

Brad's gray eyes were staring at me, but I didn't think he saw me. He was storing and wrapping his head around the information I had just shared with him.

"I think I'd like to see these jars and papers before I call it a night," Brad said.

We climbed the stairway together. It was nice knowing that we would walk up this staircase for the rest of our lives. In the turret, I unscrewed the cap of one of the jars and handed it to Brad.

"Are they in any order? Is this the first one?" Brad asked.

"I have no idea. Whatever is written here are things your grandmother wanted to say and share with somebody, probably a family member."

Brad flipped through a few pages scanning through each one. "I don't see anything here to get excited about. Aunt Lillian is right. It's mostly telling about Grandma's garden, what she planted and how it's thriving."

"I want to bring my rocker over and put it up here. It's so restful. Was your grandmother a restful person?"

"We all loved to be around her when we were kids. Johnny was talking about it today. He hates that he didn't get back here before she passed. She always had a soft spot for Johnny. He got all of us in trouble, but that never bothered Grandma. She'd say, 'Johnny Whitlock, I know that somehow this is your fault, and if I catch you acting up again, you're not coming back to this house.' Then she'd give Johnny the biggest piece of cake or pie." Brad yawned.

"I've got to call it a night and get back to Jason's. Are you coming back down?"

I shook my head. "I'm going to stay up here a little while. It's relaxing."

Brad reached for me, and I leaned against him. He kissed me gently. "Take care, Jo. Don't wander out of sight of the house. You and Aunt Lillian need to stay together. There's a killer out here, and I have no idea who they are or why they murdered Doc. When are Joseph and Ashley coming back?"

"Tomorrow. Alaina will be back tomorrow evening. I believe she's spending the weekend here with your aunt. She wants to help us get this work done, and the kids and I have a revival this weekend."

He kissed me again. "You'll get it done, Jo. I believe in you."

I listened to him walking rapidly down the steps and the front door closing behind him. After a moment, I heard the sound of his car starting and driving down the road.

I turned off the lights and leaned on the edge of one of the open windows. The stars were crystal clear tonight. "God," I breathed. "Please don't let this be one of those unsolved cases. What is hidden in the darkness let it come to light."

The following day, Joseph and Ashley arrived. Lillian had been working with her vegetables, so Joseph and Ashley went to the garden to talk to her. After a short while, she followed them inside the house, and I heard them going through dresser drawers in her bedroom.

The formal living room looked a mess. There were boxes and more boxes. One section was going with Lillian. One group donated to charity. Another area was trash. The latter was the smallest pile. Lillian couldn't bear to throw away much.

I sighed. At least we were getting something done. I only had a few pieces of furniture to move. Mostly, I had lived out of a suitcase for the last twenty years. Whatever I had bought for Alaina's house could stay with her.

I had an old roll-top desk that belonged to my dad, and I wanted to put it upstairs in the turret. I thought there was room for a keyboard too. I would never be able to play like Ashley, but I could play enough to write music for our songs. Joseph was doing more of the music scores, but I liked composing too. I might get plenty of inspiration sitting up in that turret. I imagined when autumn came, and the leaves dropped off the trees and shrubs, one could see the river from there. I sighed again, contentedly this time.

My cell phone rang. I pulled it out of my pocket. It was the church where we were holding revival services on Friday through Sunday night. Joseph was scheduled to preach, and our group would be singing.

One of the longtime members had died in the church, and the funeral would be this Saturday. My heart sank when he told me they would have to cancel. I assured the pastor that I understood, and with my calendar in hand, we rescheduled for later in the year.

I put the phone back in my pocket and tapped on Lillian's bedroom door.

Joseph opened the door.

"I'm afraid we just got canceled for the weekend," I informed him. "There's been a death at Calvary Church, so they must postpone the revival. They did reschedule for the fall."

Joseph shrugged. "It happens."

"It will give us more time to make a bigger dent in all of this packing," Ashley said positively. "We've got the big closet cleared out, Mamaw."

I glanced at the walk-in closet and noticed that only a few garments were hanging there instead of being full like earlier in the month.

Lillian was sitting silently in her chair. I wasn't confident she was even listening to us until she started looking for her phone and saying. "I'll call Pastor Don. He told me to let him know last Sunday if you got a cancellation. He wants to have you at our church." Her hand was rapidly moving items on the crowded bed. "Here it is." She dialed a number and began talking to the pastor. Then she handed her phone to me. "He wants to talk to you."

I took the phone hesitantly. "Pastor, this is Jo Elliott. I appreciate you wanting to book us, but do you think it's too short notice? If you wanted time to advertise us coming——." I stopped as he insisted it was fine.

"It will be a lovely surprise. Your future husband gave me a CD some time ago, so I know how good your group is. And Lillian has been after me to book you. Everybody will be thrilled. I have heard good comments from all those who came to the cookout and met you and your family. Besides, I understand from Brad that you plan on making Willis Community Church your home church, so I can't think of a better way to introduce you to our little community. We will be so proud to have someone of your prominence as a member of our congregation."

I was feeling overwhelmed. Obviously, my future husband had been spreading it on a little thickly. I forced myself to go back to listening to the pastor giving me the particulars of the Sunday morning service. We discussed a time they would unlock the church so we could set up our musical equipment, and then I handed the phone back to Lillian. She thanked the pastor and hung up.

"Well, now that we've got that taken care of, we can get back to work," she suggested.

I left the room and reached the turret with a tape measure. I wanted to see how much space I had for the desk, keyboard, and rocker.

I found a straight-back chair in another bedroom and brought it into the turret. Sitting in it wouldn›t be comfortable, but I wouldn›t have to stand.

I eyed the jars residing under one of the windows. I pulled one of the glass jars over and unscrewed the lid. Carefully, I lifted out the papers. I wondered how old they were. I flipped through a few pages, but there were no dates on any of them. I settled back in my chair and started reading. I was searching for the page that Lillian had found. As Lillian had thought, most of what her mother had written was gardening information. She told what she planted and the seeds she sowed and gave progress reports on how everything grew. In about half an hour, I discovered what I was looking for. I laid the other papers on the floor and continued reading.

"*Today, I planted peas. Ernest says it is too early, but what does he know? He›d let us all starve because he›s still mad I lost this last baby boy.*"

I turned the paper over. "*He always wants a boy. He has no use for girls. They're not as valuable as boys, according to him. He curses me up one side and down the other when Doc Graham says it's another girl. I can't help what the good Lord gives me. The baby I just lost was a boy, and Ernest was fit to be tied. He said I would lose the boy baby, and he needed sons to carry on the Edwards name. He says Eugene is no good. He says he's a mama's boy. I felt like telling him I thought it would be better if there were no more male Edwards if they were all like him.*

I hate him. I think I've always hated him, but I will never get over seeing him throw Rosemary down the stairs because she got under his feet. I heard her cry and came running, but it was too late. There lay my little girl at the foot of the stairs –dead. I looked up at that old devil; if looks could have killed, he would have died. I have never hated anyone like I hated him at that moment. He stomped down the steps and out of the house. He never even stopped to look at his daughter. I held her in my arms for the longest time.

Violet and Ernest were at school, and little Lily was in her bedroom. She came out of her room when she heard the screaming and crying. I sent her back to her room until I could get hold of myself.

I carried the baby next door to Doc. He laid her on the table, checked her, took his glasses off, and asked. 'How did this happen, Rose?'

I wanted to tell him the truth. So badly, but I couldn't. I wanted him to call the police and arrest Ernest for murder, but I knew no one would believe me. My husband has friends in the sheriff's department and the court system. He said she had broken her neck. I just said she fell down the stairs. I was crying.

He said, 'Where is Ernest?' I said he took off. He couldn't handle it.

The doctor patted my hand and told me he'd take care of everything. He called the funeral home for me, and I arranged to have her buried at the cemetery at Willis Community Church with the rest of the family. Ernest should have taken care of it. I was sure he would be the sorrowful father at the funeral- the old devil!

I went back to the house, went upstairs to Lily's room, lay beside her, and held her tightly. Poor little thing was scared half to death. She didn't understand what was happening.

She did ask me once if Rosemary was like her pet parakeet that had died, and we had buried him in the yard. I managed to tell her, yes, Rosemary was with Jesus.

I lay there and thought about how much I hated my husband. I don't know if Doc believed my story, but he would never say anything. How can I live with a man who has killed his own child? But how can I leave? Good people stay together till death do them part. I have three other children to think about. It wouldn't do any good if I up and died. Then who would take care of my children? That day, I promised myself and God that Ernest wouldn't have any more children to kill or mistreat."

I turned to the next page. It was about planting potatoes, beets, carrots, and other root crops. It was the last I could find of anything personal.

To say I was shocked was putting it mildly. I felt confident that Lillian knew absolutely nothing about this. How in the world was I going to share this with her? I was unsure of the wisdom of allowing her to read this journal. I thought she instinctually knew that illuminations from these pages could hurt her.

I was still sitting there when I heard Brad enter the front door. He went to his aunt's room, and I heard him ask Joseph where I was. In a few minutes, I heard him bounding up the stairs.

He took one look at my face and realized something was wrong. Wordlessly, I handed him the papers I had been reading. He stood over by one of the windows and read. As his eyes moved over the pages, I saw his jaw tighten and some color drain from his visage. He stood there a moment after he finished reading, staring out of the turret windows.

I got up and went to him, placing my hand on his arm. "Brad?"

He looked at me then. "So my grandfather was a murderer? How am I supposed to feel about that?" His features had turned hard.

I tightened my hold on his arm. "Brad, I know this is a shock, but you're not your grandfather. You already knew he was not somebody you could admire."

Brad was staring out the window again. "I didn't know he was a killer either. How do you think that makes me feel that my job requires me to put away people like him, and my grandfather got by with murdering his little girl?"

"Brad, please don't make his guilt yours."

"I doubt he ever felt guilty. His kind don't."

"I feel so sorry for your grandmother. I don't know how she managed to stay with him."

"People didn't divorce back then like they do today. There was nowhere for a woman to go with her kids unless they had a family to take them in. As far as I know, she didn't have any family. I expect she felt trapped." Brad swept a hand through his sandy hair as he regarded me. "Are you certain you want to marry into a family like mine?"

Brad was a good man, and knowing his grandfather was a killer was shocking. I sensed he needed reassurance. I decided to use humor.

"Are you trying to renege on your promise to marry me?" I asked jokingly.

There was a spark in his eyes. "Not on your life," he said firmly.

I put my arms around him, and we stood close together for several moments, not speaking. Finally, I looked up into his soft gray eyes and said. "I'm sure if I could go back far enough, there are plenty of heathens in my family pool."

"Well, at least we're too old to bring up children," Brad returned.

I laughed. "If we were both young, I wouldn't think twice about having a family with you."

He kissed me and then pulled back, resting his hands on my shoulders. "I've got some news too. That's why I stopped at the house. I'm on my way down to the campground. Johnny is going to be upset, but I can't help it. Somebody called the sheriff's office and informed us about one of his campers. The guy has a criminal record. He's still down there, so I have to interview him."

"What kind of criminal record?"

He grimaced. "For murder. He was charged, but the jury didn't convict him. They didn't think the prosecutor proved his case to the point where there wasn't any reasonable doubt. I read the case files. To be truthful, it was shoddy police work. At least, that's how it looked to me.

He claimed it was self-defense, but the problem was the man he killed he had had problems with before. He had made threats."

"But what motive would he have to kill Doc?" I wondered aloud.

"I don't know, but it looks like he knew Doc. This man's name is Harvey Pemberton. His family had a business in one of those deserted shops in Willis. It was a hardware store. He moved away from here years ago. He's about seventy, but he was born and grew up here."

I sighed. "What a mess!" I looked up at Brad, a troubled expression on my features. "What am I supposed to do with this gardening journal? I don't know if your aunt could deal with this revelation. She's taking Doc's death hard."

"If I had my way, I'd say burn it," Brad retorted. "You know, when I asked you to marry me, I thought I wanted to protect you, take care of you, and love you. Instead, here I have dragged you in on another murder case. And if that isn't bad enough, you must discover that my grandfather killed his daughter." He rubbed his temples with his fingers. "I feel like somebody has punched me in the stomach."

"Well, if it's any consolation to you, since the good Lord seems to place me in the direct path of all these murders and evil characters, this is where I'm supposed to be right now. The truth is, I can handle it if I have God and you. The kids and Alaina help, but it's not the same. Knowing that I am not going through this alone makes all the difference. Because God gave me you- I can deal with it."

A slow smile spread across my dear fiancé's face. He grabbed me to him again. "I just don't want to lose you because of all this mess." He whispered against my hair.

"The way things are going, if I quit being with people who never got me involved with murders, I wouldn't have many friends left," I said teasingly. "Seriously, Brad, I'm not going anywhere." I gestured towards the jars. "What do you want me to do with this?"

"Go ahead and read them if you want. I will have to decide if Aunt Lillian needs to know this about her father. I don't think she cared much for him, but she's eighty-two and has had one bad shock with Doc dying. Now, I'm going to have to tell her he may have been killed by a fellow born here. I don't know how much she can handle."

The door opened downstairs, and I heard Alaina's voice, "Mom! Is anybody home?"

I startled. "Is it that late? Alaina wasn't supposed to be here before evening."

Brad checked his watch. "Four o'clock. I've got to go too. Don't wait up for me, because I probably won't get to see you until tomorrow. I'm going down to the RV Park to check out Mr. Pemberton, and then I'm going to Doc's place. Maybe I can dig up something useful in them about Harvey Pemberton. It will take a lot of time to go through them all, but it has to be done. I'm glad we covered everything in the warrant, or we'd have to apply for another one. At least there's no one to complain. Doc was the last member of his family."

I frowned. "Who inherits then?"

Brad shrugged. "I'll have to look for a will while I'm in his house. Knowing Doc, he may not have had one."

"That sounds about like him," I agreed. "Well, just get back here when you can."

He grimaced. "I'm sorry, Love, I'm so busy right now. Where are you all this weekend?"

"At Willis Community," I informed him.

He raised his eyebrows. "How did that come about?"

"We had a revival canceled due to a death in the church, so Lillian called her pastor, who had heard our music when some wonderful guy gave him a CD and suggested that Willis Community would be our home church."

Brad grinned. "Wonderful guy, huh?"

I grinned back. "Don't let it go to your head."

CHAPTER SIX

The next few days were busy. Doc had prearranged his funeral, so service was held for him in the Willis Community Church as soon as the coroner released his body. Doc had planned everything; the choice of hymns, even the color and type of flowers he wanted on top of his casket. He loved roses, so a beautiful spray of red roses blanketed his coffin—the church filled with people and blooms. Doc had been a part of the community's life for nearly three generations and was well-loved. We all went to the service, and I got to check out the church we would be singing in on the weekend.

Sunday was a beautiful spring day. All of us arrived at the church early. Brad helped Joseph carry in all our musical equipment. Joseph always forbade Ashley from carrying anything.

I adored the interior of the big brick church. The original floors and walls were made of beautiful wood. There was an organ that appeared to have been there for years. The enormous stained glass window in the front of the church behind the choir box and pulpit displayed its brilliant colors with the sun shining through it. The stained glass was a picture of Christ, the good Shepherd, and He was holding a lamb in His arms.

Pastor Don showed me around the church with evident pride. In the foyer, a large plaque hung with the names of significant benefactors. He pointed out the Edwards' names-Albert, William, and Ernest. The original building had been erected shortly before the Civil War. It was rebuilt and restored around the turn of the twentieth century. I tried to suppress a cringe when I saw Ernest Edward's name. No money would erase the fact that he had willfully murdered his daughter, in my opinion. I noticed happily that Dr. Graham Masters and Doctor Arthur Masters were also listed. The pastor caught where I was looking and said sadly.

"We will miss Doc. He has been a part of this church for so long. He was always here and always had a part. He was a trustee and a board member for years and years. Everybody loved him."

"Somebody didn't," I said ruefully.

The pastor nodded. "I'm sure whoever did that horrible deed will be swiftly found. Our police are good. I wouldn't want you to think that we have a lot of violence around here. Not since the Civil War, anyway. I have made quite a study of the history of this area."

"I enjoy history," I shared.

He seemed pleased. "Maybe the wife and I could have you and Brad over to the parsonage and discuss it. I have a few books in my library detailing this church's history and the county's. You might want to borrow some of them."

The guys had finished setting up, and I went up on the platform to join the others and test the sound.

The cathedral-style ceiling gave the building good acoustics. We should sound well. Brad stood in the back of the church with the pastor to listen.

Aunt Lillian arrived later, electing to drive her car to church. Alaina, who greatly liked her, had traveled in with her.

I regarded my daughter from the platform. She wore matching blue pumps, a silver cross necklace, and earrings in a lovely lightweight blue suit with a white blouse.

Johnny Whitlock arrived right after her, and it was pretty evident he was attracted to her. Lillian introduced her, and in a few minutes, they talked together like they had known each other forever. I grimaced. I hoped Johnny was a good guy. Brad liked him. He always had, but I was a mother, and my standards for my daughter might be superior to his.

The pastor's wife, Elsie Franks, came sweeping in the door and directly to me. "Jo, about today; I couldn't believe it when the Reverend told me we could get you this Sunday. I was certain we would have to wait months. I put the announcement on social media and called everyone I could think of. We should have record attendance." She turned and surveyed the congregation critically. "I see your daughter has come too. She is such a pretty woman. You must be so proud."

Her exuberance was infectious. I found myself getting excited about the service.

"We're glad to be able to come," I said graciously.

"And I see your Brad back there talking to everyone. You know, I have a wonderful idea. Now that Doc has passed, poor dear, we have a vacancy on the church board. I think Brad would make a wonderful addition. I must remember to mention that to the Reverend."

She hurried away as if the thought would leave her before she could tell her husband. I wondered if she ever referred to the pastor by his first name and grinned.

It was time for the service to start, and I sat with my family in the front pew, which was our custom. Brad came up and sat beside me with his arm around the back of my bench. Alaina had stayed back with Aunt Lillian. I had noticed before I was seated that Johnny Whitlock had managed to find a spot in the same pew as Lillian and Alaina. Forceful man, I thought.

I turned my attention to the service. It was a more formal setting with responsive readings, the Gloria Patria, the Apostles Creed, and the Doxology. The organ music filled every nook and corner of the building. I liked it. We did all kinds of denominations in our singing ministry, and the different worship styles interested me.

When the pastor turned the platform over to our group, I put murders, weddings, and Alaina, out of my mind and concentrated on presenting God's Word in the words of a song.

Forty-five minutes later, we had completed our program to a standing ovation from the audience.

Joseph, Ashley, and I exchanged glances. It does give one a good feeling, but I was always careful to give praise to the Lord and not to us.

I talked to the congregation as they walked out the front door. Brad stood beside me and conversed with everyone too. Joseph and Ashley took care of the product table. I was not too fond of sales, but Joseph and Ashley were great at it, especially Joseph. When Lillian and Alaina came by me, I noticed that Johnny Whitlock was walking right behind them.

"I've asked Johnny to go with us out to eat," Lillian informed me. "I thought we'd go into Morrisville if that were okay with you and the kids. You've cooked so much lately. I thought it would give you a break."

"That's fine. I'm sure everyone will enjoy that. I don't think anyone made any other plans."

"I've invited the Pastor and his wife as well," Lillian continued. "I'm sorry, Jo. I hope I haven't overstepped. I'm so used to being on the planning committee here at church I got a little carried away."

I laughed. "It's okay, Aunt Lillian. I'm always ready to go out and eat. We usually eat out a lot."

She smiled. "That's all right then."

It made a large party at the restaurant, and we had to wait about thirty minutes before we were ushered to our table. Lillian had chosen a good restaurant, and we all enjoyed it. Johnny Whitlock had managed to snag a seat beside Alaina. I noticed Joseph was observing him closely. He never missed much. I felt assured Alaina was in for some questions when we got home. Sure enough, Joseph said he and Ashley would ride back with Lillian leaving Brad and me together.

Brad had been paying attention too. "I think Alaina has someone interested in her," he commented.

"I noticed. Does Johnny Whitlock always go to that church, or was he there because we were?"

Brad regarded me carefully. "That sounds like skepticism. Don't you like Johnny?"

I shrugged. "I don't know Johnny. He seems okay. I'm just a little overprotective, where Alaina is concerned. I don't want her to get hurt."

"Alaina's a big girl. She can make her own decisions." Brad sounded decisive.

"I know, but I'm her mother."

He patted my hand. "I think Alaina can take care of herself; if she can't, Joseph will take care of her. I imagine she's being teased about Johnny about now."

I half smiled. "Oh, Joseph was noticing, all right."

Back at the house, Alaina was looking a little harassed. "Are you all right?" I asked her.

"I'm fine. And don't you start." My usually calm blonde daughter was slightly heated. "I've heard enough about it from Joseph."

"Was he giving you a hard time about Johnny Whitlock?" I questioned innocently.

Her blue eyes snapped at me. "Mom, don't act like you don't know what I'm talking about. Just because I'm talking to some man does not mean I'm going to run off with him."

"I should hope not. You barely know the man."

She pointed her finger at me. "Mom, I mean it. End of discussion."

"Yes, madam," I said meekly.

Of course, none of us were surprised when Johnny Whitlock showed up that evening, and the two of them walked down to the gazebo and sat down there and talked until dusk.

"What do they have to talk about?" Joseph grumbled. "They've been down there forever. It's not like they even know each other."

"I imagine that's why they're talking-getting to know each other," Brad informed him.

"Well, I don't know that I like some man being after Mom." Joseph declared firmly. "I'd like to know more about him, myself."

"I think she's old enough not to need your permission," Brad returned. I saw Joseph's face and decided to take the temperature down a degree or two.

"Joseph, your mom's got good instincts. She may not even be interested if she gets to know Johnny."

"Your mom has always had good sense," Ashley interjected. "She never interfered with us. Let's step back from this."

Joseph relaxed slightly. "I'm still going to keep an eye on him."

Lillian came into the room as he spoke. "My friend, Lora Hutchins, is coming over tomorrow to help us go through some more stuff. I don't think we need her, but she volunteered, and I didn't have the heart to tell her no. She's a somewhat irritating woman, but she has been a friend for years. Plus, she's a hard worker."

"How irritating?" Joseph wanted to know.

Lillian frowned. "She's one of those people who will get in your face and tell you you're wrong if she thinks you are. She's got a little too much of a holier-than-thou attitude."

Joseph was looking disgusted. "Ashley and I were planning on staying, but maybe we should go back with Mom. She's going back to work."

"I could use your help, Joseph," Lillian told him. "I can handle Lora. I don't let her browbeat me."

I sighed. It looked like tomorrow was going to be another interesting day.

And it was! Alaina hugged me and started home very early the following day.

Much to Joseph and Ashley's disgust, Lora showed up at seven in the morning, ready to go to work. I had been awakened early by Brad's phone call. He always called before he left for work. He warned me that he would probably be back late that night.

I went upstairs to find Joseph, Ashley, and Lillian working in the kids' bedroom. Lora was organizing everything. A short, fat woman with cropped gray hair, she pressed her lips in a firm, stern line that made one think this woman would not take nonsense. Her blue eyes were set a little too close together, and overall, she looked unpleasant.

"I don't know how you've all been managing," she said in her high-pitched voice. "I have never seen such a lack of organization. I would have never believed it of you, Lillian. You organize perfectly for the church, but this house is junked up full of stuff you plainly don't need."

Lillian observed her mildly. "It's my life, Lora. I can keep what I want."

"Well, all I can say is it's a good thing this is happening now and not waiting until after you die to leave it for these poor children to look after." She shook her grey head in disgust.

"It's my life, Lora, and I'll thank you for keeping your opinions to yourself." Lillian's voice had an edge.

"Well," she pouted. "If you want me to leave, you only have to say so. I've got other things to do."

Lillian sighed. "It's okay, Lora. We'll get it done. Some of this stuff can stay here in an empty bedroom. I can't take everything. I know that."

Joseph decided to be kind. "If we all work together, I'm sure everything will go smoothly."

Lora surveyed him and the closet and drawers skeptically. "It's going to be a job." She stared at Joseph. "You're probably not used to hard work, traveling around singing all the time."

I intervened. "Joseph does a lot of the driving and the carrying in and out of equipment. I think you will find him used to hard work. There's much more to this than just getting up and singing."

"Well, I'm sure I wouldn't know about that, but I've been talking to the women at my beauty shop, and they had never heard of your gospel group. You said Sunday that you had been singing for twenty years and composed your own songs. Somebody asked me how come you have never had a hit song or sung with big groups in convention centers. They said they would have heard of you if you were anybody important."

I could tell Joseph was ready to pounce, and I raised my hand to forestall him.

"We don't care about being celebrities. We have chosen to stay in the church world. We are about ministry, not number one songs or singing in big auditoriums." I said tersely. "Believe me; I have worked harder traveling around this country singing than doing anything else in my life. We're not on vacation; we're working."

"I always found I needed a vacation after traveling," Aunt Lillian piped up.

"I wouldn't know about that. I never had a lot of time for vacations," Lora replied. "I had to work, and then I had Mother and Father to care for until they died."

"As far as that goes, I took care of my mother, too." Lillian volunteered.

"At least I didn't let mine fall down the steps." Lora retorted. "I'm not saying that was your fault Lillian, but it was terrible that no one did anything to stop her from climbing the stairs in the first place."

I thought Lillian would throw her out on that remark, but she merely replied.

"If you knew my mother like I did, you would know she did whatever she wanted, including going up and down the stairs." Her hand rose and fell. "I remember one time I wanted to go on a Ferris wheel at the fair, and my grandmother, Christine, said I shouldn't. It wasn't safe. I might fall out while it was up in the air. Mother said, 'well if she falls out doing something she wanted to do, she will die happy.'" She looked at us with defiance. "I got to ride the Ferris wheel. It was the first time and not the last."

"I like roller coasters myself," Ashley confided shyly. "And so does Joseph."

"Mom and Mamaw always let me ride them," Joseph confirmed. "The higher they are, the better I like them."

"I'd think there were more important things to do than ride on cheap thrills," Lora said, pulling everything out of the dresser drawers and placing it all on the bed.

"I think everyone needs to take time to enjoy life," Lillian replied. "We all don't like to do the same things."

"I think everybody needs to concentrate on being more holy myself," Lora answered. "I'd think we'd all be better off if we prayed more and read the Bible more. You can't be in church seven days a week, but you can read and pray seven days a week. I try to become more holy every week."

"And are you? Becoming more holy every week, I mean?" Joseph asked.

She glared at him. "I'm pretty sure you are being sarcastic, which I don't think is very Christ-like at all!"

Lillian intervened this time. "Oh, Lora, I'm sure we're all aware of how holy you think you are. I'm surprised the Lord hasn't taken you to Heaven to sing with the angels by now."

Lora looked abashed for a moment. "I can't sing," she admitted.

Lillian got to her feet and put her hand on Joseph's shoulder. "Joseph, I need you to help me pack up my car. I called the apartment manager this morning, and my place is ready to be occupied. I want to take a load over there today. It will free up some space." She turned to face Lora. "As for you, my dear, I suggest you go at once and take singing lessons. You need to be prepared. I think the rest of us are done for today."

She started out the door, and the three of us followed her, praying to hold in our laughter until we got outside.

I helped Joseph and Ashley carry out boxes and place them in Lillian's car. Lora left right after them. Ashley stayed with me while Joseph drove Aunt Lillian to Morrisville to her new apartment. The day was comfortable-weather-wise. Ashley wore white shorts, and I wore navy capris with a red and navy top. I had decided I had quite enough of Lora Hutchins.

"Let's walk down and look at this campground of Johnny Whitlock's," I suggested

Ashley and I walked mostly in silence for a few minutes.

I felt her glance over at me. "Do you think Joseph's Mom is interested in Johnny Whitlock? Is that why you wanted to walk down here?" she asked.

I laughed. "I don't know." I was treating the subject more casually than I felt.

"There wouldn't be anything wrong in it if she were."

Ashley was staring straight ahead. "I didn't mean that. I know Joseph is a little upset about it. I think he thinks things are fine the way they are."

"In that case, he must be perturbed with my marrying Brad."

She smiled shyly at me. "Oh, no, Joseph thinks a lot of Brad. It's just this is his mother."

"Well, I'm his grandmother. I want to think he cares about me."

"He does, Mamaw. It's just different with his mother."

"Joseph doesn't like to think about someone finding his mother attractive." I slipped my arm through hers. "It will all work out the way it is supposed to."

The campground was within sight. A big white sign in dark green letters read Cherokee River Park, owned and operated by Johnny Whitlock. I could see a police car parked in front of the office.

As we approached, raised voices reached our ears. Two men were standing beside the vehicle. One of them was Brad. The other man was older. He was overweight, and from my vantage point, his face was red and breathing heavily. He was swinging his arms, and I could tell he was agitated even from a distance.

"I'm not putting up with it," the stranger shouted. "I know how you police operate. I've been through it before. I wasn't guilty then, and I'm not guilty now. This is nothing but police harassment."

I couldn't hear Brad's answer, but he seemed to have himself under control. If he noticed me coming, he showed no evidence of it.

Brad's hand was on the door handle of the cruiser. "If we have more questions, we know how to reach you, Mr. Pemberton. We appreciate your cooperation. You are free to go."

"You can forget about cooperation. You upset my wife something awful. You can talk to my lawyer if you have any more questions." He stomped back into the campground.

Brad watched him go and then turned to us.

"Hello, ladies."

"Hi. So that is Mr. Pemberton."

"Yeah, that's Harvey Pemberton."

"He seemed to be pretty upset," I commented.

Brad grimaced. "He is. I had to question him. He didn't like it. His wife liked it less. She cried and went on until I had to ask to talk to him outside their fifth wheel. He walked back with me and expressed himself very forcibly about his opinion of me and the entire police force. He said he and his wife had made friends in this park, and what were people to think when the police showed up questioning them."

"In other words-what, what will the neighbors think?" I guessed.

Brad nodded. "Are you girls out seeing the sights, or was there a purpose in your walking down here."

"Joseph has taken a carload of your aunt's boxes to her new apartment. Ashley and I had had about all we could stand from your aunt's friend, Lora Hutchins."

"I've met her before. That's the holy one, right?" There was a twinkle in Brad's gray eyes.

"So she says," I answered calmly. "I have my doubts."

"I distrust anyone who has to advertise their holiness," Brad said shortly.

"Can I ask you if you think this Harvey Pemberton is guilty of killing Doc?"

He shook his head. "I don't know. He's got a bad enough temper, but I don't know what motive he would have. He said he hadn't given Doc a thought in years-didn't even know the man was still alive. He just remembered the river, and when they saw an advertisement, he thought he'd like to come back to the area and spend a few days." He rubbed the side of his face, and I wondered if he was getting a headache. "That could be true. I'm going back to Doc's house. Another officer is meeting me there, and we'll secure Doc and his father's medical files. They'll be safe at the sheriff's office, and I might find something to tie Pemberton to this. I don't know if we will find anything, but we have no right to hold Harvey now. There's no evidence. He's going to stay here for a few more days. I've got all his information."

The door to the office opened, and Johnny Whitlock strolled down the steps to where we were standing.

"Are you done stirring up all my campers," He asked Brad. "Mr. Pemberton came in the office this morning blustering and mad."

Brad had folded his arms across his chest. "He's got a temper. I know I made him mad, but it's my job to find out the truth. I want Doc's killer. I can't help it that Pemberton's got a record. I have to check him out under the circumstances."

Johnny nodded. "I know. You are just doing your job. It's okay. Just don't cost me any more business than you can help." He turned to Ashley and me. "Alaina get back all right?"

"Yes," I answered shortly, and he grinned. He had a cute grin. "You've got a pretty daughter, Mrs. Elliott."

"I think so," I said coolly. Johnny went back to talking to Brad, and I surveyed him closely. He looked close to Alaina's age. His brown hair curled neatly back. His face and arms were suntanned, and he had a tall, slim look. His eyes were puppy dog brown, and there were laugh lines on his face around his mouth and eyes. He looked easygoing.

Ashley hadn't said anything, but I knew she wanted to go from the looks she had darted at me.

I said loudly. "We're going back to the house, Brad."

Brad smiled. "Okay, Jo. I'll see you tonight."

They were still talking when we started back up the highway. I glanced back through the campground. It was laid out neatly and, at the moment, had quite a few campers and RVs. I noticed a bathhouse and laundry room, and it looked like the other building was the clubhouse. If the parked trailers were any indication, it looked like the Cherokee River Park was thriving. I imagined a lot of thought had gone into putting the place together.

Lora came back after Lillian and Joseph returned but left before supper. She said she had to get home and feed her husband. Lillian, who saw her out the door, raised her eyes toward the ceiling and murmured, "Thank God!" She didn't notice me standing in a doorway, and I silently slipped back into the kitchen to hide a potential giggle.

Brad was late that night. I had gone up in the turret. Alaina had brought over my rocker, and I had settled in it and picked up the gardening journals. I continued to read. I had dragged a lamp up the stairs. The turret was all unpainted wood on the roof, but the wood was beautiful. The walls were wood also, and the windows undraped and open. The floor had the same plank wood. I liked being surrounded by all that wood. Someone had installed a white ceiling fan at some time, and it had a whining sound that was rather soothing. I flipped through some pages looking for something more interesting than gardening advice.

Near the end of a page, I found some writing in a different pen.

"I don't know how much more I can take. If I didn't have the garden to occupy my mind, I would have gone crazy by now. I talked to Doc Graham and told him I was having trouble sleeping. He wanted to give me some pills, but I didn't want to start doing that. I told him I would get by somehow.

All Ernest and I do anymore is argue. It's not good for the kids. They either go outside or go to their rooms to escape it. I caught Violet sobbing in her room, lying on the floor, just shaking. I got her in bed and sat beside her for a good while. She told me she just wanted to run away from home. I asked her where she would go, and she said anywhere her father wasn't.

I don't know what I would do if it weren't for Doc Graham. His son, Arthur, came home from medical school the other day. He seems like a fine young man. He helped me bring in the firewood. It was so cold, and the snow was peppering down. Eugene was trying to help, but he's still little.

I don't have to worry about Ernest helping. He won't. I can't talk to anybody at church, not even the Pastor and his wife. They all think Ernest is wonderful. He is faithful to the church, generous with his money, and an upstanding citizen. Little do they know what a devil he is at the house! Nobody but Doc would ever believe me if I told him what he was really like. I try to keep the children away from him as much as possible. As it is, he slaps them around.

The other night, Violet spilled her milk at the supper table. Ernest slapped her over the head. She never shed a tear, just dropped her head and stared at her plate—poor little thing. I have no family who would take me in. I'm stuck here."

I looked up and outside at the growing darkness. As much as I liked this house, it had certainly not been a happy home when Brad's dad and Lillian grew up here. I felt so sorry for children that didn't have the advantage of a loving home and parents. I wondered what I would have done if I had been in an abusive marriage with a man who mistreated my children. I was finding it difficult to imagine. Josh had always been so good with Alaina. He had been a good father. Alaina's husband, Tim, had been excellent with Joseph. What little I knew of Ashley's parents made me think they were good people. It must be terrible to live in that fear and hopelessness.

I looked at my phone. It was nine o'clock. I heard the front door open and sat quietly, waiting for Brad to come searching for me.

He entered the turret in a few minutes, and I rose to my feet, and we held each other silently for a few minutes.

"I found some more of your grandmother's notes. Her desperation for her children and her fear for them is awful. I can't imagine living like that year after year." I informed him.

"He was an old devil by all accounts," Brad said quietly.

"I've been trying to imagine what I would do in that situation."

"Back then, there weren't any choices."

"From what she says, everybody else thought he was wonderful," I told him. "That would make it harder."

"A street angel and a house devil, I guess," Brad said bitterly.

I sat back in the rocker, and he stood against the wall, his arms folded.

"Well, we had to bring Harvey Pemberton in tonight for questioning. We suggested he not leave town for the moment. Johnny's not a happy camper."

"You found something?"

"Yeah, Doc and his father kept very detailed notes. Doc wrote that Harvey Pemberton had threatened Doc that he would kill him if he caught him around his house again.

This wife he has now is a second wife. Harvey was living here with his first wife, and she complained to Doc that her husband was abusing her and she was afraid of him. Doc went to try to talk to him, and he threatened him with a shotgun. There was a scene in downtown Willis on the street, and Mr. Pemberton was going to knock Doc down. Some other guys got involved and protected the doctor. Doc wouldn't press charges, and that was that. The Pemberton's moved away then, but not before people had stopped going to his dad's hardware store. He ended up closing the store, and apparently, Harvey Pemberton blamed Doc for slandering his family, so they lost their business. It's all in black and white. I feel sorry for this wife, but we had to question him."

"Do you think he did it?" I asked.

Brad shrugged. "I don't know, Jo. It fits. He could have held a grudge that long, I guess. I want more evidence that he was at Doc's place. It's early days. We'll figure it out."

I was to remember that later.

CHAPTER SEVEN

Lora Hutchins returned the next day to give us her
"help." She never stopped talking and criticized everything
Lillian, Joseph, and Ashley did. She had a better plan, an
improved idea for everything.

I escaped to the garden where the flower beds were
growing. Lillian had shown me how to fertilize and mulch
everything. That was keeping me busy. It also made Lillian
happy as she could not keep up with it and still pack up
her things

I ventured back into the house when hunger pangs
overcame me. I could hear raised voices standing outside
on the back porch. It sounded like it was tense in the place.

I entered the den to find Lillian sitting in a Queen
Anne chair, looking through papers, and ignoring what
was happening around her. Lora was expressing herself forcefully, and Joseph was getting heated. Ashley
watched him, ready to intervene and defend her husband
if necessary.

"What's going on?" I asked on entering the room.

Lillian never looked up, but Lora turned in my direction, and I could see her face was red. I hated to think about what her blood pressure numbers were.

"I have just been explaining to your family how awful I think it is that the police are harassing poor Harvey and Dotty Pemberton down at the campground. They have gone so far as to question the poor man just because he was charged with murder years ago, and they are at it again today. He was acquitted, so it is obvious to me that they made a mistake and are making another one now. I said I couldn't help it if you were marrying Brad Edwards; I think they are just persecuting that poor man."

I frowned. "Do you know the Pemberton's?"

"Of course, I know Harvey Pemberton. I grew up with him. I'm a little older than him, but I remember him. I was best friends with one of his sisters, Elizabeth. We were friends until she passed away."

"And I said Brad and the sheriff's department would not be questioning him if they didn't have good reason to suspect him," Joseph said.

Lora looked at Joseph like she didn't like what she was seeing. "Just because Doc Matthews left some papers detailing the problems between his family and the Pemberton's doesn't mean anything. If we went around arresting everybody for having problems with people, all of us would be in jail."

I stared at Joseph and knew it was on the edge of his tongue to ask her if she had problems with anyone since she was so holy. I shook my head, and he remained silent.

"I don't know the Pemberton's," I admitted. "But I did get to know Doc, and I liked him a lot."

"I did not quarrel with Doc," Lora said. "I try to get along with everyone. I think that's what a good Christian should do. If I have a problem with someone, I go to them just like the Bible says." She finished filling a box and sealed it with tape. "I intend to stop by the campground before I go home this evening and see the Pemberton's. Of course, I don't know her, but I knew all his family, so I thought maybe I could comfort her. She has no one else around here. She doesn't come from here. And it would be wonderful to see Harvey again."

"That's very nice of you," I commented mildly.

That seemed to satisfy her, and we talked about other things.

Joseph followed me into the kitchen, where I started fixing sandwiches for lunch.

"I'm surprised someone hasn't smothered that woman," he said in a low tone. "She has about driven me crazy this morning. I don't know how Aunt Lillian stands her. She never stops talking, and it's all about how wonderful Lora Hutchins is."

"I think Lillian just ignores her," I said dryly.

"She's hard to ignore." Joseph returned.

Lillian came into the kitchen and rolled her eyes. "Do you think God would forgive me if I say I don't know how somebody hasn't murdered that poor old woman?"

I looked at both of them. "Have you left poor Ashley in there to deal with her?"

Joseph appeared horrified and left the room.

Lillian sat down at the table, and I handed her a ham sandwich with lettuce, tomato, and mayo. The potato chips were on the table, and I poured her a glass of iced tea.

"Has she always been like she is now?" I asked, slicing more tomatoes and preparing more sandwiches.

Lillian's hand rose and fell. "I think she's getting worse. I went to school with her. She was what we called a tattle-tale. She was always reporting everybody to the teacher. She still runs to the preacher when she hears anything she thinks shouldn't be. The pastor's wife won't answer the phone when she sees Lora's number, but don't say I said so." She sighed. "She's always liked to know things about everybody, and if anybody can dig up dirt, I'd say Lora was the best at it. When we were children, if she learned anything about us that we didn't want our parents or teachers to know about, she made a point of letting us know she knew."

"I'm surprised you're friends with her if she aggravates you this much," I commented.

Lillian got a look. "The truth of the matter is I feel sorry for her. The friends she has had in the past have dropped her. I'm probably the only friend the woman has. She's really to be pitied."

Joseph and Ashley came in together and sat down at the table.

"Is Lora eating with us?" I asked.

Joseph shrugged. "I asked her, but she said she was on a roll, and if we didn't keep at it, we would never get done before August."

"She thinks we take too many breaks," Ashley informed me. "She says it's unnecessary to go into detail about where everything came from and who gave it to you."

"Well, maybe we can eat in peace," Lillian suggested reaching for the chips. "She has been unusually trying this morning."

It was a cloudy day, and the house was comfortable, so I decided to help inside. There were a few dishes in the large china cabinet that Lillian wanted to take with her. I was carefully packing them in newspaper and placing them in a box. Lillian and Lora were in Lillian's office library. I told Joseph and Ashley to take a break, and they walked down to the river. How much more could Joseph stand of Lora Hutchins?

As days do, this one passed. Lora promised us she would return in the morning, and we gratefully watched her go out the front door. We all breathed a sigh of relief.

"Can't you tell her we don't need her or something?" Joseph asked Lillian.

"I may have to," that woman replied. "She was starting to agitate me this morning when she started in on the police, especially when she was talking about Brad."

"Did she say more about Brad than what I heard?" I questioned.

"Oh, she was really against him," Ashley assured me. "She said she didn't know what a nice woman like you would be doing marrying a policeman."

"And then she asked if you weren't a lot older than Brad?" Joseph put in. "I asked her what that had to do with anything, and she said she wouldn't do it. She would be afraid that a younger husband would look for a younger wife when she got old."

Now, my temper was beginning to rise. "Brad's not that kind of man," I said flatly.

There was a half-smile on Lillian's face. "I'm surprised her husband hasn't found someone else instead of putting up with her."

"I would," declared Joseph. "I'm certain it wouldn't be holy, but I couldn't stand that."

We all laughed.

The next day was no better, except that Lora told us she had to leave promptly at noon. She had promised Dotty Pemberton she would have lunch with them. Apparently, her mission of mercy had been well received.

"Dotty is just a wonderful person," Lora informed us. "I don't know what the problem was with his first wife, and

Dotty didn't seem to want to discuss it, but I would say Harvey did well for himself this time."

"Did Harvey remember you?" Lillian asked.

Her face beamed. "Oh, yes! He was very pleased to see me. He remembered Elizabeth and me being friends. I told him that everyone here did not think he did this horrible thing."

"Do the police still think he killed Doc?" I asked.

She stared at me. "I don't know what the police think. Since you're engaged to Brad, you would know more than I would about that."

"Brad doesn't tell me everything," I said quietly.

"Well, they were both glad to hear that some of us still believed in innocent until proven guilty. They went through a terrible time when Harvey was charged with murder all those years ago. I said I didn't know what to think of a system where they would try to find you guilty a second time just because they thought you were guilty once." Lora tossed her head defiantly.

"I think it would stand to reason that if you had a record of being charged with one murder, and another one turned up where you were, it would be logical that the police might want to look at you," Joseph reasoned.

"If he had been found guilty, but it doesn't make sense to me that they would immediately center in on him just because he was charged. He was found innocent." Lora proclaimed as a matter of fact.

"I think it was more than that," I intervened. "There were the files Doc had that described the threats and problems between Doc and Mr. Pemberton. I think the police justified questioning him since he was on the scene when Doc was murdered."

"Nobody saw Harvey at Doc's house," Lora argued. "I was here at the cookout. Several people went over to check on Doc that evening. You went over there yourself, Jo, I am told. Would you want people to say you killed him?"

Joseph whirled around to face the older woman. "There better not be anyone saying anything like that about my Mamaw. She thought a lot of Doc. We all did."

Lora wasn't backing down. "Then you can understand why I don't like anybody accusing my friends falsely too."

I slipped to Joseph's side and whispered that he and Ashley might want to return to the river before he said something he regretted. I watched them slip out while Lillian responded to Lora.

"Oh, you don't even know Mrs. Pemberton," Lillian said with feeling.

"I may not know her well, but when I visited their fifth wheel, it was like we had known each other forever." Lora snapped back. "And Harvey and Dotty made it clear I was welcome there anytime I felt like coming."

"I suggest we let the police sort it out," Lillian said mildly. "I'm sure they know what they're doing."

"I doubt that very much," Lora responded. "Between catching up yesterday, we talked about old times, and

Harvey shared some things with me. The Pemberton's weren't the only people around here that had some issues with the Masters. And last night after supper, when I was thinking it over, I believe I may know some things that may point in a different direction. I'm not one to gossip, so I'm not going into it, but Doc may not have been as lily-white as you all think."

Lillian got to her feet and towered over the shorter woman. "I don't want to hear any more about it. Doc was my best friend, and Brad is my nephew. I have no doubt he is a fair and competent deputy. I don't like anybody accusing my family either, Lora." Her tone was firm.

The color was rising on Lora's face. "Well, I'm sure anyone would take up for their own family, Lillian. All I'm saying is that there may be more to the story."

"There's more to most stories than what gets told," Lillian reminded her. "Let's get busy. This fussing isn't getting anything done."

Lora left promptly at noon. Lillian followed me into the kitchen and watched me make toasted cheese sandwiches for everybody.

"Well, at least we won't have to put up with Lora the rest of the day," Lillian said. "Have the kids come back from the river? I saw you whispering to Joseph and figured you had rescued Joseph."

"Not yet," I replied. "Joseph needed to cool off. He was getting angry."

"Joseph is very protective of you," Lillian commented. "I liked seeing that."

"Well, he's my only grandchild, and we work together, so we are close."

"He's a good singer and guitar player. I meant to tell you how well I thought you did on Sunday." She got a look on her face. "I was proud of all of you and that you would be part of my family. But don't tell Lora. I'm sure that pride is a sin. I'm not feeling too holy today."

I grinned at her. "I think it says a lot about you that you haven't refused to be her friend. I'm not sure I could have done that."

Lillian's hand rose and fell. It was a gesture I saw her do quite often. "I tune her out half the time. That probably helps."

I sat down at the table with the toasted cheese sandwiches. "Do you think Lora knows something about Doc's murder, or was she just trying to make herself sound important?"

"Who knows? She can find out things. She talks so much, you can't imagine how she has time to listen, but she has been known to solve some minor mysteries."

"Such as?"

"Oh, like who stole the apples out of one of the orchards or who was shoplifting at the Pemberton Hardware. Simple stuff like that." Lillian bit into her sandwich as she spoke.

I frowned. "This is a whole lot more serious than that. We're talking about murder. Someone did kill Doc. If she goes around hinting that she knows something, the real culprit may believe her, and she could be a target."

"I doubt that she knows anything," Lillian said. "She would just like us to think so."

Joseph and Ashley came back in, and all of us decided to give the house a rest, and we went to the backyard. Joseph and Ashley helped carry the bags of mulch, and I spread it on the beds I had weeded. Lillian pulled up a lawn chair in the shade, sat, and watched us. It was a peaceful afternoon, and even though we were working, it was relaxing. The gardens were shaping up nicely. I was learning what all the plants were and feeling more confident about caring for them.

"After reading some of your mother's gardening journals, I am more interested in growing all these flowers," I informed Lillian.

She had her eyes closed, resting, but now those fine grey eyes opened to stare at me. "Oh, are you reading them? I had put them out of my mind."

"I've read some of them. You were right. It was mostly gardening."

Lillian closed her eyes again. "That's what I imagined. Mother was an avid gardener. Father fussed about it, but it pleased him when people stopped and bragged about how beautiful everything was."

"She must have been a wonderful person."

113

"She was. She took a lot off of my father. Of course, back then, people never thought of getting a divorce, and she had us children, to think about. I remember the arguing quite well."

"Violet and Eugene probably felt the same way." I ventured, unsure of how far to travel on this path.

"None of us liked to be at home when Dad was here," Lillian told me.

"I'm surprised you love this house so much," I said.

She opened her eyes again and surveyed the grounds. "Well, I was only five or six when Dad died. Violet was a year ahead, and Eugene was two years older. We were all still small. Life was much easier after that, and Mother would have made any house a home."

I thought about that as I continued working. I imagined Brad was correct in not sharing what I had found in the journals. It didn't seem to me it would do any good and could cause significant harm.

It was nearly six o'clock before we quit for the day. Joseph and Ashley went upstairs to shower and change. I took a glass of tea and went up to the turret to sit and rock and survey our hard work to see if it met with my approval. I felt some pride in a job well done. I wondered if Grandma Rose had come up here after tending the gardens and sat contemplating her work. At least after her husband had died, she could do that in peace.

I heard the kids come out of the shower, and I went to get some clean clothes and shower myself. On the way to the bathroom, I heard Lillian's phone ring, but I ignored it.

When I came downstairs twenty minutes later to start fixing supper, I found her in the kitchen sitting stony-faced at the table. She didn't even realize I was there until I touched her shoulder.

"Aunt Lillian, are you all right?" I asked gently.

She looked up at me and back down to the table. "That was Pastor Franks," she said. She got up, went to the kitchen sink, and stared out the window.

"Did he want something?" I asked tentatively. She was acting oddly.

She turned to face me, and I noticed her face was gaunt, and her color wasn't good.

"He wanted me to know. They found Lora Hutchins dead in her car about a mile from her home."

I was shocked. "Did the poor woman have a car wreck?"

She shuddered. "No, someone smothered Lora with a pillow she had in the back seat!"

CHAPTER EIGHT

"Smothered!"

I saw Joseph and Ashley standing in the doorway. I knew from Joseph's face that he was thinking of how little he had liked the woman, and now she was dead.

My mind was on Doc. "Just like Doc," I said softly.

All three of them looked at me. Joseph and Ashley exchanged troubled glances, and Lillian said.

"Do you think it's related somehow to Doc, Jo?"

I shrugged. "I don't know, but if Dora were smothered….." My voice trailed off.

"Pastor Don didn't know many details." Lillian shared. "He just knew that she had had car trouble on her way home, or so she told her husband when she called him on her cell phone. He told her he'd come and get her, but when he got there, she was dead."

Lillian struggled to her feet and started towards the back door. "Don't bother fixing me any supper. I don't think I could eat right now." She went down the steps, and I watched her cross the yard towards the river from the kitchen window.

Joseph and Ashley sat down at the table.

"What are you thinking, Mamaw?" Joseph asked from behind me.

"I wonder if the two murders are tied together in some way," I answered him absently.

"But why would anybody want to kill her?" Ashley questioned. "I mean, I know she was difficult to like, but people don't get killed just because they're hard to like, do they?"

A faint smile touched my lips. "If they did, I'm afraid there would be many more murders."

Joseph raised one eyebrow. "What are you thinking, Mamaw? I can almost hear the wheels turning in that brain of yours?"

"Well, I'm wondering if she went to see the Pemberton's as planned and whether she talked about knowing something that might point to someone other than Harvey Pemberton. If that information got to the wrong person, and that person was guilty, he could have acted. Until now, Harvey Pemberton is the only one the police are looking at. No one was considering anyone else. That might threaten a guilty person." I surveyed my family closely. "We already know how people will react if they feel threatened. We saw that at Hoover last year."

Joseph grimaced. "All too well. And here we are again." He grinned at me. "I thought you didn't want to be involved in any more murders."

"I'm not involved. Well, in a way, I am," I amended my statement. "If it concerns Lillian, it concerns me because she is Brad's aunt. Doc was her best friend, and Lora was a friend, however disagreeable she could be. Aunt Lillian is going to take this hard. It's two blows close together."

"Well, maybe Brad will have some information for us when he gets home," Ashley said hopefully.

We ate a quick supper and went out on the front porch. Settling in the swing, I shared with Joseph and Ashley what I had found in Brad's grandmother's gardening journal. I hadn't had a chance to share it with them without Lillian being around.

Understandably, they were horrified.

"The man threw Rosemary down the stairs and broke her neck?" Joseph asked incredulously.

Ashley shuddered. "I'm going to think of that now every time I climb that beautiful staircase."

"Wasn't it investigated at the time?" Joseph asked.

I shook my head. "They treated it as accidental. I don't imagine the police were ever involved. Grandma Rose went to Doctor Graham Masters next door. He asked her what had happened, but she was too afraid of her husband to tell him the truth. I felt he may have suspected something, but he had nothing to go on, and she would never tell. She was pregnant at the time, and she lost the baby. It was far enough along that she knew it had been a little boy."

"She lost two children nearly the same time, didn't she?" Joseph said. "That would be rough."

"I don't know how she stood to live with him after that," Ashley observed.

"I don't think she wanted to, but divorce was still a bit of a disgrace in those days, and she had nowhere to go. Things have changed a lot since then. There are options for women now."

"Thank God!" Ashley breathed. "I know Joseph would never be like that, but if he were, I'd like to think I had a way of escape."

"You don't have to worry," Joseph informed her. "My mother and Mamaw would probably kill me for you."

We laughed together.

"I tell you what I am interested in around here," Joseph said, "is where that treasure is that Brad's great, great grandfather buried during the Civil War. Now, that interests me."

"Who told you about that?" I asked, knowing I had not.

"Aunt Lillian did," Ashley told me.

"Does she believe the story?" I asked her.

"She seems to. She said she and Violet, and Eugene used to search everywhere. It has yet to be found. So it's still here somewhere."

"I've been thinking about it," Joseph continued. "They probably hid it away from the house. That would be the first place the soldiers during the Civil War would search. I want to hunt some more if we ever get everything packed up and moved."

"Go for it," I encouraged him. "You'll never know unless you try. Of course, it may be just a story."

A few minutes later, Brad pulled up and parked in front of the garage. His eyes swept over us critically. "Have you heard the news?"

"Yeah, Pastor Don called Aunt Lillian," I told him. "Do you know any details?"

He sat down in the swing beside me. "I was one of the officers that went out on the call. Her husband notified us as soon as he found her. She had broken down on a lonely stretch of road. She was lucky she got her cell phone to work out there, but she did make a call. Between the times she called her husband, and when he got to her, someone else had stopped. Whoever did it was in a hurry. They didn't bother to throw the pillow in the back seat. She had put up quite a fight from the evidence, but whoever it was overpowered her. It looks like it could be a robbery gone wrong. Her purse was rifled through, and her husband said she was carrying a couple of hundred dollars. He said she liked to have cash on her. She didn't like bank cards. The money was gone."

"Is that what you think?" Joseph asked him.

"I don't know. I know Mrs. Hutchins has been here for the last couple of days. Should I be thinking of something else? Do you know something I don't?"

I took over. "Mrs. Hutchins implied today that she had some information that might involve someone other than Harvey Pemberton in the murder of Doc."

His eyes narrowed. "Did you believe Mrs. Hutchins? Did Aunt Lillian?"

"Aunt Lillian said Lora always liked to learn things about people and let them know she knew." I suspected my visage was troubled.

"That could make her a target to someone, all right," Brad commented. "Where is Aunt Lillian?"

"Down at the river, I think. Aunt Lillian may be at the gazebo. She wanted to be alone," I told him.

"I think I'll go talk to her." He reached for my hand and pulled me up beside him, and I followed him off the porch.

We found Lillian in the gazebo, staring out at the river. She was sitting serenely in the glider. She heard us approach and forced a smile when we walked inside the white summerhouse.

"Checking up on me?" she asked.

Brad sat beside her in the glider and put his arm around her. "Are you holding up? I know she was a friend of yours."

She grimaced. "I've been wondering how I'm supposed to feel. The poor thing didn't have many friends. She got on everybody's nerves with her holier-than-thou attitude. I guess I feel guilty that I don't feel as sad about Lora as I do Doc."

"It wasn't the same kind of friendship. You don't need to feel guilty at all." Brad assured her. "I've been around her enough to wonder why you were friends with her in the first place."

"I felt sorry for her, I guess," Lillian answered him.

"Her husband's the one I feel sorry for," Brad said bluntly. "The poor little man looked like he couldn't call his soul his own. I've never seen anybody as browbeaten as he was. He didn't even know how to answer questions without looking back at her to see what he was supposed to say."

"So they killed her the same way Doc was?" Lillian asked him.

He nodded. "It may be a robbery gone wrong. I told Jo and the kids that her money was gone out of her purse. It is a lonely stretch of road where her car broke down. There are no houses there; very little traffic and really nothing but trees."

"If it's that far off the beaten path, I suppose that means it was somebody local?" I queried.

Lillian and Brad exchanged glances. "Probably so," Brad admitted.

"So it could be the same person who murdered Doc? Especially since it's another smothering," I pressed.

Brad passed a hand through his sandy hair, and I discerned he was worried. "It could be. We haven't tied the two together yet."

"Do you still think Harvey Pemberton killed Doc?" Lillian asked.

"Aunt Lillian, I don't know. We're investigating. What happened this evening just occurred. I'm not the only cop on the case. I don't know." Brad told her.

Lillian stood up. "I want you to find Doc's killer. I don't care who it is. I want him caught." Her words were stern.

"We'll get him, Aunt Lillian." He slipped one arm around Lillian and the other around me. "I want you two to be more cautious. I don't think you should be coming to the gazebo by yourself. Somebody has killed two people. It could be a stranger from the campground. It could be someone we know. I want you all to play for safety." He looked from one of us to the other.

Lillian nodded, and I said. "We'll be careful, Brad."

He looked satisfied, and we headed for the house.

The following day we awakened to heavy rain falling and gloomy grey skies. I got up early and went to the turret. The trees and shrubs were dripping with water, and I could smell the fragrance of the old-time shrub roses, and somewhere there was a honeysuckle vine, its perfume filling the air. I reflected on God and the beauty of His creation. Then I remembered how Lora Hutchins had been alive yesterday morning, but today she was gone.

I sighed and went downstairs to find Lillian sitting in her chair behind her desk in her office, staring into space. She focused on me when I entered the room.

She forced a smile. "I was thinking of Doc," she confided. "I am glad I am moving to Morrisville. It wouldn't be the same living here without him next door."

I sat down in a chair across from her desk. "I wonder if Lora Hutchins knew something somebody didn't want her to know. I suppose it could be a random killing, and someone just passing through killed her." I was thoughtful.

Lillian gave a bitter laugh. "Nobody passes through here. You have to want to come to Willis for some reason. We're off the main track."

"She hinted that she might know something," I continued.

Lillian's hand rose and fell. "Lora always thought she knew more than she did. She always went around acting like she knew something none of the rest of us did. She was very irritating, but I am sorry she died as she did. I wouldn't wish that on anyone."

"This might be one time she probably should have kept quiet and taken her suspicions to the police," I said frankly. "I learned from the case in Hoover that talking where a murderer can hear you is very dangerous."

Lillian regarded me fondly. "Brad was apprehensive about you. He said you were having a rough time dealing with all of that."

I nodded. "It got to me."

"And yet you're marrying a cop. Are you sure about this, Jo?"

I smiled. "I'm very sure about marrying Brad. If I weren't, Lora would have upset me a lot more. I am older than him, but he has chosen me to be his wife, and I think it's up to us to know what God wants for our lives."

Lillian looked satisfied. "Brad's happy. He's feeling a little guilty right now because he has to work so much.

The sheriff's department here is not large, and it's all hands on deck when something like this happens. Not that people around here turn up murdered all the time, although you might think so with two unsolved murders. I can't remember when this has happened before."

Pictures of a little girl thrown down the stairs and lying dead at the foot of them flittered into my mind. I wondered what Lillian would say about that murder if she knew it.

Aloud I said, "Brad doesn't need to worry about being with me all the time. I'm not some young thing who doesn't want her fiancé out of her sight."

"That's probably a good thing." A frown wrinkled her forehead. "Do you think they'll ever find out who killed Doc? Do you think it was Harvey Pemberton after all these years?"

I shrugged. "I don't know who the guilty person is, but I know Brad won't stop investigating until he finds out the truth, and neither will I. I feel very strongly about that. Doc was ninety-seven, but I wouldn't have cared if he were a hundred and seven. I want people to live until God decides to take them. I don't want someone else making that decision."

"It's not for us to make," Lillian stated firmly. "I wonder if it is Harvey. Do people carry grudges for decades? I'd think the memory would fade after a while."

"It depends on the person. It's like any other emotion-if you keep feeding it, it keeps on living." I said philosophically.

"I guess you all saw that when Harold Ashton was killed," she said shrewdly.

I nodded. "But then I met Brad, so something good came out of it."

Lillian put her hands on her desk and pulled herself to her feet. "Breakfast, I think, and I will cook some eggs and bacon. I don't want you to think I am totally helpless in the kitchen."

I laughed. "I would never think you were helpless at anything."

She came slowly around the desk and hugged me. "I am so thankful for you and your family, Jo." A spasm of pain crossed her face. "Arthritis is acting up this morning. It's a rainy day. That always makes it worse."

"Do you want to take the day off?" I asked, concerned.

She shook her head. "No, I've got to get into Alaina's room. It's been a throw-all. It's got my parents' and grandparents' things in there. I just boxed everything up and pitched it in there. I've been putting off going through it. Since Doc's death, I have felt a bit vulnerable. I'm not sure what I'll find there and whether I can handle it right now."

"If you'd like to wait, it's okay. We can't possibly use all of these bedrooms." I assured her.

"Well, if Johnny Whitlock has his way, you won't need one for Alaina," Lillian said astutely.

I stared at her. "You think Johnny is seriously interested in Alaina? I thought he was only flirting."

"Oh, I think he is interested," Lillian said brightly.

"Is he a Christian, Lillian?" I asked and then grimaced. "I'm sorry. I sound like Lora with her holiness."

"He comes to church, so I guess he is," Lillian replied.

I didn't answer. I knew many people who went to church but weren't disciples of Christ. I recollected some who turned out to be murderers.

CHAPTER NINE

We all attended Lora's Hutchins funeral. It was not nearly as massive as Doc's, but Lora didn't have as many friends. Pastor Franks' sermon was gracious and caring, and I would have never learned from his words that Lora had aggravated him more than just a little. I noted that Brad had been right; Lora's husband seemed lost. He was thin and looked very frail. His family had to help him do everything, and I felt sorry for him. I hoped he would have someone there for him after everything was over.

While on the road that weekend, I discovered that Alaina had been talking to Johnny on the phone most nights, so things were getting a little more intense.

Joseph was not happy. Ashley attempted to calm him down, but he was not listening to her. I suggested that maybe he would not be excited about anyone dating his mother, but he tossed that idea aside. Joseph remembered his father very well, and I didn't suppose anyone would ever measure up to him. He informed me that he wasn't so immature to expect his mother to grieve for his father all her life; she had the right to find happiness too. I was thankful to hear it. Sometimes I wondered if he understood that.

Joseph and Ashley returned to Lillian's with me, only to discover Alaina sitting in the den with Lillian. She had taken a vacation week to come to help us was what she said she was doing there. I doubt if any of us believed her, and especially not when Johnny Whitlock just happened to come by. They made dinner plans while Joseph sat there brooding. Lillian and I exchanged glances, and we moved toward the kitchen. At the sink, we conversed in low tones.

"I told you," Lillian said.

I was staring out the kitchen window. "I can't make Alaina's choices for her, Aunt Lillian. I just wished Joseph would lay off. He got mad at us when we criticized anyone he was dating."

"It's his mother," Lillian said as if that explained everything. "When I found out Doc's father had been interested in my mother, I about blew a blood vessel. Mother wasn't interested, and Doc Graham carried a torch for her for the rest of his life. This thing with Johnny may blow over too."

We spent the day in the bedroom Alaina was staying in. I began to think Lillian had thousands of pictures. She had packets and packets of letters and cards that had belonged to her mother and grandmother. Lillian was struggling with what to do with all of it. I could tell she wasn't ready to discard any of it.

After much discussion, I sat down on the bed beside her.

"Aunt Lillian, why don't you box all of this up and leave it here? It won't be in our way. I don't think you can or should throw any pictures out. Can we bring a box at a time over to you when you get settled in Morrisville? Then you can go through everything at your leisure and won't have to feel rushed. How does that sound?"

"It sounds heavenly," she responded with a smile. "This is just getting to be too much. Let's go downstairs, and let me sort out what dishes and pots and pans I want. There should be plenty for both of us."

Having solved the current problem successfully, I followed my family downstairs. I noticed that Lillian was holding on to the stair railing tightly. I suspected she was worried about falling. Arthritis had been bothering her a lot lately.

Alaina went out to dinner with Johnny Whitlock. Brad came home in the middle of our supper. Joseph wasn't saying much, and Ashley was watching him worriedly. Aunt Lillian and I tried to keep the conversation moving, but it was a struggle. I met Brad's eyes with frustration on my face. He sat at the table and began putting food on his plate.

"How's everybody's day been?" he asked conversationally.

"We got a lot done," I volunteered. "Aunt Lillian has decided to box up a lot of stuff and leave it here. I told her we don't need all this room. We can take it to her apartment as she wants, and she can go through all the cards and pictures when she has more time."

Brad nodded and smiled at his aunt. "Sounds like a good plan to me."

Joseph finished eating and pushed his plate back. "Is there any news about Doc's murder?"

Brad shook his head. "Not at the moment. The analysis of the pillow showed that someone had used it to smother Doc. Whoever did it probably wore gloves. I would think every criminal in the world would know to do that by now."

"What about poor old Lora?" Lillian questioned. "Do you know any more about her death?"

"Not much," Brad admitted. "There were no tire marks on the side of the road, so whoever it was must have stopped on the blacktop."

"Or they could have been walking," Joseph supplied.

"If they were, it means it's somebody local," I said thoughtfully.

Brad looked at me. "We're treating it like it is local. The road is off the main track."

"I guess a serial killer could have been passing through and got the urge to kill," Joseph offered. "But I think it has something to do with her acting like she knew something about Doc's death."

"Whether she did or not, it's dangerous to talk like you know something when there's a killer loose." Brad was firm on that point.

131

"So you think somebody took her seriously," I queried.

"Don't you think her death proves that, Mamaw?" Joseph asked.

"I know there are mentally disturbed people who kill just because they want to kill," Brad said, "But overall, I think there is a reason for most murders. You have to find out what it is. Most murders are for money, passion, or to protect one's interests."

"What do you mean by passion?" Joseph inquired.

"I mean deep feelings of jealousy or some other emotion. Most of those types of killings are the spur-of-the-moment kind. Somebody's anger overpowers them.' Brad explained.

"So basically, you're saying that you all think that Lora was killed by the same person who killed Doc?" Joseph continued.

"If she died because of something she knew that made her dangerous to Doc's killer, then yes," Brad responded. "If it had happened on one of the main roads, we might entertain thinking it was a stranger, but as it is, no."

"Are you still looking at Harvey Pemberton?" Ashley threw in.

"We are, but his wife swears he was with her when Lora Hutchins died. When we told her about Lora's murder, she seemed genuinely grieving. Harvey wasn't showing much emotion, but I could tell he didn't like it. Of course, he liked it less when we questioned his whereabouts." Brad pushed his dinner plate back from him. "I have decided that we will have to go through all of Doc and his Dad's medical files and see if there are any answers."

Lillian cleared her throat. "Well, you might not find anything there."

Brad looked at her with narrowed eyes. "Why not?"

Her hand raised and fell. "Because neither one of them put everything down in their records."

"And how do you know that?" Brad's voice was stern.

Instead of answering him, she turned her head towards me. "How far have you got in my mother's journal?"

I frowned and glanced at Brad. "Well, I haven't had time to read all of it," I said, trying to sidestep her inquiry.

Brad was watching his aunt. "You may as well tell her what you've read, Jo. I think she already knows."

"If you mean do I know that my father threw my baby sister down the stairs, which resulted in her death, then yes, I knew about that." Aunt Lillian's voice was calm. She might have been talking about the weather.

I stared at her. "You knew? But how?"

"Doc told me; or rather he confirmed what I already suspected." She rose slowly to her feet. "Let's go sit in the den. This chair is getting uncomfortable."

I started stacking the dishes, but Lillian stopped me. "Leave them. We'll do them later."

I followed her obediently to the den. Joseph and Ashley took the love seat, and Aunt Lillian sank into her Queen Anne chair. Brad moved a footstool over for her to rest her feet, then settled on the sofa beside me.

Lillian began speaking. "It's like this. I was only five when Rosemary died, but I came out on the landing right after it happened. Mother was cradling my little sister in her arms and crying like her heart would break. She sent me back into my room. I could see Rosemary wasn't moving, so I suspected she was dead. When I got older, Eugene, Violet, and I talked about it, not in front of Mother but between us. Of course, our father was gone by then, but Eugene and Violet believed that Dad had killed Rosemary."

"That's a terrible burden for a child to bear!" I exclaimed.

"When Dad died, Violet and Eugene never shed a tear. Doc told me that. His father had told him when he was dying. They came home from school, and Mother told them Dad was gone, that he had had a heart attack. It was odd. Doc said that after Mother told them, Eugene and Violet continued their chores like nothing had happened." Lillian was reminiscing as she spoke.

"Where were you?" I asked gently.

"I had gone to be with my Grandmother Christine that day, so I wasn't there. Grandma let me stay the night with her, so I didn't know until the next day."

"How did you feel about it?" Brad inquired.

Her hand rose and fell again. "Things would probably be better without him. At least, that's what Violet and Eugene said. I usually agreed with whatever they said. It was a lot better. There was peace in the house then."

Brad was frowning. "So you are telling me that Doc's dad covered up a homicide?"

A faint smile touched Lillian's lips. "Doc and his father were true friends to my mother. He loved my mother and wanted to protect her. Doc's father suspected my father had something to do with Rosemary's death, but he never said anything until later. After Dad died, Mother told him the truth. He wasn't surprised, Doc told me. It would have been tricky proving it back then unless Mother admitted it. I think she was afraid of Dad."

"I don't blame her," Joseph threw in. "If he didn't mind killing his daughter, she probably wondered what he could do to her. And then what would happen to her children."

Lillian nodded. "That's what she told me years later. Mother said he had all the people around Willis fooled into thinking he was some saint. She didn't think anyone would believe her story. Dad had made friends in high places in the county. My mother never shed a tear when my father died of a heart attack. Everybody just thought she was very private and didn't want to show her grief publicly. She was private, but I think she was more relieved than anything else. I don't believe Mother ever mentioned my father's name after his funeral. No, I take that back, Violet mentioned him once, and Mother said, 'let's forget him. He's gone.' That was all that was ever said."

Joseph commented. "It's good that you weren't a cop back then, Brad. That would have been a mess, you having to arrest your own grandfather."

Brad released my hand that he had been holding and walked across to one of the large floor-to-ceiling windows on the side of the house. "I'd come closer to breaking his neck instead of arresting him, but you all didn't hear me say that."

"Did this have anything to do with Violet leaving home as soon as she was of age?" I asked Lillian.

Lillian closed her eyes in remembrance. "Violet was never happy at home. I would say she hated her father, but she had a lot of fights with her mother too. She was a bit of a rebel and didn't like any rules. Mother was strict but kind. Violet wanted to do what she wanted to do."

"Sounds like she had some of her Daddy in her," Brad commented.

"She did," Lillian agreed. "She could be very hateful to Eugene and me. We tried to stay out of her way."

Brad came back over and sat down by me. "Are you sure you want to marry into this family?"

I smiled and took his hand. "Of course."

He smiled back and squeezed my hand. "Where's Alaina?"

Joseph grimaced. "Out with that Whitlock fellow."

Brad grinned. "Maybe we'll have a double wedding," he teased.

Joseph gave him a smoldering look, and Brad quickly changed the subject. "I was thinking today about our wedding. Aunt Lillian, if it's all right with Jo, I'd like you to take my mother's place as the groom's mother."

Lillian brightened visibly, and I murmured. "What a wonderful idea." I looked at Brad. "I don't have a mother either, you know."

Brad frowned. "Is there someone who has been like a mother to you? Maybe in one of the churches, you all have been going to for years."

I grinned suddenly. Do you know who I would really like to have that honor?"

"Who?" Joseph said. "You're up to something. I know that look."

"I don't know if she'd do it, but I would like Maude Ashton to stand in for my mother."

"Maude Ashton!" Three voices sounded together.

Then Lillian questioned. "Who is Maude Ashton? Is she connected to the Ashton's, I know?"

Brad overcame his astonishment enough to burst out laughing. "Jo, you are full of surprises, aren't you?

He patted my knee and answered his aunt. "Maude Ashton was Harold Ashton's sister-in-law. She about drove us crazy while trying to solve Harold's murder. I never saw such a closed-lip woman. Jo had her melted like butter by the time she was done. She sings Jo's praises to everyone." He turned back to me. "I think that's a wonderful idea. I think she would be flattered. I must go over there and pack up what I want to keep. You could go along and visit Maude Ashton while we're there."

"And we need to talk to Pastor Jim Abbott," I reminded him.

"Yeah, I remembered you wanted him to marry us. I do too. He was my pastor when I lived in Alcott." He turned to Lillian. "You'll like Pastor Jim and Sue."

"Where were you thinking about being married?" Lillian asked.

Brad and I exchanged glances. "What do you think, Jo? We haven't talked much about that?"

"I like a church setting," I admitted. "But to tell you the truth, I would love an outdoor wedding in this backyard somewhere. Maybe closer to the gazebo if there is enough room for people to sit down there."

Lillian was gratified, and Brad reached over and kissed me. "It sounds good to me. We won't have to limit who comes in that big backyard."

"Well, neither of us is interested in a big wedding. I had that with Josh, and Brad had one with Audrey. I want to keep it simple and inexpensive. I'm asking Marcella to do the decorating and the food" (referring to one of my oldest friends). "Of course, Alaina and Ashley will stand up with me if that is all right with Mr. Edwards."

Brad grinned at Joseph and Ashley. "How long do I have to think about it?"

They laughed, and Brad said. "Of course, that's fine. I will have to decide whom I want for my best man."

"Joseph, will you walk me down the aisle and give me away?" I asked my grandson.

"Of course, Mamaw, since it's Brad, I'd be happy to do that for you," he responded.

Lillian sighed. "I wish Doc was still here to enjoy this happy occasion. It doesn't seem right. I have included him in everything this family ever did and his father before him. Now there are no more Masters." Her voice sounded sad.

The front door opened, and Alaina and Johnny entered together.

"Have I walked in on a family reunion or what?" Johnny was grinning.

"We're talking about our wedding, Johnny," Brad told him. "I've been so busy at work, and Jo has been trying to get the house cleared and the gardens finished, so we haven't been planning as we should have. Time is getting away from us."

I was studying my daughter while Brad spoke. Her color was bright, and there was a sparkle in her eyes that I hadn't seen since her husband, Tim, had died. The way the two of them looked at each spoke volumes. My daughter was falling in love with Johnny Whitlock, and if I were not very badly mistaken, Johnny felt precisely the same way.

It was not a comfortable evening, thanks to Joseph's stony silence. We all retired early, except for Alaina, and she and Johnny sat on the front porch a long while conversing.

I was still awake, taking the opportunity of reading more in Grandma Rose's journal. I hadn't found any more earth-shaking revelations, but I was learning a lot about growing different species of flowers, herbs, and vegetables.

Brad's grandmother's journal was very detailed. My thoughts kept drifting back to Alaina and Johnny. Brad dismissed our current family situation as being none of our business. She was my daughter, so I didn't quite see it that way. I didn't want a breach between Joseph and his mother. They had always been close. I could tell Ashley was concerned. She loved that our family was so attached, and I didn't think she wanted anything to disrupt that serenity. I could hear laughter occasionally from the front porch since I had my bedroom windows open, but I couldn't hear any words. I didn't make it a point to eavesdrop on my daughter, so I wasn't attempting to listen. It wasn't until I heard Johnny's truck start up and Alaina come into the house that I breathed easier and went into a restless sleep.

The following day, the rain was coming down in bucketsful. I had planned on finishing the mulching of the flower beds today, but that wasn't happening. I sat at the breakfast table for a long time with a cup of hot tea that was getting colder by the minute. I have never been a coffee drinker, but when I sipped the lukewarm tea, I made a face and drained the cup in the kitchen sink.

When Joseph strolled into the kitchen, I was trying to decide whether to say anything to him about his mother and Johnny. His blue eyes looked sterner than I ever remembered seeing them.

"What?" I asked.

"I'm going to ask Brad to check out Johnny Whitlock," he announced. "It's not so much that I mind Mom having a boyfriend. You're right, Dad's gone, and he isn't returning. I don't know what it is, but something about him doesn't sit right with me."

I looked up at him. "Are you sure you would like any man your mother might date?" I asked directly.

Joseph moved uneasily around the table. "Ashley asked me that too." He hesitated in answering me. "I don't know, Mamaw. I've been thinking about it, and the closest I can get to explaining it is that I've just got a feeling about him. I think it is all a façade-a smoke screen."

I surveyed him closely, remembering a time when I had a feeling about someone that the rest of the family couldn't see. "Well, Joseph, if that's how you truly feel, and it's not just you getting your back up because Johnny's not your dad, I'll support looking into him. But," I cautioned. "I think we need to do it quietly. Your mother has a right to her privacy too. And, do you think you could stop looking like you'd like to do murder when we're all together?"

Joseph's face eased into a grin. "I'll try. As Ashley says, I could be wrong. I'd hate to misjudge someone. I don't like it when someone judges me falsely."

I started washing the breakfast dishes. "No, we don't want to be like Lora Hutchins; bless her little heart. Now that someone has murdered her, I have to live with the guilt of wishing she had stayed home instead of coming over here to help."

Joseph grimaced. "I know. I'm dealing with that too. At least I didn't say everything I thought. I could think of all kinds of comebacks for what she said."

I laid a damp hand on his arm. "I'm glad you didn't either. I had to bite my tongue several times, but it's terrible she has been killed, and I wish we could find her murderer and Doc's too. It's rather alarming to think someone is smothering people left and right around here."

Joseph arched an eyebrow. "I've caught myself looking behind me a few times after dark." He poured himself a glass of iced tea. "Have you read anything else interesting in Grandma Rose's journal?"

"Not since we talked about it the other evening. I am learning a lot about all the plants she put out around here. It's quite an education. She loved perennial flowers."

"You haven't dug up any more jars, have you?" Joseph asked teasingly.

"No, thank Heavens, and I haven't found any buried treasure either," I assured him.

"I'd love to know if that story is true," my grandson said. "Do you think it's in the house or outside somewhere?"

"Outside," I answered promptly. "The house Albert Edwards built here is long gone. Ernest built this one at the turn of the century. They started from the concrete foundation on up. I don't think it is in the house."

"You're probably right," Joseph agreed. "The house would be the first places soldiers would look."

I finished with the last dish and turned to face him. "But then again, it could be just a story-a legend that never really happened."

"What do you think, Mamaw?"

I shrugged. "I don't know. I imagine there were a lot of people hiding their valuables during the time of the Civil War. I think Brad's grandmother believed it."

"Do you think I could get Brad to check Johnny Whitlock out?" my tall, slender grandson asked.

"Let me ask him. I don't think he would mind. Just don't let your mother know we're doing it. She'll be mad at all of us."

"I won't," Joseph promised. I noticed his features had lightened when he left me.

I jumped when I heard someone pounding on the front door. I went through the den to where Joseph had joined Ashley sitting on the floor, going through more boxes. I could hear Alaina and Aunt Lillian's voices from upstairs.

"Who in the world is that?' Ashley wondered. "It sounds like they're trying to break the door down."

Aunt Lillian and Alaina had heard it too, and they came out on the upstairs landing.

"Did a meteor hit the house, or is that somebody at the front door?" Lillian asked.

"I'm going to see right now," I answered her. Outside on the front porch stood a man that I recognized.

"Mr. Pemberton, I believe," I said to the red-faced man who stood there.

"Yeah, I'm Harvey Pemberton. Is Deputy Edwards here?"

"No, he's at work," I responded.

"He's not at work. I've already been to the sheriff's office, and he was out. I figured I'd catch him here."

Lillian came down the stairs to stand beside me. "Hello, Mr. Pemberton. I'm Brad's Aunt, Lillian Edwards. I don't know if you remember me or not."

His face lit up, and he pulled off his cap. "Yes, Madam, I remember you. I didn't know if you still lived here after all these years or had moved away. I just heard your nephew was taking over the house for him and his new wife."

"This is Brad's fiancée, Jo Elliott," Lillian introduced me.

I had been studying Harvey Pemberton while they talked. I could see worry lines around his eyes and a note of stress in his voice. "What can we do for you, Mr. Pemberton?" I asked politely.

He switched his gaze from Lillian to me. "Well, Madam, Deputy Edwards seems to think I'm guilty of murdering Doc and this poor old Lora Hutchins. Mrs. Hutchins had become friendly with my wife and me, and we both enjoyed her visits. As I told the police, Dotty and I were together at the campground when someone killed her. As for Doc Masters, I admit we had our problems back in the day, but I was young and hot-tempered. That's all water under the bridge now. I'm not one to hold grudges for fifty years. I've lived my life, and I imagined he lived his. I'm sorry these two people have been murdered, but it has nothing to do with me, and my good wife is about to have a breakdown worrying about the whole affair. I told her they didn't have enough on me to arrest me, or they would have already done it. If it were left up to me, we'd go home, but Dotty wants the police to clear me before we go. We're retired, so it doesn't matter, but I wouldn't say I like staying and having people looking at me funny like maybe I am guilty. You may have heard we have been through this before, so I know how it works. Dotty remembers all that and does not want to go through it again."

"That's understandable, Mr. Pemberton," Lillian reassured him. "But we don't know much more than you do. As far as we know, they are continuing the investigation."

"Well, now, Madam, I think that is where I might be able to help you. That's why I'm trying to find Edwards. He's been pretty decent about the whole thing, unlike some of these cops, so I thought I'd like to talk to him." He switched his cap from one hand to the other. "You see, when Lora was at the camper the other day, we talked this all over. We were sitting under the front awning, and some other campers were coming by walking or on bicycles. Lora happened to mention that she recognized one of the couples. She said they used to live in Willis. That came to me last night, and this morning when they came past, I stopped them and found out who they were."

"Who were they?" I asked curiously.

"They were the Coxes-the ones who used to have the five-and-dime store beside my dad's hardware store in Willis. I remembered them after they told me who they were. It's been a long time since I saw them. You remember them; I'm sure, Miss Edwards?" His attention had gone back to Lillian again.

"Oh, yes, I do remember them. Mrs. Cox was always so helpful when you came into the store. All the clerks were always trying to help you find something. It wasn't like it is today back then. Now, you're lucky if you can find anybody to check you out in these shops." She frowned. "I seem to recall Donald Cox having an awful temper."

"That's right. Donald did. I never knew what it was all about, but I know he and Doc got into it once over something, and Lora said her dad had problems with him too. That had something to do with where the property lines were. You might remember her people and the Coxes lived side by side on those two farms. It got pretty nasty. Donald Cox let his cattle get on Lora's dad's property, and they destroyed the garden, and I don't know what all. I thought Deputy Edwards might want to know that other people might have had it in for Doc Masters."

"I think he would be very interested," I told him.

"Yes," Aunt Lillian affirmed. "We'll be certain to tell him about this."

Harvey Pemberton walked off the porch carefully. He appeared to have a limp in one leg, but he managed to get in his truck and drive back down the road.

Aunt Lillian and I stood in the foyer and looked at each other.

"And what do we think about that?" she asked.

"It's interesting," I admitted. "It's also frustrating. How many people who used to live here are camping down the road in Johnny Whitlock's campground? It seems to me it's homecoming week."

"I think Johnny advertised in trade magazines hoping that people who used to live here would see the ad and want to come back for a visit." She frowned slightly. "You know, I don't recall Doc having trouble with the Coxes. I could be wrong."

"So you think Harvey Pemberton is trying to take the focus off him onto someone else?" I asked.

She shrugged. "I don't know. Harvey might be capable of that. I never knew the Pemberton's that well. I remember going with Mother to their hardware store a few times, and Mr. Pemberton, Harvey's father, would always give me a piece of peppermint. He was always good to Mother. Well, we can tell Brad about it and see what he makes of it," Lillian decided. She peered out the front door. "Goodness, the rain's still coming down. It's for sure you can't get anything done outside today. I was hoping to carry another load to the apartment, but Joseph and I would look like two drowned rats if we did."

"There's plenty to do on the inside," I returned absently. What would Brad say about Harvey Pemberton's story? I knew Brad was fair, so I felt sure he would check it out. It looked like Brad was on the right track, that whoever killed Doc and Lora had some tie to the Cherokee River Campground.

CHAPTER TEN

Later in the week, Brad took a day off from work, and we planned the trip back to Alcott. It was bittersweet. Brad and I had met there when we found his former father-in-law lying shot on the front pew of Grace Community Church. He had been a deputy sheriff in that county and was briefly suspected of the crime. It was the first time my family and I had been involved in a murder investigation, but it was not the last time. Now, here we were again. I would have never believed it. Murder seemed to find us whether we were looking for it or not.

Brad looked across at me. "A penny for your thoughts. You're very quiet."

A faint smile crossed my lips. "I was thinking how we'd met at Alcott. Do you think we would have time to stop and see Pastor Jim and Sue?"

"I planned on stopping there and at Maude Ashton's," Brad responded. "Most of my stuff is out of my apartment. Another guy from the sheriff's department has picked up the lease. I'm leaving him the furniture. It's not anything we can use. I've lived like a bachelor for so long that I never cared about furnishing the place. It was just some-where to sleep and shower."

"Aunt Lillian's leaving most of her antique furniture with us. It's adorable," I shared. "I never expected to have anything so grand."

"I guess I never realized until later how valuable some of my grandmother's and aunt's furniture was. I knew it was a nice place to spend my summers when I was a kid. Grandma Rose and Aunt Lillian always made it seem so welcoming." Brad admitted.

"Despite your grandfather's legacy, it has a homey feeling," I commented.

"That was Grandma Rose's influence. I meant to tell you when I brought you to my aunt's the first day. That picture of Grandpa Ernest wasn't on the wall by the stair-case when she was alive. Aunt Lillian put it up after she buried her mother. I was surprised she hung it back up." Brad shook his head. "I don't know why she did."

"Maybe she thinks it's time to put that behind her," I reasoned. "Ernest Edwards is her father." I made a face and continued. "I try not to look at him when I go up or down the stairs. He looks evil to me."

"Grandpa Ernest was a piece of work by all accounts," Brad responded. "I've only got a couple of boxes to pick up at the apartment, and then we'll go over to the house. You can look it over and see if there's anything you think we'll want or need. I've got to box up some legal papers and stuff like that. I'll stick it in the room with Aunt Lillian's boxes. I'll need to go through it at some point. Jeremy may want something out of it."

"Have you heard from Jeremy?" I asked him, referring to his dead wife's son. I shot him a sideways glance.

Brad's face tightened. "Not a word. I guess he doesn't want to hear from me."

"I'm sorry about that, Brad," I said softly. "It's not your fault."

"It feels like it is," he answered shortly.

"Aunt Lillian is taking Audrey's furniture, isn't she?" I questioned.

"Yeah, it's good furniture and will fit better in her apartment. She's taking her Queen Anne chair in the den with her footstool. That's her favorite chair."

"She's taking some dishes. I think they were her mother's."

"Well, there are enough dishes for all of us," my fiancé contended.

"Have you talked to that Cox man that Harvey Pemberton told us about?" I asked, changing the subject.

Brad's jaw tightened again. He thought it was too hard for his aunt to deal with having lost Doc, and he still remembered how devastating the case in Hoover had been for me. When I told him about Harvey's visit, I knew he wasn't happy he had come to the house and talked to his Aunt Lillian and me. Brad didn't want Lillian and I involved in the case.

"I talked to Mr. Cox," Brad finally replied. "He said this was the first time he had been back in this area in years, and he had forgotten all about it. So it's another dead end. There's no evidence."

In Alcott, Brad had his key to the apartment and walked on in with me following behind him. It was a bachelor's apartment. It was far from neat. There was nothing there I needed or wanted. Brad and I carried the few boxes out of the bedroom closet where Brad had stored them, left the key on the kitchen counter, and drove on to the house Audrey had lived in briefly when she had returned to Alcott. As far as I was concerned, Aunt Lillian was welcome to the furniture there. I was glad to leave and go to Pastor Jim and Sue's house.

They were waiting for us on their wrap-around porch. I noticed that Sue had planted flowers across the front and in boxes on the porch railings. Both stood up from the white wicker furniture and came down the steps to the car to meet us.

Pastor Jim and Brad embraced and slapped each other on the back. Sue hugged me tightly. "Oh, Jo, it is so wonderful to see you!" She held me off from her. "You look great! Love suits you." We laughed together, and she hugged me again.

Pastor Jim had turned to me. He embraced me gently. "Jo, it's great to see you. I can't begin to tell you how happy Sue and I are about your upcoming marriage to Brad."

"Well, we were wondering if you'd be willing to marry us," Brad asked him.

Pastor Jim and Sue exchanged glances.

"Would I? I'd be honored." Pastor Jim was beaming ear to ear. He looked at me. "I figured you had a home church pastor you would want to marry you."

I shook my head. "No, I met Brad while I was here with you all. We thought it was only appropriate that you do the wedding. We are trying to keep it simple. We have decided to be married in Brad's Aunt Lillian's backyard. It looks like a paradise, and there's plenty of room for a few guests. My daughter Alaina and Ashley will stand up with me, and Joseph is giving me away. Brad still hasn't decided who to have as a best man, but it will probably be one of his cop friends."

"I'm thinking about asking the Sheriff, Jason Pierce, to stand up with me. We've been friends a long time," Brad contributed. "We've been so busy trying to get the house ready, and Aunt Lillian moved to her new apartment; we thought we'd better be thinking about the wedding."

"When were you planning on having it?" Pastor Jim asked.

"The first Saturday of August," I answered.

Pastor Jim looked at Sue, and she said, "I don't remember anything scheduled for that weekend except regular services."

"We were thinking about two o'clock," Brad told him. "If it should happen to rain, the alternative location will be at the Willis Community Church. That's the church where my Aunt Lillian's a member."

"Have you had lunch?" Sue asked. "I could fix us some sandwiches."

"Not yet," I admitted.

Pastor Jim started up the porch steps. "Well, come on in. Sue will put something together for us. She made a big bowl of potato salad last night so we can have that with the sandwiches." He grinned. "We sure are glad to see both of you. It's been a while. I think you're coming to sing this fall, aren't you, Jo?"

"I've got you scheduled," I said cheerfully.

Inside, I helped Sue prepare turkey and ham sandwiches with tomatoes and lettuce. "Let's use paper plates and save on washing dishes," she suggested.

With potato salad and iced tea, we had plenty. Hearing Pastor Jim pray again was heartening, and I reached for Brad's hand when he prayed for us and our upcoming wedding.

We sat around talking after lunch until Brad glanced at his watch.

"We better be heading back," he said, standing up. "We've got another stop to make while we're here."

Pastor Jim grinned. "I bet I know who that is."

"Is it Maude Ashton?" Sue asked.

I nodded, and Brad said."I have asked my Aunt Lillian to take my mother's place as my mother. Jo wants to ask Mrs. Ashton if she'll fill that spot for her."

"Oh, that is so sweet," Sue exclaimed. "And she will love it! You know, she's slowed down a bit. She's not raising as big of a garden as she used to, but her flowers are still beautiful."

"She is getting up there," Pastor Jim reminded us. "But she loves you two. That's for certain."

I hated to pull out of their driveway, but I was looking forward to seeing Maude Ashton. We arrived at her house to see her porch overflowed with pots of red, purple, and white petunias. Yellow marigolds lined the sidewalk, and fuchsia, red, and pink impatiens were everywhere under the flowering shrubs. Somebody had painted the house recently and put on a new metal roof. I almost didn't know the place.

Brad and I walked up the front steps together. Brad knocked on the screen door. We heard the key turn in the lock in a few minutes, and the door swung open. There Maude Ashton stood, not looking a day older than when I had met her a few years earlier. She was wearing a floral blue house dress and clapped her hands together when she recognized us.

"I never dreamed I'd see you two today!" She unhooked the screen door and invited us in.

I gave her a big hug, and so did Brad.

"Come on in. Come on back to the kitchen. I've been cooking some chicken and dumplings."

"I can smell them," I said, breathing in the aroma.

"I can still take care of myself," the little woman insisted. We followed her to the kitchen and sat down at the table. She beamed at us as she stirred the dumplings and served us iced tea and some of her homemade chocolate chip cookies. "I hear through the grapevine that wedding bells are fixing to ring," she commented, sitting down at the table with us.

Brad and I exchanged glances.

"That's one of the reasons we stopped by today," I said. "Brad has asked his Aunt Lillian to take his mother's place as the groom's mother, and she has agreed. My mother has passed too, and I thought it would be nice if you would stand in for her as the bride's mother."

A smile broke across Maude's wrinkled face. For an answer, she pulled herself up, came around to my chair, and put her arms around my neck. "I'd be proud," she whispered, and I could see the glint of tears in her eyes.

"Well, it will be in Brad's Aunt Lillian's backyard on the first Saturday of August. I will make sure you can have a ride over. Maybe Pastor Jim can bring you." I said.

"I'll get my daughter to take me," she stated firmly. "I'll tire out before Pastor Abbott is ready to leave." She smiled faintly. "I'm not as young as I used to be."

"You'll love my Aunt Lillian's backyard," Brad told her. "She's crazy about flowers too. I don't know how many beds she has, but it's beautiful. Jo has been working hard taking care of all of it."

"We'll turn you into a homebody yet," Maude pronounced. "I'll look forward to seeing that."

"I may have to call on you for advice," I said. "I'm learning a lot. We had a neighbor who was a retired doctor that I thought I could rely on for gardening advice, but someone has murdered him."

She regarded me closely and shook her head thoughtfully. "You're still getting yourself messed up in murders, aren't you?"

I managed to look abashed. "Well, I don't mean to. I think murders seem to follow us around."

She looked at Brad. "And I guess you're working on the case. I heard you had moved."

He nodded. "Yeah, I'm trying to work on it. We don't have much evidence."

"And then a friend of his Aunt Lillian's was killed one afternoon recently," I added. "Both were smothered, but we don't know by whom."

Maude smoothed the apron in her lap. "I have no doubt one or the other of you will find out all about it." She smiled a little at Brad. "It will probably be Jo."

He laughed. "I wouldn't vote against Jo," he admitted. "I hate to cut this short, Mrs. Ashton, but we've got a long drive back to Willis." He got to his feet, and so did I.

Maude rose slowly to her feet, and I hugged her tightly. "I'll get back to you closer to the wedding. It's the first Saturday of August, so write it down."

Maude took her calendar off the wall and wrote the wedding on the August date.

"Now, I won't forget it," she said.

I smiled at the little woman of whom I had become so fond. "Thank you for helping to make our day a special one."

She was her blunt self. "I would have never thought when we first met that you would have ever wanted me to stand in for your mother at your wedding. It's interesting how things turn out."

"Well, that was a very trying time for you and many other people around here," I reminded her. "But it all turned out all right."

She shook her head sadly. "A lot of lives were ruined," she said, then brightened. "But you and Brad are getting married, so something good came out of it. There's never a cloudy day, but what there's a silver lining."

It was a typical Maude Ashton reaction to life. We left with her standing among her flowers on her front porch, waving at us.

I sank back gratefully into my car seat. "It just makes me happy seeing her," I told my fiancé. "It reminds me of Harold's murder, but I would have never met you if that hadn't happened."

"God has ways of making His plans happen," my future husband said.

We stopped and ate on our way home. Home had a nice ring to it. I imagined my family and Lillian could manage without me for one evening.

At the house, we sat out in the driveway for a few minutes looking at the beautiful structure lit up in the dark by floodlights.

Brad reached for me, and we sat quietly for several minutes, holding each other.

"You know you have made me the happiest I have ever been in my whole life," Brad whispered against my hair.

"It's been a long time since I've felt this contented with my life," I responded. "I am very blessed to have you. I feel complete somehow."

We kissed and went into the house.

To our amazement, the entire family was sitting in the den together. I had expected Lillian to have called it a night by now, but she was lounging in her favorite chair. Johnny Whitlock was sitting on the sofa beside Alaina. Lillian looked pale, and Joseph was pacing up and down the room. Something had happened. That was for sure.

Brad took in the situation with a glance and asked. "What's up?"

Joseph stopped pacing and answered him. "We were all out in the backyard tonight, and somebody took a couple of shots at us; that's what happened. And they nearly hit Aunt Lillian. The bullet whizzed by her."

Brad dropped to his knees beside Lillian's chair. "Are you all right? He didn't hit you?"

She shook her head, her face still strained. "I'm fine. I can't imagine who would do such a thing."

Brad looked up at Joseph. "Did it seem they were trying to hit Aunt Lillian or one of the rest of you?"

Joseph shrugged. "I couldn't tell. I just knew it came from the direction of the river. Someone might have been showing off."

"That's a poor way to show off," my daughter, Alaina, said, jumping into the conversation. "I've never been so scared in my life. It wasn't just one shot; it was two. I made Joseph go through the entire house to ensure he hadn't hidden inside the house."

Brad stared at the man sitting beside Alaina. "And just where were you when all this was going on?"

"Well, I wasn't doing the shooting, if that's what you're asking," he said defiantly.

"I called Johnny," Alaina said in defense. "I thought we needed another man up here."

Joseph got a look on his face, but I gave him a warning frown, and he was silent.

"I've never had anything like this happen in all my eighty-two years of living here," Lillian insisted. "I've never felt afraid here, even when I've been by myself. And for the life of me, I can't imagine why anyone would want to kill me. That's ridiculous."

Brad patted her hand and stood up to his feet. "Did any of you call the police?" he asked sternly.

"We all ran to the house and stayed away from the windows," my daughter informed him.

"I called them," Johnny disclosed. "Right after Alaina called me. They came out, and Joseph and I showed them where we were sitting and what direction the shots came from. It was getting dusk. We didn't find anything along the river bank."

Brad nodded and went upstairs. In a moment, he was back wearing his gun and going out the back. I put my hand out and started telling him to be careful, but I second-guessed myself and decided I had better get used to him going into danger. If I couldn't deal with that, I should have never agreed to be his wife. He was a cop, after all.

I sat down beside Ashley on the loveseat. "Well, is everybody all right, other than being scared?"

"We were just sitting out in the yard talking," Ashley told me. "It was terrible. Joseph ran to Aunt Lillian when the bullet flew by. It was close." She shuddered.

"It must have been somebody who didn't know much about guns," Lillian volunteered. "I remember when Doc's dad got killed in that deer hunting accident. That man had never been hunting, but he shot and killed Doc's father."

"Yeah, Doc told me about that," I said. "He said he didn't go deer hunting and didn't take all the pills the doctors wanted to give you nowadays. He thought he'd live longer." I stopped realizing that he hadn't lived very long after that statement.

Joseph raised an eyebrow. "Well, he didn't live much longer, did he? It's getting a little creepy if you ask me. Two people have been murdered by smothering, and now someone takes a shot at Aunt Lillian; at least, they threatened her. What in the world is going on around here?"

"I just hope it's nobody connected with my campground," Johnny spoke up. "That's all I'd need. It's bad enough the police are questioning the Pemberton's. I tried politely suggesting they might want to move on, but Mrs. Pemberton wants his name cleared before they go."

"I can understand that, but we don't know how long it will take for this case to be solved," I said, considering. "Are the Pemberton's going to stay there for six months?"

Johnny shrugged. "Who knows? Some of the other campers are getting nervous. Now, I understand that Harvey Pemberton is trying to focus the blame on another family there- the Coxes."

"Well, somebody had to kill Doc," Joseph asserted, "and Lora Hutchins."

Brad came back inside the door and looked at all of us, and we stopped talking about the murders.

"Find anything?" Johnny asked.

Brad shook his head. "It's too dark to search very well. I'll look again in the morning before I go in to work. There wasn't anybody hanging around that I could see." He glanced at Johnny. "From the sounds of things, I'd say someone was using a rifle. I don't suppose you'd know if any campers carry rifles or shotguns?"

"Beats me. I don't go through all the campers to check for guns," Johnny answered. "I would imagine a lot of them carry. I would if I were out on the road traveling."

"I hear you," Brad said. "Well, I think we're safe enough for tonight." He turned to Joseph. "Would you mind helping me get some boxes out of the car?"

Joseph followed him out the front door, and I got up and went out behind them.

I walked up to the car. Brad was talking to Joseph in a low voice.

"Keep an eye on things tomorrow," Brad was saying. "I don't like this. I've called the Sheriff, Jason, and he told me to come in late tomorrow and look around some more. The guys they sent out are new to the job, so they could have missed something. In my opinion, whoever shot at you all, probably knew exactly what he was doing. I imagine he wouldn't have missed if he wanted to hit one of you. Do you think he could have been shooting from a canoe or tube?"

Joseph shrugged. "I don't know. It was too dark to see. I just wanted to get everybody in the house-not run towards the river to see if I could see the shooter."

Brad smiled faintly. "You did the right thing. I wouldn't have expected you to go investigating. Just watch out tomorrow for everybody while I'm at work. It's probably a one-time happening, but we don't know. That's the problem. I'm not willing to take that risk with it being my family we're talking about."

"That means no working out in the yard tomorrow, Mamaw," Joseph instructed me.

"I'll stay inside," I promised.

Brad appeared satisfied. "There's a gun up in Jo's room, but don't use it unless you absolutely have to. If there's a sign of trouble, call the police. Don't try to take the law into your own hands, any of you."

"Got you," Joseph said.

"You're the only man here, Joseph, so it's up to you to protect these women. Johnny can't be down here and running his campground simultaneously," Brad concluded.

"Well, I expect him to show up anyway. He'll say he's looking after Mom," Joseph said sarcastically.

Brad laughed. "Johnny's okay, Joseph. He doesn't take much seriously. He always was a happy-go-lucky guy. It's just his way."

"If you say so," Joseph muttered and walked back to the house.

Brad and I stood there looking at each other.

"What are you thinking?" I finally asked.

Brad covered his face with his hands, obviously reflecting. "I don't know, Jo. I suspect if they were down by the river or in that vicinity, they were probably using a rifle, possibly a bolt action. It sounds personal to me if it's not some random shooter who doesn't know what he's doing. I don't like how close those bullets got to Aunt Lillian, but I can't think of any reason anyone would want to take a shot at her. They could have hit her if they were proficient at all with a gun. Maybe they were trying to frighten her. And none of this seems to tie in with Doc and Lora's murders. I hate to admit it, but I'm flat out of ideas." He looked down at me. "What do you think? Your instincts are good."

I hesitated. "Has Joseph said anything to you about checking Johnny Whitlock out?"

He frowned. "Johnny? Why?"

"Just a feeling Joseph has about him that something isn't right," I explained.

Brad stared at me, and I knew he saw Johnny as the boy he had run around with when he came to his Grandmother Rose's. "All right. I'll do some investigating. It can't hurt. I'm checking everybody out that crosses our radar. I don't like trying to find dirt on folks I partially grew up with, you know."

I put my hand on his arm. "I know, but we've got to find out who killed Doc and Lora and what this was all about tonight. Have you considered it is surrounding your aunt? Doc was her best friend, and now Lora. She and Aunt Lillian were friends, too, although not as close as Doc. Now, someone has taken a shot at her. It almost looks like it is something to do with your aunt."

He gave me a long look, and then placed both hands on my shoulders. "Jo, you be careful and watch over my aunt." His gray eyes were searching my green ones. "If this is something against my aunt, she is in danger, and the rest of you could be too." His hands tightened. "All I want to do is take care of you and keep you safe. I'm beginning to think that is going to be a harder job than I anticipated."

"Alaina could have told you I was a handful," I teased him.

He laughed. "It's okay, but we better pray because I can't understand what's happening here."

"So, you don't think Harvey Pemberton had anything to do with it?"

He lifted his hands from my shoulders. "There's not enough evidence. There is no evidence he was at Doc's house or in his yard. He could have been, but so could other people. Doc habitually sat on a big rock on the river shore and talked to everybody who came by. With the campground open, that's a lot of people." He shook his head. "For somebody that claimed not to like people, he sure liked to talk to them a lot."

"I know. I talked to Doc one time down there. As far as Lora Hutchins goes, I can't see Mr. Pemberton murdering her. He seemed to like her coming by the campsite."

"His wife certainly did. Dotty Pemberton liked Lora. That was obvious. And there is no motive there either."

I looked at him. "Brad, I don't think we've got all the puzzle pieces here. Something is missing. When we find out what that is, we'll better understand who killed these two people and who took a potshot at your aunt."

CHAPTER ELEVEN

Brad searched the property the following morning. I watched him from my position in my rocking chair in the turret.

Alaina was returning home, and she had promised she would come and tell me goodbye before leaving. I gathered she planned on stopping at the Cherokee River Campground to tell someone else goodbye.

Right now, my focus was on Brad and his diligent search of the backyard. He vanished from my sight when he went down the slope to the river. I could see the top of the gazebo with its rooster weather vane, but that was all. In about ten to fifteen minutes, he was back in my sight. He looked up and saw me sitting in the turret and waved. I waited for him to make the journey up the stairs. He came into the turret and grinned at me.

"I believe this is your favorite room in the whole house," Brad teased me. "You'll want to sleep here next."

"There's not enough room," I told him, surveying the small turret. Alana and Joseph had brought over my roll-top desk, the keyboard, and the rocking chair, but there wasn't a place for anything else.

He laughed and gazed out the window. "I didn't see any evidence of anything-no shell casings or anything to indicate anybody had been on the property. There should have at least been shell casings. Of course, they could have picked them up and taken them after the fact. There are too many footprints down at the river, but then there are people from the campground walking up and down the bank daily. I'll get a report from the officers who came out here yesterday. Just stay away from the windows today as best as you can."

I kissed him goodbye and sat quietly, meditating on this new mystery we were entangled in. I barely heard Alaina's footsteps on the stairs.

She was frowning when she entered the turret. "Mom, I know you love it up here, but don't you think you're a bit of a target."

"I'm staying back from the windows," I told her. "It's probably my favorite place in the whole house."

She sat down in the chair that went with the desk. "I don't like leaving with all this going on, but I've got to get back to work." Her face showed her concern.

I smiled at her. "We'll be all right. I'd feel better if we could find some pattern to the whole thing. There's nothing to connect Doc's murder with Lora's or vice versa. Since somebody shot at Aunt Lillian last night, I'm beginning to wonder if somehow everything is connected with her."

"What do you mean?" my blonde daughter asked.

"Well, Doc was Aunt Lillian's best friend. They had been friends all their lives. He had been good to her mother too. Lora was her friend too, sort of, anyway. It is easy for me to understand how Lora got herself killed. She was very aggravating; although I shouldn't say so since the poor thing is dead."

"If I didn't know Joseph better, I might be tempted to think he smothered her," Alaina admitted with a faint smile. "He was certainly put out with her and all her holiness."

"I think it just about got to Lillian," I responded. "She told me she felt sorry for her because she didn't have any friends. I think that last day, her sympathy had about run out."

"I take it Brad didn't find anything of interest out in the yard?"

I shook my head. "No, he's concerned about all of us." I paused. "What does Johnny Whitlock think about this?"

"Mother, I hope you're not starting on Johnny like Joseph." Her voice had raised a little.

"I wasn't going to say anything about Johnny. I don't know him," I returned. "I wondered if he had any ideas about who could have killed Doc and Lora."

Alaina seemed mollified. "He doesn't seem to have a clue, but you know he hasn't lived him in years. He was just a boy when his parents moved from here."

"Are his parents still living?" I asked curiously.

Alaina shook her head. "No, I asked him that. They died some time ago."

I studied her face. "Alaina, are you interested in Johnny romantically, I mean?"

A slow flush crept up in her fair face. "I might be," she admitted. "Johnny's a lot of fun." She looked down and laced her fingers together. "You know I've never gone out with anybody since Tim died." There was a bit of defiance on her face when she lifted her head to look at me. "I am still young, and it's been quite a few years. I will be lonely now that you are marrying Brad and moving away. Joseph and Ashley have their own lives, and you know how much time you all spend away from home."

I smiled reassuringly. "I'm not finding fault. Just make sure what you want is what God wants."

"I will, Mom. Right now, it's just nice having some-body interested in me." She came over and hugged me. "Anyway, I've got to go. Call me and let me know what's going on, so I don't worry."

"Will do," I promised and listened to her light footsteps go down the stairs.

Joseph and Ashley were my next visitors. Ashley sat on the keyboard bench, and Joseph claimed Alaina's chair.

«Well, did Brad find anything out back?" Joseph asked.

I shook my head. "No, I don't think so."

"Well, I thought the three of us could talk this over. Aunt Lillian says she's lazy this morning. She is drinking her coffee and reading her newspaper."

"She's all right, isn't she?" I asked, concerned. "After all, it's not every day she gets shot at."

"She's all right, Mamaw," Ashley answered me. "I think there are just too many things happening all of once."

"Did you all see the Abbotts and Maude Ashton yesterday?" Joseph asked.

"We did. Pastor Jim is going to marry Brad and me, and Maude Ashton will stand in for my mother, so I guess you will sit beside her at the wedding since you are giving me away, Joseph."

"That's fine," he said. "Has Brad picked his best man yet?"

"I think he's going to ask Sheriff Jason Pierce," I informed him.

I felt a little tension leave the air and surmised that Joseph was afraid he was going to ask Johnny Whitlock. I wasn't one to dance around topics. "I asked Brad to check out Johnny Whitlock," I volunteered.

Joseph looked relieved. "Good. I think it pays to be safe. If he's clean, we'll know it; if he isn't, we'll know that too. If Mom goes off the deep end over him, somebody better look into him."

I could tell Joseph was taking this being the man in the family today very seriously.

"Mamaw, who do you think killed Doc and Mrs. Hutchins?" Ashley asked me curiously.

I shrugged my shoulders. "I can't figure it out. We don't have enough clues to solve the puzzle."

Joseph got up and started pacing from one window to the other. "Okay, what do we know?"

"We know that Doc was smothered in his hammock sometime during the evening when we had the cookout," Ashley said.

"We know there were thirty people here at the picnic, and any of them could have slipped over there without being noticed." Joseph continued.

"And we know there's a campground full of people about a mile down the road, and they all tube and swim in the river and walk up the river bank," I added.

"That gives us plenty of suspects," Joseph said.

"And we know that Doc had some issues with one Harvey Pemberton back in the day." I threw in.

"That was over how he was treating his first wife," Joseph said. "Does anyone think that would be a reason for him to come back years later and do Doc in?"

"Don't forget Harvey's father's hardware store ended up closing over the whole mess," I remembered.

"I can't see it myself," Joseph reasoned. "I would think if Harvey were going to do anything to Doc, he would have done it when all of that was going on. He's moved on with his life and married someone else. It just doesn't make sense. I know he was charged with murder elsewhere but was found innocent. I can understand the need to question him under the circumstances, but I don't think he did it."

"And then the Cox's had some issues with the Pemberton's also," Ashley contributed.

"That was Harvey's father, wasn't it?' Joseph inquired, frowning slightly.

"I think so," I replied thoughtfully. "But Brad said he doesn't think there is anything there."

"Well, somebody killed Doc and Lora," Joseph insisted. "They didn't smother themselves."

"And there has to be a motive," Ashley contributed. "People don't go around smothering people for no reason. At least they don't unless we're dealing with a homicidal maniac."

"That's always a possibility," Joseph said seriously. "We've never run into one of them yet or a serial killer."

I stared at him. "I should hope not," I said sternly. "It's bad enough what we have had to deal with; deacons dead in pews and young women stuffed in our RV bays."

"Well, those cases got solved, so I imagine we will figure this out between us." Joseph sounded confident. "I just wish we had more to go on."

"I don't know if Brad has read any more of Doc's files, but I think that's a good place to start," I said, thinking aloud.

"Aunt Lillian said he didn't put everything in writing about his cases," Ashley mentioned. "So it could have something to do with something he didn't put down."

"Yeah, his father certainly didn't keep a record about Ernest Edwards throwing his daughter down the stairs," Joseph pointed out. "We know she broke her neck and died as a result, but there are no medical or police records about that."

"There're all kinds of people who could have killed Doc," I said slowly, "But what we don't know is how many of them had a motive. Doctors know a lot of family secrets. People used to talk to their family doctors back when he was practicing, but they don't always want those secrets revealed. As for Lora, if she were killed because she hinted to everybody, she might know who killed Doc and why; someone might have got nervous."

"I can imagine all kinds of people having a motive for killing Lora Hutchins," Joseph said under his breath, but I still heard him.

"Aunt Lillian felt sorry for her, Joseph,' I chided him softly.

He looked at me, started to say something, and then thought better of it.

"Or some homicidal serial killer may have seen her parked, broken down along the highway, and killed her too," Ashley said.

"Well, I think the police have ruled out the Pemberton's, at least Harvey, and I can't imagine why Dotty would kill either of these two. Brad doesn't seem to think the Cox man had anything to do with it, either. Mr. Pemberton told the police he didn't even know Doc was still alive. Both families thought it would be nice to camp by the river where they had been raised. I don't see that either of them have ulterior motives myself."

"Something has occurred to me," Joseph said, sitting back at the desk. "Have either of you thought of the possibility that this has something to do with Aunt Lillian? I hadn't thought about it until she was nearly shot last night. Sometime in the night, it came to me that she could be the focal point. She and Doc were close friends. Lora was a friend, and now somebody has taken a shot at her. At least we think it was her the shooter was aiming for."

I leaned back in my rocker. "I mentioned that to Brad this morning. The same thing had occurred to me."

"But why, Joseph?" Ashley asked, clearly perplexed. "Why would anyone want to take out Doc and Lora just because they were friends with Aunt Lillian?"

Joseph and I exchanged glances.

"That doesn't make a lot of sense when you put it that way," I said.

Joseph snapped his fingers. "Maybe it does. I think Mamaw is right. I think Brad should go through all of Doc's files. Maybe Doc had to go because of something he knew that would identify the killer if he were still here to tell on them. Perhaps someone is after Aunt Lillian. And Lora Hutchins was just in the way because someone feared she knew something. What is it they call that-collateral damage?"

"It would take a calculating person to devise such a plan." I wasn't sure I liked the sound of it.

"Well, if I'm right, I think whoever it is would be calculating," Joseph pointed out. "What about this? Maybe this person knows or thinks he knows where the Albert Edwards treasure is. They want Aunt Lillian out of the way, and probably imagine you and Brad, Mamaw, wouldn't want to live here if something happened to her. It would allow them to search the property at their leisure."

I was impressed. "It's a good theory, Joseph, but I don't think most people even believe in that story. That was supposed to have happened over a hundred years and fifty years ago. If there were anything to find, somebody else has probably found it by now."

Joseph shook his head adamantly. "I don't think so, and neither does Aunt Lillian. I've talked to her about it."

I frowned. "But what good would it do someone to kill Aunt Lillian to get the treasure? They don't need to kill her."

"Well, maybe they want to scare her out of here. If they wanted to kill her, they could have done that last night." Ashley suggested.

"Maybe they want to scare all of us out of here," Joseph said. "It would be easier to search the place if all of us were gone."

"I don't see that we are getting anywhere," I said at last. "But I think Doc and his father's medical files should be gone through. I think Brad is doing that."

Joseph and Ashley left the turret, and I sat there and stared out across the yard. I wanted to finish the beds, but I had promised Brad to stay inside today. I was getting the hang of growing herbs and perennial flowers and shrubs. It looked like a Garden of Eden, but now there appeared to be a serpent in the garden. He was shadowy and crafty. I just couldn't put a name and face on him yet.

CHAPTER TWELVE

The house phone rang at about eleven that morning. I heard Lillian answer it, and then Joseph raced up the stairs to bring me the phone.

"It's Elsie Franks, the pastor's wife," he mouthed, handing me the receiver.

"Hello, this is Jo Elliott."

"Jo, I'm so glad I caught you." That vivacious woman said. "I was wondering if you and Brad were busy this evening. I wanted to invite you over for supper."

I was thinking rapidly. I wasn't sure Brad would want to leave the house this evening after what had happened the previous night, but then Joseph would still be here.

"I'll call him and see if he is going to be working late," I told her. "What time would you like us to be there?"

"Would six be all right? That's when the Reverend and I usually eat."

"Let me call Brad and get back to you." I hung up and noticed that Joseph was still standing there.

"Can you keep an eye on things tonight if we go to the Franks?" I asked.

"Sure, Mamaw," he said. "It might be a good idea. They've been here for thirty years, so there would not be much about this area that they wouldn't know about."

"Pastor Don told me he loved history and had several books on the history of Willis. Something interesting might turn up," I reasoned. "Let me call Brad and run this by him."

I went downstairs to see if Lillian would feel safe with just Joseph and Ashley there. Brad was fine with our plans. He thought he ought to get off at the regular time that evening.

"Of course, I'll be fine. I'm not going to be run out of my own home," Lillian stated defiantly. "It will take more than a couple of shots. Besides, we don't know if they were shooting at me or somebody else. For that matter, they just may have been randomly shooting. Did Brad find anything when he searched the yard this morning?"

I shook my head.

She stared at me. "Well, I've lived here for eighty-two years, and I'm going to stay until I get moved to Morrisville. The idea that someone can make me leave until I am ready is ridiculous!"

I grinned. "That's the spirit, Aunt Lillian."

"Besides," she confessed with a grin. "I've got a gun too, and I know how to shoot it. Eugene taught both Violet and me how to shoot. Mother insisted on it. She wanted us to be able to defend ourselves."

"Are you a good shot?" I asked curiously.

"Not as good as Violet was," she admitted. "Violet was a crack shot."

Joseph had decided in my absence that he would fix dinner, and he and Ashley were in the kitchen preparing when Brad and I left for the Franks' residence.

The Franks lived in a brick house beside the church. It had always been part of the church property and was the parsonage. The front porch overflowed with geraniums and petunias. There wasn't much yard, but someone had planted red salvia along one side of the sidewalk.

We climbed the steps to the porch, and Pastor Don met us at the door.

He was all smiles. "We're so glad you could come this evening. We meant to have you over before now, but we got busy, and of course, we knew you all had the house to go through." He gestured with his hand for us to walk in. "So, now, you're here, and that's all that matters."

The living room was neat, with a couple of packed bookcases among the furniture. Brad sat down with the pastor in that room while I made my way to the kitchen, where Elsie was setting the table.

"Want some help?" I asked graciously.

"No, no, I've got this," she said, hurrying over to the stove to stir something in a pot. "It is so good of you to come with such short notice. The Reverend has been quite anxious about these murders. We're just a little country community. We aren't used to such goings on as this."

"I think all of us are upset about Doc and Mrs. Hutchins," I assured her. I wondered what she would say if she knew about Lillian being shot at the previous evening, but I wasn't about to share that news.

"Doc was such a treasure. I find it hard to believe anyone would want to hurt him. Of course, you didn't know him well, but he was a dear. As for Lora, she could be difficult, but as the Reverend says, she's gone now, and we must try to remember her good points." Elsie finished setting the table and smiled at me. "I'm going to put the food on the table, and you go get our two gentlemen."

I went back into the living room to find the pastor discussing with Brad the possibility of selecting him for the church board. Brad seemed honored but non-committal.

"Let me think about it," Brad told him. "I'm not saying 'no,' but right now we're so busy at the sheriff's office over these two murders, I'd hate to say 'yes' and then not be able to be at the meetings."

"We understand. Of course, we do. You give it some thought and some prayer too." He looked up at me as I entered the room. "I guess my good wife sent you to get us."

I nodded, and the three of us walked back into the kitchen and seated ourselves around the table.

Elsie Franks had outdone herself. She had a beef roast, mashed potatoes, gravy, fresh green beans seasoned just right, and garden-raised tomatoes and cucumbers. There was the inevitable iced tea to go with it, and she had baked a blackberry cobbler with vanilla ice cream for dessert.

Brad and the Franks had coffee, and I elected to have another glass of iced tea. Elsie refused my help cleaning up and sent me back to the living room with the men.

"It will only take me a few minutes, and then we can visit. I have a dishwasher, so I'll fill it up."

Pastor Don showed me some of his books about Willis in the living room. We went into his study and found the walls wholly filled with bookcases. His desk sat in the middle of the room, and it was neat and sparsely covered. Just a light and some pens graced the desktop. He seemed to know where every book was. He was very organized.

"I've collected books all my life," he was saying. "But some of my favorites have been about this area. Willis was well-known in the county back in the day. It was a large community, not like it is now. It's sad to walk down Main Street and see all the closed-up buildings that used to be thriving businesses. Mrs. Franks says we can't live in the past, but I'm afraid history has always been my passion."

He handed me one of the books titled "Willis in the Days of the Civil War." This book has some information about Albert Edwards, who bought the place you have now and built a stone house on the property. That stood until the turn of the twentieth century when your grandfather Ernest Edwards built the present house."

"Do you know anything about the money Albert Edwards was supposed to have hidden around the time of the Civil War?" I asked.

He smiled. "I have heard that story. Lillian insists that it is true, that her mother told her, and that William Edwards, Rose's father-in-law, had recounted the tale to her. To my knowledge, it has never been discovered."

"Where do you think he would have been likely to hide it?" I queried.

He shrugged his thin shoulders. "Probably not in the house, or someone would have found it. I always imagined it was in the ground somewhere; or maybe in the cellar or cistern. The cellar was under the smokehouse, but it fell years ago. It was still in use when Rose Edwards was bringing up her kids, but I thought I heard that Lillian had some excavator cover it up. I couldn't say about the cistern, but with the smokehouse gone, it would have dried up long ago. You see, the rain ran off the smokehouse roof into the eave sprout and the cistern."

I saw. I had avoided going to that part of the property due to my recent bad experiences with cellars.

"When I was a kid visiting here, my friends and I tried to dig up the entire yard before my grandmother put a stop to it," Brad commented.

"It's an interesting story and could be real as many people hid their valuables around that time. Nobody knew for sure which side would be the victor at the beginning of the Civil War. People were divided around here on their loyalties. Having two sons fighting on opposite sides in one household wasn't unusual. I pray we never have another mess like that in this country."

Elsie entered the room and sat in one of the two recliners. "Well, that's done. I hope you all got enough to eat."

"It was wonderful," I told her, and Brad said we appreciated the invitation.

"We've been talking about the supposed treasure that is hidden somewhere on the Edwards property," her husband said, bringing her into the conversation.

"I heard about that," his wife said, "But after all of this time if it has not been found, I would think it wasn't going to be."

"You never know," said her husband. "Stranger things have happened."

"What I want to know is if the police are any closer to finding the murderer of Doc and poor Lora Hutchins?" Elsie Franks questioned, looking at Brad.

"We've eliminated some possible suspects, but unfortunately, we're running out of theories," Brad answered. "Somebody has covered their tracks well."

"That is too bad," Reverend Franks said sadly. "It is never good for the guilty to go unpunished."

"We loved Doc dearly," Mrs. Franks continued. "But everyone knows doctors are privy to information the rest of us don't have. We wondered if maybe it was something like that. People like to keep their secrets, well, you know, secret."

"I don't know," Brad said bluntly. "We're still investigating."

"Lora Hutchins talked too much, and it even got back to us that she had made her brags that she knew why Doc had been killed." Mrs. Franks seemed agitated about it. "I tried encouraging her to keep silent about it, but she wouldn't listen to us either."

"Now, Mrs. Franks, we must be kind. The poor thing was murdered too." The pastor said, gently rebuking her.

"I know, but everybody knew what she said, and if the murderer is around here, he may have heard about it too." She looked at Brad. "Do the police still think it's someone local, or are they thinking it's a stranger passing through?"

"We're looking at everything," Brad said evadingly.

"How is Lillian holding up?" the pastor asked, moving the conversation in a different direction.

"She's doing okay," I spoke up. "It's hard for her because she knew them both so well."

"Lillian showed real Christian charity to Lora," Elsie commented. "I've always admired her for that."

"Would it be possible to borrow any of your books on the history of Willis?" I asked.

"Of course, of course. Let me get two or three that I think you might be interested in. You keep the books as long as you like." The pastor hurriedly got to his feet and retreated to his study.

About thirty minutes later, armed with three books, Brad and I left the house and started back to Lillian's.

"I think we got invited to supper so Mrs. Franks could find out what the police were doing in this investigation," Brad said, and I could tell he was a little annoyed.

"Probably," I agreed. "But it is interesting to know what everyone is thinking. People seem to believe that Doc's murder had something to do with something he knew about someone. And Lora's murder was caused by her telling everyone she knew who it was."

Brad looked at me for a second and then laughed. "That pretty well sums it up in a couple of sentences," he said. "But what am I supposed to do with that?"

"Read some more of Doc's and his father's medical files, I guess." I put my arm through his. "Let's go home and see what the rest of the family is up to."

CHAPTER THIRTEEN

The rest of the family was playing dominoes. Joseph and Ashley were very competitive, so I could hear their raised voices walking up the steps to the front door. Brad left, and I played a game with them before bed.

I didn't sleep well. Something was tugging at my mind. I couldn't put my finger on anything, and my dreams were crazy and shadowy. Nothing made any sense. Nothing added up.

The following day was sunny and clear. I had decided, shooters or no shooters, I was going to finish the flower beds in the backyard. I was too near completion to stop now. Joseph declared he would help me and left Ashley to assist Lillian in the house. I knew he was attempting to keep Ashley out of danger and be my bodyguard. While we worked, I told him about the conversation with the Franks from the night before. Joseph spaded with his hands, but those shrewd blue eyes also kept watch. When we stopped for lunch, I decided we were done.

"I don't think even Grandma Rose could find any fault with these beds," I said proudly.

Joseph was staring into the horizon. "Let's walk over and look where that old cistern and cellar were." He suggested.

I got a look on my face, and he said. "Now, Mamaw, that's in the past. You are going to have to get over that."

I sighed. "You're right. Let's go. I'm not sure Brad would approve, but I don't want you going by yourself. I think it's close to Doc's property line."

We walked across the yard like we didn't have a care in the world. I was trying not to think about cellars or bullets flying by.

Sure enough, there was an area where a building had been torn down, which I suspected was the smokehouse, and the cellar had been concreted over.

It didn't look like anyone could have gotten in it for years. The cistern was beside it and still had the hand pump, although it was covered in rust. There was a heavy wooden lid that I doubted was the original.

"I wonder if I could get the lid off and look inside?" Joseph was thinking aloud.

"Go ahead," I encouraged him. "You won't be happy until you do."

Joseph lugged on the heavy lid, and I ended up helping him. Together we pulled the cover off and peered down into the darkness. Joseph threw a rock down into the cistern and heard it clatter against the concrete bottom.

"No water in it anyway," Joseph said. "I'd like to get a ladder and go down in it."

"Not today, you won't." I was firm about that. "I expect we'd better get back to the house."

We pulled the lid back over the cistern. We were close to Doc's house. The old stone structure looked forlorn with Doc gone. The grass was knee-high, and the garden had gone to weeds already. It gave me a sad feeling. I would have to get Brad or Joseph to mow it. I felt like we owed Doc that much.

Brad came home earlier today and motioned me to go to the turret. Before he arrived upstairs, I had already climbed up and was scrutinizing my handiwork.

I turned when he entered. "What's happened?" I asked.

"I started looking into Johnny Whitlock," he shared. "He left here with his parents when he was nine years old. He went into the army after high school. He didn't do that well academically in high school, and he got in trouble in the army and got a dishonorable discharge. I haven't got all the facts on that yet. Anyway, he ended up on the streets as an alcoholic. Then, all at once, he does a total about-face. Some street mission got hold of him, and he changed his life. I talked to the minister who runs the mission, and he said it was wonderful how Johnny had come to know the Lord and became an entirely new person."

"That sounds like a good testimony to me," I said, watching him.

"It did to me too. The minister told me that when Johnny's mother passed away, she left him some money, and that's how he bought the campground here. I guess

Joseph can stop worrying about Alaina getting involved with Johnny. He looks clean. He's got a record for being drunk and disorderly, petty stealing, and that sort of thing. It looks like they slapped him on the wrist and sent him back on the street." Brad seemed pleased about it all. "I didn't like the idea of my old friend not turning out right, but now we know."

"I'll tell Joseph if you want me to. I think he'll be relieved. You can't blame him for wanting to look after his mother." I pointed out.

Brad smiled. "I don't. I would feel the same way." He ran a hand through his sandy hair. "It just doesn't help with the cases I'm looking at. If I didn't know better, I'd think whoever killed Doc and Lora just disappeared into thin air."

I couldn't get to sleep that night. I kept rolling and tossing. Finally, in exhaustion, I got up and mounted the stairs to the turret. It was peaceful. I didn't turn on the lights. I just sat there in the dark. The windows were open, and I could hear bugs hitting the screens. Night sounds were around me. There was a full moon, and the yard seemed full of shadows. I moved my rocker against the wall and decided to risk a light from the floor lamp I had carried upstairs.

I picked up one of the Mason jars and unscrewed the lid. I could do something useful and read Grandma Rose's journals. It didn't appear I was going to get any rest. I sighed. I read about growing tomatoes, peppers, and corn.

It was more of the same. But then I discovered another section written with a different ink.

I straightened in my chair, and I was more awake than ever.

'Ernest was gone all day over at the courthouse paying the property taxes," I read.

'So we had a little bit of peace today. The children are in school, except Lily, and I sent her to his mother's last night. Yesterday, Ernest and I had a huge fight. He said he ought to put us all out on the street as little good as we all were to him.

I tried to talk to his mother, but I realized today that she is afraid of him too. He has a terrible temper. His father, William, is gone, and he was the only one that could do a little something with him. I know he took up for the children and me a few times when he was living, but there's no one I can count on anymore. I thought about talking to the preacher, but he thinks Ernest is a great person. Besides, Ernest is on the church board, and if the preacher did anything against him, he would see to it that he was fired. I don't want that.

What am I to do? I have no friends that I can go to. Ernest saw to that. He found fault with any woman friend I made. Doc Graham is the only one I can talk to, but he doesn't know what to do either. He says he can't get involved with family disputes, and I can see his point. Graham's the only doctor around here and he must treat everyone equally.

Ernest would say something was going on between Doc and me if he got involved, and there's not. As God is my witness, I have always been faithful to Ernest. I have a clear conscience about that. I almost wish he would run off with some other woman, but he likes to have a good reputation. If people only knew what he was really like?

I don't think I will ever get over seeing my baby daughter lying dead at the bottom of those stairs. I think about it every time I go up or down those steps. God, help me. I don't know what to do."

I looked up from reading and stared across at Doc's old stone house. I blinked my eyes and looked again. I could see a shadow moving outside the back door. I rapidly put out my lamp and started down the steps reaching into my pocket for my cell phone. Quickly, I dialed Brad's number. He answered on the second ring. He didn't sound like he had been sleeping.

"Brad," I said softly. "Somebody is sneaking around Doc's back door."

"Can you tell who it is?"

"No, it's too dark. I can't tell if it's a man or a woman, but I think it's a man."

"Okay, Jo, I'm on my way. Don't any of you go over there." It was a command.

"They may be gone by the time you get here," I complained.

"We'll have to chance it. I'll call it in," Brad answered. "There may be a patrol car out that way. Whoever it is may not think any of you are awake and believe they have plenty of time to look around."

I heard him knock on a door, and the sheriff answered him.

"Jo says someone is trying to break into Doc's house," Brad told him. To me, he said, "Jason's coming with me. I've got to go, Jo. Can you watch out of the turret and keep an eye out until we get there?"

"I planned on it," I told him.

"Check in if anything changes," Brad said, and I heard the click as he hung up.

A bedroom door opened downstairs, and I went down to see Joseph and Ashley in the hallway.

"What's going on?" Joseph asked.

"I was up in the turret and saw someone trying to get in Doc's back door," I informed him. "Brad's coming over with Jason."

Ashley was holding onto Joseph. "We heard you talking," she explained.

"Yeah, I called Brad as soon as I saw somebody trying to get in Doc's house."

I started back up the steps to the turret. "I've got to keep watch up here."

I heard Joseph and Ashley come up behind me. The three of us knelt on the floor and peered out the window towards Doc's stone house.

For a few moments, we didn't see anything. Then I stiffened. I caught a glimpse of light. Someone was inside the house with a flashlight.

Joseph had seen it too. "Somebody's in there. Maybe I ought to go over and scare them off."

I grabbed his arm. "Brad said no one was to go over. The sheriff lives between here and Morrisville, so they should be here any time. Brad doesn't want us involved. It's a police matter."

Joseph's lips tightened. 'I don't want whoever that is getting by with it just because there are no cops around."

I understood his frustration. "I know, Joseph, but we are not police."

"Before Brad, we wouldn't have thought twice about getting involved, danger or not," Joseph fumed.

I could feel my temper rise, and he said quickly. "Of course, I guess we could get into trouble."

I saw movement on the road and two men moving toward Doc's house. They were both holding guns, and one of them was my Brad. I reasoned they had parked the cruiser down the road and walked in.

As we watched, Brad moved to the back of the house while the other cop entered from the front. The sound of glass breaking hit our ears, and a dark figure flew out of a side window and headed toward the river. I heard Brad yell, "Stop!" but the intruder never slowed. He was moving swiftly. I didn't imagine Brad expected him to come out by the side of the house, so the guy had a good head start.

Brad and Jason ran across the yard, and we watched until they were out of view. We saw the two return from the river about ten minutes later.

We went downstairs just as Brad and Sheriff Jason came through the front door.

Brad wasn't happy. "He got away whoever he was."

"I didn't get a good look at him," Jason admitted. "He must have been going out the window when I turned the key in the lock."

"It was a man. I'm pretty certain of that," Brad commented. "At least he moved like a man. He was fast. That's for sure."

"What would someone want in Doc's house?" Joseph wondered.

Brad and I exchanged glances. "Probably those medical files," I said to Joseph. "You got them all out, didn't you?" I questioned Brad.

He nodded. "Yeah, we've been going through them. There are a lot of files, so it's going to take a while. Police work is like that-painstakingly."

"Well, it seems we are looking in the right direction anyway," Joseph said slightly smugly.

The sheriff raised his eyebrows, and Joseph explained. "We've been talking, and we think Doc was killed over something he knew that would identify the murderer. It's just a theory, but I think I'm right."

Brad smiled grimly. "I suppose you also think somebody was gunning for my aunt the other night and wasn't just a crazed shooter?"

"Yeah, I think so." Joseph was meeting him eye to eye.

Brad looked at me. "May I ask what you were doing in the turret at one o'clock in the morning?"

"I couldn't sleep. I've been reading your grandmother's journal." I said abashedly.

"And I suppose you two heard Jo calling me?" Brad questioned, looking at my grandson and his wife.

They nodded, and Brad continued. "Well, let's hope we don't wake up my aunt."

"It's too late for that. Who can sleep around here?" We all turned to see Aunt Lillian standing in the doorway in her bathrobe and slippers.

Brad made a face, and she looked from Brad to the sheriff. "What's going on now, and why are you two here in the middle of the night?"

The sheriff responded to her. "Jo saw someone trying to break into Doc's house and called us. He was still in the house but got away from us when we arrived."

Lillian stared at them. "Whatever would anyone want in that old house?"

"It's been suggested they were looking for Doc's medical records," Jason told her. He grinned at Brad. "It looks like your new family are all investigators."

Brad gave a short laugh, but it rang hollow, and I knew he was concerned about us.

"I'll get someone from the sheriff's department out in the morning to see if there are any fingerprints or other evidence. I figure we gave them a good scare tonight." Jason told Brad.

To us, the sheriff said. "I suggest you all go back to bed. I don't think anybody's going to try anything else tonight."

It was still another hour before I got to sleep. My thoughts were all over the place. I felt like I was trying to put a jigsaw puzzle together without any of the significant pieces. "Lord," I prayed, "help us to figure this out."

Aunt Lillian was still talking about the intruder in the morning and seemed surprised that anyone would try to break into Doc's house.

"He never kept a lot of money over there," she said thoughtfully. "I can't imagine what they wanted. I wonder if we are not getting some undesirable people down at that campground. We never had all this going on before they reopened that place."

The kids and I looked at each other and then at her.

"Are you saying you think it's some random person from the campground? Why would that person kill two people they didn't know?" Joseph sounded puzzled.

Lillian's hand rose and fell. "I don't know. It's about as good of a theory as any other I've thought of." She turned to Joseph. "Let's take some more stuff over to Morrisville today. I need to get out of here for a little while."

"Sounds good to me. Mamaw, will you and Ashley be all right?" Joseph questioned.

"We'll be fine," I answered for Ashley and me. "I think I may take it easy today. I did too much yesterday and didn't get much sleep last night."

Ashley needed some laundry done and decided she'd get all the sheets and towels washed while she was at it.

I escaped to my turret. I had to admit the yard looked great even if I had done most of it. I wondered how much it had all cost. The plants would have been much smaller when Lillian and her mother had first bedded them. It was important to me to keep the garden up to the high standard those two ladies had begun.

I went back to reading Grandma Rose's journal. I skipped through some of the pages hoping to find more personal notes. The woman could write scores of papers on gardening, and I suspected that was a form of escapism for her. I was curious to read how she coped with a nearly impossible situation.

The phone rang downstairs, and it didn't sound like Ashley was answering it.

"Let it ring," I thought. "It's probably just some telemarketer."

Finally, in near exasperation, I opened up the other jar. There were fewer sheets of paper in this jar than in the first one. I settled back in the rocker and began to read. The first pages were more of the same -gardening and more gardening. Finally, I came to another section where she was sharing personal things. Mostly, it was a woman crying out of her desperation. I could read it in every line. It was a woman who loved her children and wanted them raised in a peaceful, safe home. After the death of Rosemary, I didn't think she felt that her home was safe or peaceful. She was struggling with what few options she felt she had. There were no women's shelters or safe houses back then. Her husband had effectively cut off all avenues of escape with friends or family. Her parents were deceased, and her mother-in-law would not dare help her as she was scared of her son, also. Divorce would make her a target. She didn't think anyone would believe her if she told the truth about her husband. Doc Graham Masters might back her up, but that would ruin his career. She had no doubt, and I ultimately agreed that Ernest Edwards would have destroyed Doc's medical practice. She wasn't the sort of a woman to have a lover. She was stuck with no way of escape. Even if she died, there were still her children to think of. Who would take care of her children?

And this woman, more than anything, was a mother who loved her children.

I turned the page and stopped rocking. There in big letters were the words: ***TODAY I KILLED MY HUSBAND!***

CHAPTER FOURTEEN

The papers slid out of my hands and hit the floor. I don't know when I was so shocked. How would I ever tell Brad or Aunt Lillian what I had discovered? Not only was his grandfather a murderer, but so was his grandmother-this woman who was like a paragon of virtue to her daughter, Lillian.

My next thought was, is murder ever justifiable? The Ten Commandments ruled that out with its startlingly direct "Thou Shalt Not Kill." What would I have done in her shoes? How far would I go to protect Alaina, Joseph, and Ashley? I got up and began pacing the floor like Joseph.

Forgotten were the instructions to stay away from the windows. All I could think of was that poor woman who had fallen down the stairs five years ago and died at the age of ninety-six. How long had that woman lived with what she had done to keep her children safe? Eugene would have been around eight, so we were talking about sixty years or so at least. I sat back down in the rocker, feeling dazed. I had to get myself together before Joseph and Lillian returned, and Brad came home tonight.

I picked up the papers from the floor and began searching to see if there were more. To my amazement, the next page started again on gardening. I flipped through some more pages until I found what I was looking for.

"It has occurred to me," she wrote, *"that someday someone in the family might want to know the rest of the story. Was I right or wrong to kill Ernest? I don't know. It doesn't much matter now. He is dead. The two oldest were at school. I sent the youngest to my mother-in-law. She has a habit of showing up without warning, so I thought it best to keep her occupied.*

I fixed dinner for Ernest just like always, but unknown to him; I had put Monkshood root in his food. I had carefully dug some out and replaced the soil exactly as it was. He grumbled as he ate like always. Said something tasted bitter. (It would.) Nothing ever suited him anyway. He said my cooking had made him nauseous in a very short time. He wanted me to get the doctor, but I knew he was out on calls and not home. Later, his breathing became labored. I touched him, and his skin was cold and clammy.

I sat there and watched him. I knew enough about the plant that I was aware that his heart would slow and stop. He died staring at me with those accusing eyes. He never knew what was wrong with him.

I finished my dinner and went over to Doc's. He wasn't home. I waited until he returned and told him I thought Ernest had had a heart attack. I didn't drive, so I couldn't go for help, not that I wanted to. Doc had a phone, but he had locked his house when he had left. Ernest didn't see the need for a phone with Doc next door.

When Doc returned, he came to our house and pronounced him dead. I asked him if he thought it was a heart attack, and he looked at me strangely, but then he said, 'yes, that was what it looked like to him.' As he did with Rosemary, he made all the arrangements for me.

When the children came home from school, I gathered them around me and told them their father had gone to Heaven. (God forgive me!) Neither of them cried. Eugene said something about things just happening. For a little boy, he is very smart. When Lily returned with her grandmother, she let me hold her and never said a word.

Grandma Christine wanted to try to comfort me. She said she knew what it was like to be a widow. Grandma Christine did, but I was sure she had never met one as happy as me! She and her husband, William, were very close by all accounts.

Everybody behaved very nicely during the wake and the funeral. People felt sorry for me, and I let them all be sympathetic, but inside I was shouting for joy. I was free!"

I turned the paper over, but there was nothing else but a footnote at the bottom of the page.

"I am burying these papers in mason jars out by the Monkshood plant. It seems like a good place to keep them.

Maybe someday, someone will find them and judge me or feel my pain. It won't matter which. I am at peace."

And then there was her signature Rose Edwards.

I wondered if she had indeed been at peace. Undoubtedly, she had been a woman of morals. How had she managed to live with what she had done? I placed the papers back in the jars and returned them to the corner of the turret.

I was still sitting there when Lillian and Joseph came back. Ashley had been busy and got all the laundry done. I went to the kitchen to begin supper. I was being too quiet, for Lillian was watching me.

"Are you all right, Jo? You aren't talking very much." She commented.

I forced a smile. "I'm fine, Lillian. Just a little exhausted. I didn't get much rest last night."

She was still studying me. "Well, maybe you should go to bed early tonight. You do look tired."

Brad came home while we were still at the supper table. I handed him a plate, and he sat down beside me.

He smiled at me. "How was your day?"

"Okay," I said, attempting to be non-committal.

I didn't think he entirely believed me, but I dropped my head so he couldn't see my eyes.

Brad turned to his aunt. "Aunt Lillian, I have some news for you," Brad announced.

She laid her fork on her plate. "I hope it is good news. I've had about all the bad news I can handle."

Brad was helping himself to another pork chop. "These are good, Jo." He began cutting up the chops into bite sizes. "You'll never guess what we discovered today among Doc's medical files- Arthur Masters' files, that is."

Lillian's hand rose and fell. "I couldn't begin to guess. You'll have to tell me."

Brad was chewing on his pork chop. He waited a moment. "Well, in the middle of all those files, we found Doc's will." He pointed his fork at his aunt. "And you are the only beneficiary."

I heard Ashley gasp, and Joseph raised one eyebrow. Lillian sank back in her chair. If she knew about it, she gave a good imitation of being surprised.

"Me? Why would he leave everything to me?"

"Well, who else did he have to leave it to?" Brad pointed out. "You were the closest thing to family he had. It was written twenty years ago, and I guess he had never wanted to change it."

"Is it legal?" Lillian wanted to know.

"It's a legal will. It's handwritten and signed. He got a couple of men from church to witness it. At least that's who they told me the two were at the sheriff's office. Both of them are deceased now. But it would hold up in court if that's what you're asking." Brad told her.

"What am I going to do with another house?" Lillian asked fretfully. "I'm just getting this one sold, and now I'm stuck with another one."

"You could sell it," Joseph suggested. "Money's always a good thing to have."

"True," Lillian agreed. "But it would have to be someone good. I wouldn't want just anyone moving in beside you all," she said, looking from Brad to me.

"I don't know exactly how much Doc had in the bank," Brad continued. "He had already prepaid his funeral expenses, so that was no problem, but we did find a bank book today. It had a few thousand. The house and land would be worth something, but the furniture didn't look much good when I went over the place."

Lillian shook her head. "Doc didn't care much about what the house looked like inside. All he cared about was what the outside looked like."

"I was thinking yesterday we needed to mow and do some weeding over there," I mentioned.

"You'll need to take the will to the courthouse and get probate started," Brad told his aunt. "Unfortunately, that's going to have to wait until we get his murder solved unless your lawyer takes it to court and gets a judge to sign off on it."

Lillian's face displayed her sadness. "I would rather have Doc than his money or his house," she said sorrowfully.

"We all would," I said softly. "But Doc must have loved you a lot to leave everything to you."

"Just like I was his wife," Lillian murmured. "He loved me. I know that. I loved him but didn't think I would make a good wife." She arose from the table, and we heard her bedroom door close a few minutes later.

My face was probably a study. All I could think of was the confession I had read earlier. ***Today I killed my husband.*** How much misery had Ernest and Rose caused their family because they were miserable? Lillian had refrained from marrying because she didn't want it to turn out like her parents' marriage. Violet had run away from home with someone she apparently had not married and never returned. None of the family knew whether she was dead or alive. Eugene had stayed away from his home and seldom brought his wife. Rosemary's life was cut short by a tyrant of a father. And Rose; what price did she pay? How had she suffered?

I stood over the kitchen sink, washing dishes and drying them without seeing them.

I didn't know Joseph and Ashley had left the room until I turned to face Brad.

He had come up behind me and put his arms around me.

"Okay, I know you well enough by now to know that something's happened today." He said gently. "Are you going to share it with me or not?"

"Let me finish the dishes, and then I'll meet you in the turret," I whispered back.

His gray eyes searched my face. "Okay," he said finally.

Joseph and Ashley were in the den watching television. I finished straightening up the kitchen and started up the staircase. Brad was standing in the turret gazing out the windows. He turned when I entered the room.

"You did a good job on the gardens, Jo. Grandma Rose would be proud of you." He was smiling, but the smile faded when I handed him the papers where Grandma Rose's confession was written.

Today I killed my husband. I would see that line in my dreams, I thought.

The color left Brad's face. He stared at me for a long moment, then looked back down at the paper he still held in his hand.

"You'd better go ahead and read the rest of it," I said gently.

He continued to read. I went and sank into the rocker chair, watching him. Different emotions flittered across his features. I knew him well enough by now to be able to read some of them.

When he finished, he sat down on the keyboard bench, his shoulders hunched.

I went to him and touched his shoulder. "Brad, are you going to be okay?"

He slipped his arm around my waist. "I know murder's wrong," he said thoughtfully. "I've helped to put a couple in prison myself for killing someone- one of them- more than one person. But reading this and knowing all the circumstances, I can't honestly say I wouldn't have done the same thing. I hope I wouldn't because we can't have people taking the law into their own hands. Was it wrong? I'd have to say, 'Yes.' Would I have sympathized with her? Again, I would say, 'Yes.' He looked up at me. "Does that offend you?"

I shook my dark head. "Not a bit. I've thought a lot about it this afternoon and evening. If someone killed my child that callously and mistreated my other children, I don't know what I'd do, Brad. In today's world, there are shelters and laws to protect a woman, but back then- she had nowhere to go. It's obvious she was worried about what would happen to her three remaining children growing up in that atmosphere. I think she was afraid your grandfather might hurt her or one of the other children."

"So now I know both of my grandparents are murderers," Brad reflected. "I'm glad I didn't know this before I became a cop. I might have made a different choice."

"Why? You're a good cop."

"The problem is we don't get to make judgment calls like this. In reality, it was murder, and the Doc probably knew it was and covered it up. It wasn't just murder, but premeditated murder. She knew what she was doing when she prepared his dinner with Monkshood. She couldn't plead temporary insanity. A jury would still have to convict her if they followed the law." He looked at me again. "They wouldn't have had a choice."

"I don't think I could have voted to convict had I been on that jury," I said flatly. "Not knowing the circumstances."

"It's hard to tell which way that would have gone," Brad said. "Doc Graham Masters knew the truth; if he knew it, his son probably did too."

"No doubt she paid in other ways," I said, thinking aloud. "She had to live with what she had done. It makes me feel differently about that Monkshood plant."

"I've seen it bloom in the late summer and fall," Brad admitted. "It is beautiful. I wonder why Grandma left that out there. You'd think she would dig it up and destroy it."

"Maybe she wanted to be reminded. Somebody told me that she said anything was worth it for the children. She must have been thinking of that. I think she took the chance and made the horrible decision because of her children." I put my arm around Brad's neck. "The question is do we tell your Aunt Lillian?"

"No!" Brad rose to his feet and went back across to the window. "No, definitely no! I don't want my aunt to know anything about it. Hide these papers and jars somewhere."

I frowned. "Don't you think Aunt Lillian has the right to know? Do you think your Dad knew or guessed?"

"If he did, he never said. I don't know whether Aunt Lillian has the right to know, but right now, I'm deciding not to tell her, and please don't you say a word to your family either." He was observing me. "I don't think Aunt Lillian can handle any more right now. Finding out she is

Doc's beneficiary has sent her to her room tonight. I don't know what this would do to her."

I hated to mention what I was thinking. "Brad, do you think she already knows? She knew your grandfather had killed her little sister."

He frowned and rubbed his forehead with his hand. "I hadn't thought of that. If Aunt Lillian does, she needs to tell us on her own. Right now is not the right time to bring this up." He turned back to the window. "If I could only find out who killed Doc and Lora Hutchins."

I sighed. Yes, if only.

CHAPTER FIFTEEN

Lillian came to me the following day while I was eating my breakfast of scrambled eggs and toast in the kitchen.

"I'm going to Morrisville today," she announced. "I called my lawyer, and he will fit me in this morning. I have Doc's will, and I'm going to see if my lawyer can get probate granted. It's up to the judge, apparently. Tom, Tom Lufton, my lawyer, and I have been friends for years, so I called him before he left his house. Brad said the sheriff's department has no problem with my having it as I am not suspected of killing the poor man." She poured herself a cup of coffee and prepared some slices of toast. "Doc leaving everything to me is causing me more work, but I quite see that he had no one else to leave it to as far as family. I wish he would have thought of something else. He could have left it to a charity." She shook her head.

"I think he cared a lot about you," I said, sitting down at the table with her with my cup of hot tea.

"I know he did." She sipped her coffee. "While I'm there, I will get the paperwork to get this house in your and Brad's name. I haven't told Brad yet, but I'm going to deed the house to you both and have you all sign a contract to pay monthly payments to me directly. I don't need any interest, and I'm not going to charge the only relative I have a lot of interest."

My green eyes widened in surprise. "Aunt Lillian, Brad, and I don't expect you to lose money on this deal. You have to live too. We would have to pay interest to a bank or loan company."

"I know, but this is what I want to do for the two of you. It's my wedding present to you, so don't expect anything else." She grinned as she finished her words.

I stared at her. "I don't know what to say, and I don't know what Brad will say either."

"If the both of you are smart, you will say, "Thank you very much," and be done with it," she said, drinking the last of her coffee. She rose to her feet. "I'm going now. When the kids get up, tell them to wait for me to return before they start getting into things. If I'm not too tired, I may go through some more. If I am, tomorrow's another day."

I listened to her footsteps go out the front door, and in a few moments, her car started, and then that sound faded farther from the house she went.

I was still sitting at the table with my cold toast and tea when Ashley and Joseph entered the kitchen.

"You look to be in another world, Mamaw," my grandson said. "What's going on?"

"Just thinking," I returned evasively.

"Well, Ashley and I have been talking…." He stopped. "Where's Aunt Lillian? Is she up yet?"

"Up and gone," I answered. "She went to see her lawyer today."

Joseph cocked an eyebrow, and when he didn't get any response from me, he continued. "Well, like I was saying, Ashley and I have been talking, and we thought we'd like to look around the property a little more. Maybe we can see somewhere where something might be buried or hidden."

I was skeptical. "Joseph, the property's not going to look like it did back in the middle of the 1800s. There might have been other buildings here, a barn, for instance."

That didn't deter Joseph. "I know there was a barn. It was near the smokehouse, and they had a cistern to water the animals. The cistern for the house has been gone for years. It was close to this house. Later they drilled a well, and now I think they've got city water out here."

"That's more convenient than a cistern," I commented. "That depends on rainwater. You'd be out of water if you had much of a drought."

"It's hard for me to imagine depending on the rain for water," Ashley contributed. "We're just so used to going to the sink and turning on the spigot."

"I imagine Rose and Ernest and his mother and father, William and Christine, had to get by without a lot of things we take for granted today," I mused.

JOYCE IGO

"Have you learned anything new from reading Grandma Rose's gardening journal?" Joseph asked.

"She goes on a lot about gardening. I've learned a lot about that," I answered.

Joseph gave me a hard look and then. "Well, I'm getting a ladder and going down in the cistern by the cellar."

"Not by yourself, you aren't!" I insisted firmly.

"He'll be all right, Mamaw," Ashley said. "I'll go with him."

I got to my feet and started clearing the table. "All right, you two, I've got some calls to make for our singing group this morning. Try to stay out of trouble."

Joseph grinned. "Aw, Mamaw, you know we can care for ourselves."

I grinned back. "I know, Joseph. It's just that we seem to get ourselves in messes that none of us planned on."

I watched them go out the back door and, out of the corner of my eye, saw Joseph carrying a ladder out toward where the smokehouse had been. Soon trees and shrubs hid him from view. I finished the kitchen and then went to get my phone.

I sat in Lillian's office, contacted pastors where we were scheduled to sing and made some new appointments. It always took more time than I had estimated, mainly because they were all friends, and we had to catch up on each other.

An hour later, Ashley came into the house looking for me. I heard her call, "Mamaw! Where are you?"

My heart sank. I went in the direction of her voice. "Ashley, please tell me nothing has happened to Joseph."

She was in the foyer. "No, Joseph is still in the cistern. He forgot to take a flashlight, so he's using the light on his phone to look around."

I frowned. "So why did you come in?"

It was Ashley's turn to frown. "I thought I heard you calling me. It sounded like you, anyway. I thought you needed help with something. I told Joseph I heard you call and that I would be right back."

"I didn't call you."

We exchanged looks, and both of us flew out the front door and around the side of the house. We didn't lessen our stride until we reached the cistern. The lid was resting over the top of the cistern, but there was no Joseph or ladder.

"Joseph! Where are you?" Both of us were screaming the words at the same time.

At first, I didn't hear any response, but then I noticed the lid moving slightly up and down. Quickly, the two of us began pushing the heavy wooden cover back off the cistern. Joseph's dark head came into view. We helped him climb out, and he glared at us.

"That wasn't funny!" he said furiously.

"We didn't put the lid back on, Joseph," Ashley assured him.

"Well, somebody did. All of a sudden, everything went black. The ladder didn't reach quite the top, so somebody trapped me in this cistern. And if it wasn't one of you, who was it?"

I didn't blame him for being angry. "Joseph, Ashley said she heard someone calling her name and thought it was me, so she came in the house to see what I wanted."

"And Mamaw hadn't called at all," Ashley said, puzzled. "I don't know who it was, but I heard my name."

Joseph was scanning the yard. "There are so many trees and bushes around here. There are too many hiding places. If you all hadn't been here and known where I had gone, it's hard to say how long I might have been down there."

"Somebody would have found you, I would think." I encouraged him. "It looks like someone is trying to scare us, so we won't want to buy the place."

"But why?" Joseph said. "Why would anybody care if you and Brad bought it or not."

"Maybe somebody wants it for themselves," Ashley threw in.

"Well, you can't always get what you want," Joseph returned. "Just because I want something doesn't guarantee I'll be able to have it. Aunt Lillian has promised it to Brad and Mamaw. Somebody else will have to go somewhere else."

"Maybe it's someone who knows about the treasure," Ashley responded.

"If there is such a thing, the chances of finding it look to me to be dim," I said. "Brad looked for it when he was little, and so did Lillian and her brother and sister."

"Albert Edwards should have left a paper saying where he had hidden it instead of going off and getting himself killed in the Civil War," Joseph complained.

"I don't imagine he planned on getting himself killed," I countered. "For all we know, someone may have found it decades ago and never said anything."

"Wouldn't trying to get rid of old money and old coins attract attention?" Joseph asked.

"Well, if you essentially stole them, you'd probably look to sell them to somebody shady like yourself," I pronounced.

"I guess that's true," Joseph mused. "Well, they would belong to the Edwards family."

"And right now, that family is down to two-Lillian and Brad," I contributed. "And neither one of them has the treasure."

Joseph shook his head. "What a mess!"

"Did you find anything down in the cistern?" I asked, getting back to the reason he was down in the ground in the first place.

Joseph shook his head. "I looked it over pretty closely, and I couldn't see any loose concrete or anything. I hoped someone searched the cellar before they covered it up."

We walked back across the yard and around the front of the house. We got to the front porch when Brad drove up in his cruiser. To our astonishment, Aunt Lillian was in the front seat with him. I turned back down the front steps, Joseph and Ashley behind me.

I opened the passenger door. "Aunt Lillian, why are you riding around in a police cruiser?"

Brad came around to me. His features were stern and set. "One of Aunt Lillian's wheels had all but one lug bolt on her car loose. It could have killed her." He reached a hand inside the car and helped his aunt out. She was looking pale and strained.

I put my arms around her. "Are you all right, Aunt Lillian?"

She patted my shoulder. "I will be. I'm pretty shaken up. I've never been so frightened in my entire life. It's awful, feeling you don't have any control over your car." She held on to my arm, and Brad and I helped her into the house. She sank into her Queen Anne chair in the den. "You'll have to forgive me."

"There's nothing to forgive you about," Brad reassured her. "I'm just glad you're okay."

"How does something like this happen?" I asked.

"It doesn't just happen," Brad said, with anger in his voice. "I know my aunt, and she has her tires rotated when she's supposed to and goes to a reputable mechanic. I think somebody has messed with it; probably just enough that she wouldn't notice it at first."

"Where did this happen?" I demanded to know, shocked that someone would have dared.

"On the same stretch of road Lora Hutchins was on," Lillian explained. "Fortunately, I was driving slowly. When I realized something was wrong, I got off the road. At first, I thought I had a flat tire. The tire was thumping like it. I wouldn't have made it if I had gone another quarter mile. There is a steep hill with a long curve, and I would have lost control of the car. I called Brad immediately and locked my doors. He was out that way in his cruiser, or it might all have ended differently."

"Well, thank God for that!" I breathed.

"Amen," Brad responded.

"I guess I'm going to have to clean out the garage so I can put my car in it if you think somebody did something to it out in the driveway." Lillian grimaced. "It's got to be done anyway. I had the oil changed and new tires put on recently, and I've been going to the same mechanic for years, so I know they would have tightened up all those bolts." She attempted to get up but was still a little unsteady. Brad reached for her, and she settled back down in her chair. "I didn't even get to the lawyer's office."

"I'll take you when you're ready to go," I offered.

She frowned at me. "Can you go right now?"

Brad lifted an eyebrow. "Do you think you're up to it after what you've just been through? Don't you think tomorrow would be better, Aunt Lillian?"

"Tomorrow may be too late," that lady said, managing to stand to her feet this time. "If someone is out to get me, I want to ensure all my affairs are in order. You and Jo are getting this house because that's the way I want it. Come on, Jo. I'll call Tom back and tell him I'm coming in." She dialed her phone as she walked out of the room.

Brad and I exchanged glances.

"I'll follow you all into Morrisville," he said. "I hope nobody's done anything to your car." His voice was grim. "I'll look it over before you go."

I bit my lip. "Who would do something to Lillian's car, and why?" I was struggling to make sense of the whole thing.

Brad shook his head. "I don't know, but whoever it is, I think you're right that it does center on my aunt. I'm having a wrecker take the car into her mechanic shop and check it out. The problem is it's like everything else; you can't prove anyone sabotaged it."

"If she had reached that hill and curve, she might have been killed," I worried.

Joseph broke in. "That sounds deliberate to me."

"And after what happened to Joseph this morning, it looks like it's another attempt to frighten all of us," Ashley added.

Brad looked at Joseph. "What happened to you?"

I briefly told him about the cistern lid being put back on and Ashley thinking she heard someone calling her.

Brad passed his hand over his forehead and took a deep breath. "I'm not sure what to do to keep you all safe," he said.

Lillian came back into the room. She smiled at me. "Come on, Jo. Let's see if we can get to Morrisville this time. Tom says he'll see me whenever I get there.

CHAPTER SIXTEEN

I followed Lillian's directions and let her off at her attorney's office. Brad followed us into Morrisville after checking around my car and only turned off to head towards the courthouse. It was comforting to know he was behind us the thirty miles we had traveled.

"I'll call you when I'm finished," she promised. "Go look the town over since you will live near here."

I found the courthouse first thing and drove around it. Morrisville mostly had anything and everything I thought we would need. I stopped at a sandwich place and got a tuna salad sandwich and an iced tea. From my booth, I sat staring out the window.

I tried to make sense of what had been going on in our lives. I felt a great admiration for Brad's Aunt Lillian. She was a strong woman. Of course, so was her mother. Rose Edwards would have had to be strong to deal with a brute of a husband and to live with her actions in correcting the problem. Both of these women saw what needed to be done and did it. Right or wrong, and even I had to agree it was wrong to take a life; they had made the choices they did. I wondered if Rose had ever regretted her decision.

She was reminded whenever she saw the Monkshood plant or walked in her yard.

Why would she keep a visible reminder of her heinous crime? I thought I would have probably dug it up and destroyed it. I would have made certain it was out of my sight. Then, it hit me. Rose Edwards kept the Monkshood because she wanted to remember. She never wished to forget. It was a price that a mother gladly paid for the sake of her children, but the moral woman she was could never accept atonement for her sin. So she paid every day of her life! She would not forget that she was a murderer and deserved punishment. Just because the legal system had not caught up with her and meted out a penalty that had not stopped her from having her own retribution. She lived with the fact that she had taken a life that was not hers to take. She made no excuses. She accepted her fate. She gave up her life so that her children could have a life. If she had been charged and convicted, she would have gladly taken her punishment for her children's sake. She had failed to save Rosemary but was determined not to fail the other three. And she hadn't.

I left the sandwich shop in a bit of a daze. I drove back to the attorney's office and parked in their parking lot. I leaned my head back, closed my eyes, and thought.

Someone had smothered Doc. I was no closer to figuring out why that had happened than I was in the beginning. I passed my thoughts on to Lora Hutchins. I still believed her murder was because she talked too much and claimed to know more than she possibly did. Nothing Lora had said about the Pemberton's or Coxes had panned out. Brad had investigated the accusations very carefully. Somebody somewhere thought she knew more than she did. I was sorry she had died so horrifically, but I was confident that I understood why she had died.

I thought of the night I had detected someone attempting to break into Doc's house. That was probably to get at his or his father's medical files. I wondered how much of them the police had gone through. Fortunately, the sheriff's office had secured the files, and the intruder had not retrieved anything. What was in those files that were a threat to someone?

Then there were the shots fired from the direction of the river. What was that all about? Were they trying to hit Aunt Lillian or one of my family? I tried to think of any reason anyone could have to try to frighten or kill them but came up against a blank wall. Then I considered Brad's Aunt Lillian. She had been a close friend of Doc's. So close that he had left everything he owned to her. Lora Hutchins was a friend of sorts; someone had smothered her too. And Lillian had been targeted, not once but twice. First, by an unknown shooter, and then today, someone had tampered with her car, and it was just the grace of God that kept her from having a serious accident or being killed. She could be dead this afternoon instead of sitting in her lawyer's office. There was no doubt that someone had been after her. No one else drove her car.

Then there was the dirty trick someone played on Joseph and Ashley. It could have been just a prank, or maybe someone wanted Joseph out of the way, thinking two women alone would be more vulnerable. What had somebody planned for us if Lillian and Brad hadn't shown up immediately after that? I rubbed my forehead with my hand. It was beginning to ache. Why would somebody care if we bought the house? Why would anyone want to frighten us away from it?

I looked towards the lawyer's office and saw an older gentleman helping Aunt Lillian out the door and down the sidewalk to her car. I waved, and she saw me. She walked towards the car with her lawyer behind her.

"Jo, this is Tom Lufton. He's my lawyer and has been a friend for more years than we want to admit to." She laid her hand on the attorney's arm. "Tom, this is Jo Elliott, who is marrying my nephew, Brad."

The lawyer put out his hand and said. "It is very nice to meet you, Mrs. Elliott. Lillian speaks very highly of you and your family. We are so glad you will be living in our area."

"I am glad to meet you also," I returned, shaking his hand and surveying the tall, silver-haired man. His face was angular, and his sharp brown eyes wouldn't miss much.

Between the two of us, we got Aunt Lillian into the car. Mr. Lufton bent and spoke to Lillian inside the vehicle. "I'll get the papers we discussed all drawn up, and we'll set up a time for you to return and sign everything." He patted her hand that was resting on the window frame. "Just stay safe, please."

She nodded. "I'm not going to be scared out of doing what I want to," she said firmly.

Lillian was quiet riding back to the house. I did tell her about someone shutting Joseph up in the well. She was upset about that but, like me, thought it must have been a prank. Probably someone from the campground who thought it would be funny.

"I will have to set some limits on the people from the campground," she declared. "I can't stop them walking past us on the river bank, but I can put a stop to them coming onto my property, or you and Brad can."

I didn't try to force her to talk. My mind was taken up with trying to figure out what was really going on; what was hiding behind the scenes that we knew nothing about.

Brad was still upset when he came to the house that night. He tenderly inquired after his aunt. We were all sitting in the den watching television. At least some of us were. Lillian was sitting there, but from the expression on her face, I surmised she was in her own world. I wasn't paying much attention to the show either.

Brad sat beside me on the sofa, leaned over and kissed me, and said to his aunt. "Did you get everything done you wanted to in Morrisville, Aunt Lillian?"

She nodded, and he looked at Joseph and Ashley. "What have you two been up to today?"

"Joseph got trapped in the cistern," Ashley informed him.

Brad raised an eyebrow. "So you said. And what were you doing in the cistern in the first place?"

I laid my hand on his arm. "Joseph would like to find the treasure your great-great-grandfather hid on this property. He wanted to check out the old cistern."

"And I heard someone call my name and thought it was Mamaw, so I left long enough to see what she needed," Ashley continued her explanation. "Only Mamaw had never called me, and when we went back out, that heavy lid was back over the cistern, and Joseph couldn't get out."

"Did you see anyone hanging around?" Brad asked.

We all said "No" together.

Brad's pleasant features were looking grim. "It was probably someone from the campground having fun," he said.

"I didn't think it was funny," Joseph retorted.

Brad looked at him. "It wasn't, but there are still people who think it is funny to pull a chair out from under someone too."

Lillian straightened in her chair. "Have you heard from Red at the mechanic's yet?"

Brad nodded. "He tightened up all the lug nuts. Red went pale, checking out the wheel. He said you were fortunate. There's no way to prove anyone messed with it, but in my experience, lug nuts don't come loose on their own. With everything else going on around here, I think it's safe to say someone was up to no good."

"If there were anything to find, Red would find it. He's a good mechanic and very reliable. I've gone to him for years." Lillian was firm on that point. "So somebody can run me over there to pick up my car tomorrow."

"I'll do it, Aunt Lillian," Joseph promised.

She smiled at him and turned to Brad. "My lawyer will ask the judge to grant me probate on Doc's estate. He doesn't think there will be any problem." Her hand rose and fell. "I don't know what to do with it. I'm sure it's a mess inside. Doc was no housekeeper. Just what I needed; another house to go through."

"Well, there's no hurry on that one," Brad said practically. "There's not a big hurry on this one either. Jo and I don't care how much you leave here to go through later, do we, Jo?"

I shook my dark head, and Brad continued. "With everything that has gone on, you must feel overwhelmed. Don't try to do more than what you can."

Lillian's eyes narrowed and I could tell she was thinking deeply. "Well, if you all are right about this, someone is out to get me. I can't imagine why. But that is the reason I wanted to go to my attorney's today." She gestured towards Brad and me. "Tom is writing up the deed for this house. I'm putting it in yours and Jo's names with the contingency that Jo does marry you." She raised a hand to forestall the comment that was on my lips. "I know, my dear, and I trust you. It's just an added protection."

"Moreover," she continued, "as I told Jo this morning, I am setting it up so that you will pay me directly into my bank account. I don't have an urgent need for money, and I don't want you paying interest. I don't want you having to pay a loan payment to a bank."

Brad was frowning. "That doesn't seem fair to you, Aunt Lillian. You never know when you'll need extra money. I've talked to my bank, and they are willing to give us a loan."

She shook her head. "No, I want to do it my way. If something happens to me, the house will be paid for. I am making a new will and leaving everything to you two with the stipulation that if something happens to you or Jo, the other has the right of survivorship, and after you two are gone, it will go to Alaina, Joseph, and Ashley and their children. I don't have anybody else, and Brad, you don't have any children either. I am quite fond of all of you, and I think this is for the best."

She relaxed and sat back in her chair, satisfied with her plans.

We were all silent for a few moments digesting all of this new information.

Brad finally spoke. "I think I speak for all of us when we say we love you for yourself and not for what you can give us." He raised his hand when he saw she was about to speak. "Having said that, all I can say is thank you. It's far more than I would have ever expected to have."

"It's not your fault that your first wife spent it quicker than you could make it," Aunt Lillian told him bluntly, speaking plainly about her thoughts on his deceased wife.

Brad hesitated. "Do you mind telling me what you plan to do with Doc's place, or have you thought about that?"

"I thought about it a lot today," she confided. "It occurred to me that he might have wanted it back in the family. That property originally belonged to Albert Edwards. He sold that to the Masters back in the day before he died in the Civil War."

Joseph was getting excited. "Then Albert Edwards could have hidden his money somewhere in Doc's place! Do you think we've been looking in the wrong place all these years?"

We all stared at him. Lillian broke the silence. "That's a good question, Joseph. As soon as I get the keys to the house, we'll look around."

Brad stood and took a set of keys out of his pants pocket. "That reminds me. I'm supposed to give these back to you. The sheriff says you're not a suspect in Doc's murder, so he didn't have a problem with you having the keys. However, understand if you turn up anything that could help solve Doc's murder, we need to have it."

"Of course," Lillian said obediently.

"Are you still reading the doctor's files?" I questioned.

Frustration clouded Brad's face. "I've never read such boring stuff in my life. He goes into great detail over some things, and others he barely mentions. Between Doc and his father, they must have delivered every baby born around here for years. If you knew the people, it would be more interesting."

"Have you turned up any more about the Pemberton's or the Coxes?" Joseph asked.

"Not yet. Harvey's first wife was sickly. Doc seemed to feel sorry for her. He doesn't seem to have liked Harvey Pemberton any better than Harvey liked him." Brad shook his head. "There's an endless amount of paper."

Lillian struggled to her feet. "I'm going to bed. I hope I can sleep. There's been an awful lot of excitement today."

Brad looked at me and motioned toward the front porch. We waited until Aunt Lillian returned to her room and slipped out together. We sat down on the swing and rocked gently back and forth.

"Something, in this case, has got to break," Brad said softly. "This thing has the potential of never being solved. I don't want it to turn into a cold case where we don't have the human resources to pursue it."

"I still think it has something to do with Aunt Lillian," I said.

I felt him turn his head to look at me. "Have you thought of the possibility of it having something to do with the Edwards family?"

I frowned. "What exactly do you mean? You and Lillian are the Edwards family."

"I know," Brad said intensely. "I've gone over it and over it. I've listened to all of you, particularly you. What

229

if it's the Edwards property and what someone thinks is hidden somewhere on it that's the motivation in this case?"

I looked at him in the semi-darkness and realized that he was serious. "You mean someone believes the story of Albert Edwards hiding gold and silver and wants access to find it. It's a theory, all right." I stared out into the road.

"Here's what I've been thinking," Brad shared. "This all started with Doc's death. What if the person behind this is someone that Doc could identify if he lived? He might even know the motive for a lot of this. So, they take Doc out. I think you're right about Dora Hutchins. When she started claiming she had information on the case, someone got nervous and took her out. Then we have the night someone took a shot at Aunt Lillian. We were gone. They probably wouldn't have dared do that if I had been here. But you and I are gone, and we're going to assume that my aunt was the target. I think they meant to scare her. I imagine if someone wanted to kill her, they would have."

I shivered in the warm night air. "That's kind of cold-blooded, isn't it?"

Brad put his arm around me. "I think this person is cold-blooded. Of course, Aunt Lillian isn't fazed by this, being the strong-willed person she is."

"But Brad," I interrupted. "Anyone who knows your aunt would realize she wasn't easily frightened. After all, she is selling the place to us. Why would they try to scare her? That's not going to stop the sale of the house."

"It would hold it up if they killed her before she got all the paperwork done and signed," Brad said seriously. "I'm telling you, Jo. It wouldn't take anyone any time to loosen a lug bolt; believe me. Unless you caught somebody at it, it's nearly impossible to prove. Fingerprints are no help. Anybody with an ounce of sense is going to wear gloves." He stared out around the front of the house. "I guess I need to put security cameras around the place. I suppose whoever this is could think we might not want the place if Aunt Lillian was tragically murdered here."

I thought about that. "That would make me feel terrible, but this is an old house, and we already know there were two murders that took place here, and we're still buying the house. Would that make a difference to you?"

"Well, it's not going to happen if I can stop it," Brad said firmly. "Joseph and Ashley are practically living here, and you are here all day. Between the three of you, try not to let Aunt Lillian out of your sight."

"What would happen to the place if Aunt Lillian died before she signed her will?" I asked.

"It would go to me anyway, as far as I know. Aunt Lillian told me I was her heir in her old will. She's included you and your family in this new one." Brad responded. "I'm it as far as I know."

I turned to face him, leaving the comfort of his arm. "Brad, what if there is another Edwards? What if Violet is still alive or a child of hers? What rights would they have to this place and any treasure found here?"

Brad stared at me, and I could almost see the wheels turning. He stopped propelling the swing with his foot and grabbed my arms. "Jo, that could be the answer!"

CHAPTER SEVENTEEN

"But who in the world could it be?" I asked. Brad had gotten out of the swing and was pacing back and forth across the porch.

"It could be anyone," Brad said, rubbing the back of his neck. I felt for him. I knew the stress of it all was getting to him. "I don't know if Aunt Lillian would recognize her sister after all these years. If she had children, we don't know whether they are male or female. As I said, it could be anyone."

"There aren't any new people around here besides ourselves," I added. "Except for the campground. Anyone could park a camper there and go unnoticed."

"I can't very well go camper to camper and ask if they are related to Violet Edwards," Brad fumed. "Johnny would be mad at me. They wouldn't have to be in Willis, anyway. They could be in Morrisville-anywhere." He sat back down beside me. "It's just so frustrating."

"I think it's because it is more personal," I said gently. "This is your family we're talking about."

"Well, considering that my grandfather killed his daughter, and my grandmother killed him, I suppose it could be possible that one of their children could have turned out bad. My dad was a good man-honest and moral. Aunt Lillian certainly doesn't have that streak in her. I never knew Violet, and to be honest, Dad and Aunt Lillian never said much about her. I don't know if Grandma Rose ever talked to them about their sister. I can see what I can get out of Aunt Lillian, but I'm certain she doesn't know much more than we do."

"Do you think Violet would have known anything about where Albert Edwards buried his money?"

Brad shook his head. "I don't see how. Dad told me he and his sisters searched all over the property. My friends and I also looked for it, but never found anything. I always figured someone had got to it before we started looking. "

"It's too bad he didn't tell somebody. You would have thought he could have told his wife or children."

"I don't know if he told anyone or not. I remember hearing Dad and Mom talking about that one time. I was a kid and didn't pay much attention to what they were saying."

"We need to see what the place looked like at that time. Are there any old pictures? I think that room Alaina sleeps in had many of your grandparents' and great-grandparents' things in it. I'll ask Aunt Lillian tomorrow."

"When is Alaina coming back?"

"Tomorrow, I think. We're off this weekend, as it's the Fourth of July. Alaina wanted to be here for that."

Brad grinned. "And to be with Johnny Whitlock, no doubt."

I grinned back. "I can't begrudge my daughter some happiness."

"Johnny's okay," Brad asserted. "I haven't got to spend much time with him. Maybe he'll come up on the Fourth. Have you made any plans yet?"

"We usually just do a cookout- a picnic as a family," I told him. "I have no problem with Johnny coming. I know Lillian is going to miss Doc. She always included him."

"We're all going to miss Doc," Brad pulled me to my feet. "I need to go. We'll have a family conference tomorrow."

True to his word, Brad stopped before work the following day and had a family gathering in the den. He explained what theories we had come up with and how he wanted us to protect Aunt Lillian.

"We'll start going through the pictures in Mom's room today," Joseph promised. "Aunt Lillian, you'll have to help us because we won't know any of the people."

Lillian was skeptical. "I always thought Violet probably died years ago," she said. "She was the wild one in the family."

"Well, we don't have proof of that," Brad reminded her. "She might have done what you did, Aunt Lillian; she may have changed her name. I haven't exactly been sitting on my hands. I ran her through our computers again yesterday, but she's never been in trouble with the law."

"It would surprise me if she had. Violet was always a sly one. If she were up to no good, she seldom got caught," Lillian's expression told me she had no delusions about her older sister.

"Well, I'm going in to work. You all stay safe and out of trouble," Brad counseled. He kissed me briefly and went out the door.

Lillian was looking after him thoughtfully. "Well, we'd better get started on that room if Alaina is going to have a place to sleep tonight. I seem to remember some pictures of the old house up there. It's been a long time since I've gone through them. There should be some snapshots of Grandpa Albert and Grandma Rachel; I believe her name was Rachel. Alaina's coming tonight for the weekend, isn't she?"

I nodded. "Brad and I were talking about cooking out tomorrow. That's something we usually do on the Fourth."

"Sounds good to me," Lillian agreed. "If anyone wants breakfast, you'd better get it." She stood to her feet. "We've got a lot to get done today."

"I'd better eat," Joseph decided. "I don't mind working, but not on an empty stomach."

I laughed. "I'll fix us all some eggs and bacon and toast. That should keep us from starving until lunch."

Fortified by a good breakfast, we all climbed the stairs to the second floor to tear apart the bedroom Alaina had slept in. I had decided she would have to use another bedroom that night. There was one more bedroom on that floor, but it was smaller. The bed looked comfortable, so I didn't suppose it would matter.

We dragged out suitcases, boxes, and trunks full of old photos, postcards, and scrapbooks. Someone else had separated the letters and cards. We put those containers to one side and concentrated on the pictures. Some were clearer than others. They were all in black and white. Some were starting to fall apart from age. There was writing on the back of some; on others, it was anybody's guess who the people in the photographs were.

Aunt Lillian had found herself a straight-back chair, and Joseph had carried it into the bedroom for her. She was going through the photos carefully.

"This was Mother when she was young," she commented once, "and here is my father."

We all dutifully looked at the faded photo. I still thought Ernest Edwards appeared arrogant. Now that I knew more about him, it was hard to look at his picture with any interest.

Rose Edwards had been a beautiful young woman. One photo showed her with her children. Eugene was standing beside her like a little gentleman, his face solemn.

I studied Violet's face closely. She was attempting to look serious, but she couldn't hide the mischievous expression in her eyes. Lillian was holding on to her mother's arm, and I thought the little girl on Rose's lap must be Rosemary. None of them were smiling, but then the old-time photographs never seem to have anybody smiling. I noticed Rose seemed anxious in the picture. I was sure she had plenty to be stressed about.

Lillian was handing me another photo. "This is my great grandfather, Albert Edwards," she explained. "He's the one who bought the property here and Doc's place too." She laid her finger on the background. "You can see the old stone house in the background."

I observed the background with interest. "The house looks much like Doc's, doesn't it?"

"It does," Lillian agreed. "My grandfather built that house. Doc's Dad, Graham Masters, bought the property off of William Edwards, my grandfather, and he wanted a stone house like the one that used to be here. My father's idea was to build the one that's here now. I don't remember the other one, but I remember seeing these pictures."

I studied the man standing in front of the house. He looked young in the photo. I compared him to the picture of Ernest Edwards. "Your father doesn't resemble his grandfather," I commented.

"No, my father took after his mother's side of the house in looks. He didn't take after his father, William, either. Here is a picture of William and Christine with my father when he was a baby. You should see a bit of Brad in Grandpa William."

My eyes widened. "Brad's a throwback, isn't he? You can tell he's related to his great-grandfather."

"It's strange how certain things skip a generation," Lillian said. "But I've seen it happen over and over." She was sorting the pictures as she talked. "Now, here is a picture of Violet right before she left home. Of course, she wouldn't look anything like this now."

I took the offered picture and tried to imagine what kind of a person Brad's Aunt Violet might have been. She was tall and slender like Lillian. Her hair was dark, and she had a high forehead. The mischievous expression in her eyes was gone, and in its place was the same arrogance I had noticed in her father. Frankly, she looked rebellious. I handed the photo back to Lillian without comment.

As the day progressed, we took pictures showing any part of the property or the old house. By the end of the day, we were all exhausted and had put any pictures we felt might have relevance in a box by themselves. I had gotten better acquainted with the Edwards family tree.

Alaina showed up that evening, only to disappear with Johnny Whitlock shortly after she arrived. When Brad came home, he went through the box of pictures on his own.

He was frowning over one of the photos. He handed it to his aunt. "Is this inside the stone house? It about has to be because it's Grandpa William in the picture. It looks like it's around Christmas time, but that fireplace mantel looks familiar. It looks like the one in the living room."

Lillian glanced at the photo. "It's the same mantel. It's mahogany, I believe. Dad and Grandpa took it out of the house that was torn down and put it in this house. Grandpa William had made it. I remember Mother telling me about it. They had quite a time tearing it out of the wall and moving it. It was very heavy. Mother said Dad said it was cumbersome for a mantel, but it's eight feet high or thereabouts, so it weighs a lot."

"Interesting," was Brad's only comment. He laid the picture aside and continued going through the ones we had set aside. "Was there a barn on the place at one time?" he asked. "This looks like a barn to me."

"There was a barn. It was close to Doc's property line." Aunt Lillian answered him. "There was a lot of land here that belonged to the Edwards family at one time. Little by little, it's been sold off until we have what is here now. Grandpa William sold some, and then my father sold more. Nothing more has been sold until now. The barn got torn down after my father died. I remember Mother having a milk cow and chickens when we were little. After Violet and Eugene left home, the barn began falling in, and Mother had it torn down. We didn't need a cow or chickens for the two of us. It was cheaper to buy milk and eggs."

"Well, I've never shown any interest in farming," my fiancé said, "so it's probably just as well it is gone. Besides, Jo doesn't eat chicken, so what would be the point."

"I eat chicken," Joseph spoke up.

"And anything else he can find," I added. "Joseph is a human garbage disposal."

"Did Alaina get in?" Brad asked.

I nodded. "She's out with Johnny. We may need to run into Willis and get some groceries for the cookout tomorrow."

"Yeah, I was thinking about that. I'm thinking about cooking some steaks if everyone is okay with that." Brad said, surveying the room.

"We need to invite Johnny Whitlock, too," I mentioned.

Lillian was staring at the floor, and I suspected she was missing Doc. He had always attended family gatherings.

Brad got to his feet. "We'll run into Willis and see what we can find."

I went out the door with him, and in a few minutes, we were shopping at the small supermarket in Willis. It had everything we needed, and we finished in no time.

In the car, I asked Brad. "Was there something about the picture of the mantel in the old house that interested you?"

He grinned at me. "You caught that, did you? I just found it strange that they kept the mantel. They tore the old house down and destroyed it except for the mantel. And then Aunt Lillian talked about her father and grandfather, saying how huge the thing was. I wonder how heavy it is and why. That's all."

"You're not thinking Albert Edwards hid his money in the back of that mantel, are you?"

"Not exactly the back, but inside the back, maybe."

"Oh, Brad, wouldn't William or Ernest Edwards have known about it then?"

"Not necessarily. Old Albert hid it pretty cleverly."

"If there were troops around, would he have had time?"

"Well, the story was he was afraid they might come around, so I think it's safe to assume that he was preparing for that possibility."

"Brad, you're not going to ruin that beautiful mantel, are you? Aunt Lillian will have a fit."

"We can always wait until she moves if that will make you feel better." My husband-to-be consoled me.

I considered that. "I think Aunt Lillian should be in on it." I finally said. "We're going to feel pretty stupid if it's just a heavy mantel."

"I tell you what, if I manage to damage it, I'll get it fixed. But if that treasure is where I think it is, I don't think anybody will be upset about the mantel." He grinned at me. "Besides, I happen to know a little more about it. When I saw that picture of Grandpa William, I remembered something my dad had told me long ago. All of my grandfathers on the Edwards side were stone masons and carpenters. Dad went to college and was an accountant. He was never interested in being creative with his hands. He didn't want to do anything that reminded him of his father. Anyway, Dad said that his dad, Grandpa Ernest, had a little too much to drink one New Year's Eve and had pointed to the mantel in the living room and told him that the mantel was the most expensive piece of wood in the house."

"When did your dad tell you this?"

"I was an adult. It wasn't long before he and Mom had the car accident."

"And you're just now remembering it?" I sounded skeptical.

"Back then, I wasn't interested in the family's history. I was going to the police academy and dating Audrey. I wasn't thinking about the family treasure. It had excited me when I was a kid, but I figured it was just a story. I never thought about it until we decided to buy the house ourselves. When I saw that photograph tonight, I remembered what Dad had said. I don't know how, but Grandpa Ernest knew exactly where Grandpa Albert had hidden his money.

I thought to myself. "Yeah, it would be Ernest Edwards that knew.

CHAPTER EIGHTEEN

Between us, Brad and I decided to keep our theories to ourselves until after the holiday weekend. We got home in time to play a table game with Joseph, Ashley, and Lillian. Alaina still had yet to return, but I wasn't expecting her back early.

I hoped that Johnny was everything she thought he was. Tim and Alaina had been high school sweethearts, but a heart attack had taken him away from her too soon. I didn't want my daughter hurt. I wanted her to be as happy as I was with someone who loved her as Brad loved me.

The Fourth of July dawned with a beautiful sunrise and the promise of a lovely day. I made pancakes for breakfast with sausage links and maple syrup. Brad set up the grill in the backyard, and I started making potato salad and deviled eggs. Alaina had bought some fresh green beans and corn on the cob from a roadside market on her way to Willis, so it looked like we were going to have a feast.

While I cut up potatoes, onions, and boiled eggs, Alaina was stringing green beans. Joseph took the corn out in the backyard and was shucking it. Ashley was helping him.

For a time, we worked in silence, and then Alaina said. "Mom, may I ask you a question?"

I smiled. "Of course. Always."

She wrinkled her forehead. "How did you know Brad was the right one for you?"

"Well, we were both praying about it, you know. I didn't know for sure until that night in the old Graham house. That night when I thought I wouldn't live to see you and Joseph and Ashley again, I realized that I felt the same about Brad. I loved him. Of course, since then, spending time with him and talking with him, we discovered our goals are the same, the way we look at things. He is fine with my being in the music ministry. He's not asking me to give that up. The more I am around him, the better I like him."

"Would you have agreed to marry him if he had asked you to give up the music ministry?" she asked.

"No," I was certain about that. "If I have to be less than what I should be by marrying someone, then I wouldn't marry that person. I haven't minded being single. I missed your Dad, but my life has been full with you, the kids, and the ministry. Brad adds to that. He doesn't take away from it." I looked straight into her blue eyes, much like Joseph's. "Are you thinking Johnny will ask you to marry him?"

The color rose in her cheeks. "Well, I think he may be leading up to that," she finally admitted.

"Do you love him?" I asked bluntly.

"Yes, I think I do." She evaded my gaze. "He's fun to be with. He's got some little boy left in him- not that he's immature, but he likes to enjoy life. He makes me feel like a teenager. I don't think I've laughed as much as I have with him since Tim died."

I smiled. "There's nothing wrong with that. Brad makes me feel young again. Falling in love is like that. I'd pray about it. God will direct your life if you let Him. You know that, Alaina." I washed my hands in the sink and walked over to where she sat, stringing beans. I put my arms around her and kissed the top of her head. "I want you happy, and I want you to have God's best."

She hugged me back. "Please don't say anything to the others. What I feel for Johnny is special to me, and I don't want to be teased about it."

"Mum's the word," I told her, returning to my potato salad.

Aunt Lillian was quieter than usual when we gathered at a picnic table in the yard, and I surmised she was missing Doc. He had been at the last cookout. I put my arm around her and gave her a quick hug. She looked up at me and smiled sadly.

"You know what I'm thinking, don't you?" she said softly. Her gray eyes were filling with tears.

I knelt beside her. "Aunt Lillian, I miss Doc too. You have a lot of good memories of him."

She bit her lip, fighting back her emotions. "I'll be all right, but thank you for noticing and caring."

Johnny had come up from the campground and joined us. He was in a super mood. His campground was crowded for the holiday weekend, and he informed us there wasn't any room for one more camper. I tried to observe him without appearing to do so. From my perspective, I believed he cared for my daughter. His brown eyes softened when he looked at her. Would Alaina be willing to move here and find another job? I knew she loved her work at the hospital; her house had been hers and Tim's. I knew Johnny lived at the campground, but I didn't know if it were a house or a camper. Of course, he might consider making different arrangements if he married. I was so engrossed in my thoughts that I didn't hear Joseph speaking.

"Mamaw, are you here or not? You look like you are a million miles away."

I stared at him and blinked my eyes. "Huh?"

Everybody laughed.

The dinner was delicious. I loved fresh beans and corn on the cob. Brad had asked each of us how we wanted our steaks done, and he and Johnny took care of the steaks. I watched the two men conversing over the grill fondly. It would be nice for Brad to have another man in the family. Since Brad had looked into Johnny Whitlock's background, Joseph seemed to have accepted him. Ashley was happy with what made Joseph happy.

"It looks like you are going to have Alaina over here, too," Lillian said in a low tone.

"Looks like a good possibility," I agreed.

"It will be good for Brad to have someone like a younger brother, too," Lillian continued. "He never had siblings, and I don't think he was ever close to Audrey's brother."

"I don't think Audrey was close to her brother either," I returned.

We exchanged knowing glances and grinned at each other.

"I'm glad I've lived long enough to meet the woman Brad wants to marry," Lillian said. She gazed at me. "It's only a month away until your wedding day." She surveyed the yard. "There should be plenty of flowers. The Rose of Sharon's shrubs are blooming, and the roses are still plentiful. There are still a lot of different species of daisies. It should be beautiful."

"I've sent out a few announcements." I shared. "We want to keep this small and private. I sent the ones you wanted to go to your church family. Brad has invited some of the people at work. It's not like this is the first wedding for either of us."

Brad and Johnny had gotten up from the table and brought some more steaks from the grill. Brad sat beside me, and Johnny sat with Alaina across from us. Lillian was on my left side, and Ashley and Joseph sat at the end of the table.

"There are more steaks if anybody wants another one," Brad announced. "Johnny and I have worked hard on these, so eat up."

"I cleaned the corn," Joseph threw in.

"With my help," Ashley broke in.

"I bought it," Alaina told him.

"I made potato salad and deviled eggs." I volunteered.

"I sat and watched all of you," Aunt Lillian contributed with laughter.

I watched each family member in turn and thought about how blessed I was to have such a family. So many people had no one they could turn to in a crisis, no one that cared whether they lived or died.

Violet Edwards crossed my mind, and I wondered if she had ever found anyone to cherish her. Or had her bitterness towards her father kept her from enjoying a family life? I wondered how she had really felt about her mother. Did she resent her mother staying with her father? I wasn't sure she would realize how difficult it was then to leave or divorce. I wasn't sure she would care. There was marked selfishness on that face I had looked into yesterday. I felt confident it would always be what Violet wanted, that she would do what she wanted without regard for the consequences.

I gazed at Lillian, who was anything but selfish. She was a strong woman, but she had a heart. I wasn't sure Violet did. Somehow, it was a shame that Lillian and Doc had not married and raised a family. It was too bad that her mother's bad experience in marriage had caused her daughter to remain single. I supposed that was what it was. I didn't know, but I suspected fear of it being like her parent's marriage had held her back. My own parents' marriage had been happy, I thought. Josh and I had a good relationship, and so had Alaina and Tim. I glanced toward Joseph and Ashley. She had her hand tucked through his arm as they talked to Alaina. There wasn't anything going wrong with them. I contemplated the man sitting beside me cutting up his steak and conversing with Johnny animatedly. We talked a lot.

Brad and I knew what we wanted in a life partner and what we didn't. I studied his profile. Brad was still a good-looking man. I was surprised that he had been interested in me. Mostly, I had decided I would be alone for the rest of my life. It had been a complete life. The ministry kept me busy. Even though we had gone out every weekend until this holiday weekend, I had spent a lot of time at Aunt Lillian's-going back to Alaina's as needed. I tried to keep the weekdays clear in the summer months to enjoy the warm weather.

I came back to the present when Joseph announced. "It's such a hot day, Ashley and I are going to put on our swimsuits and go down to the river."

"That sounds like a great idea," Johnny said. "I'll run back down to the campground and get my swimming trunks." He looked at Alaina. "Want to come with me?"

"Sure, I'll come with you. I packed my swimsuit. The water will feel good." My daughter was glowing with pleasure. "It's a gorgeous day."

The four dashed off and left Brad, Lillian, and me sitting alone at the table.

Brad glanced at me. "Did you want to get in the river?"

I shook my head. "No, I can't swim, remember?"

He grinned. "I forgot. I'm not much for swimming either. I can, but it's not one of my favorite things to do."

"I'm going to get this food in the house since it's getting hot," I said, gathering the dishes.

"I'll help," Brad volunteered. "You sit tight, Aunt Lillian. We'll be back in a few minutes."

When we returned to the yard, Lillian was still sitting, except she had turned and was staring toward Doc's house. She turned to face us when she heard us coming down the steps. She smiled faintly. "That was a good dinner. All of you did a good job." She surveyed the yard. "I'm going to miss this place. It has been my home all of my life."

Brad and I exchanged glances.

"Aunt Lillian, I haven't talked to Jo about this, but if you don't want to leave here, you don't have to. If you are having second thoughts-….. "

She cut him off by raising her hand. "It was just a statement of fact. I am looking forward to having a small place. I'll make new friends, and as long as I'm able, I will still go to my church and see my friends there. I know some people in Morrisville. I retired at the same time as a couple of the women at the bank, so I know them. I'll be back to visit."

"You're always welcome, Aunt Lillian," I said gently.

She smiled. "I think the place is in good hands. It makes me very sad to live here with Doc being gone."

We heard Johnny and Alaina return. He sat across from Brad while Alaina went into the house to change. Joseph and Ashley came flying down the steps and ran across the yard to the river about the same time.

"Sure you all don't want to join us?" Johnny asked us.

Brad spoke for both of us. "I'm not much into swimming, Johnny, you know that."

"Well, you might have changed," Johnny said. "People do, you know."

"Do you think people change that much?" Lillian asked him.

"I think anybody who knew me would say I've changed a lot, particularly in the last few years," Johnny confessed.

Brad clapped him on the shoulder. "And we're all glad of that!"

Alaina came down the steps, and the pair started across the yard to the river. I followed them with my eyes. A good-looking couple, I reflected.

To my surprise, Brad began telling his aunt his theory about the mantel. At first, Lillian was dubious, but I could tell she was analyzing his suggestion.

Finally, she said, "Do you think you could check without destroying that beautiful wood? That mantel came out of the original house. It's very old, way over a hundred years old."

"Grandpa Albert was a carpenter, wasn't he?" Brad queried.

She nodded.

"Well, I think he would have been meticulous. He wouldn't want it to look too obvious, so I think he carefully concealed everything between the back and the front. That's why it was so heavy. I'm not going to take a crowbar to it, you know." Brad was trying to reassure her.

"Pastor Don knows a bit about carpentry," Lillian offered. "We could get him over here to look at it.

"That's fine," Brad agreed. "It's just an idea, but I want to check it out." He peered across the yard. "If it's buried, we'll have to dig up the whole place to find it. Once I remembered what my dad had told me, everything clicked into place. I could be wrong, of course."

"And you could be right," Aunt Lillian told him. "It's worth a check. It's exciting when you think about it. Let's get some lawn chairs and get more comfortable. The sun's starting to come over this table."

We brought out enough lawn chairs for everyone and settled in the shade. I glanced at the Monkshood. It was thriving. I was anxious to see it bloom. Brad had said it was beautiful. It was beautiful, maybe, deadly, certainly.

The other four came back from the river a couple of hours later. Their hair was dripping, and my blonde daughter had gotten too much sun. Her shoulders and face were red. Johnny flopped down in a lawn chair, pulling a t-shirt over his head. He didn't burn like my daughter. He had a beautiful tan. Alaina and the kids went back into the house to change, and if I knew Alaina, she would take a quick shower.

Joseph and Ashley came out first. Ashley's hair was wet, but she had combed the long hair. Alaina was the last one out, and as I thought, she had showered and redid her hair and make-up. Alaina was always going to look first class. She sat down in the chair beside Johnny, and the look he gave her told me he appreciated her efforts.

It was early evening when something happened that changed everything. We were still relaxing in the yard when I saw a woman and a young man coming around the corner of the house. She was tall and in a pair of shorts and a tank top, and the young man was in shorts and a t-shirt. He was tall like the woman and had her coloring, brown hair, and eyes. I speculated they must be mother and son.

"Who's that?" Joseph wondered.

Brad's eyes narrowed. "I don't recognize them. Maybe they've come from the campground."

Johnny was staring. "I don't recognize them, but there's quite a crowd there this weekend."

The pair of them walked steadily across the yard towards us.

"Can we help you?" Brad asked.

"I hope so," the woman said. Her voice sounded pleasant. "Somebody told me at the campground that Johnny Whitlock was here."

Brad stood to his feet. "Well, you've come to the right place." He gestured towards Johnny. "This is Johnny Whitlock."

Johnny rose to his feet, and the woman stared at him, speechless for a moment.

"There must be some mistake. This man isn't Johnny Whitlock."

CHAPTER NINETEEN

All of our mouths dropped open.

Johnny was frowning. "I don't know what you're trying to pull, but I am Johnny Whitlock."

She shook her head vigorously. "I'm not pulling anything, but you certainly are not him, whoever you are. I was married to Johnny Whitlock for five very long years, and this is his son, Aaron." She gestured to the young man standing behind her.

Brad looked from her to Johnny. "Johnny, do you know what this is all about?" I could feel the tension in him.

Johnny was moving closer to Alaina. There was a vacant look on his face as he put a hand on Alaina's shoulder. "Johnny told me you were dead," he said slowly.

"Johnny told you what?" Brad shouted. "Who are you if you're not Johnny Whitlock?"

Johnny grabbed Alaina's arm and pulled her up to his feet. "Time to fly," he said and ran across the yard, half dragging my daughter. I could see the shock and fear on her face when he gripped her arm.

I was on my feet. "Brad," I yelled. "Do something."

Brad was racing across the yard with his cell phone up to his ear calling the sheriff's department. I was right behind him, and Joseph was beside me.

However, it would be too late. I heard Johnny's truck starting up before we ever got to the front of the house and go flying down the road. Brad was describing Johnny and his vehicle to the sheriff's office and jumped in his car. He yelled at Joseph and me as he started the vehicle. "We'll get her back, Jo. Don't worry, pray."

I held my hands to both sides of my face, scared for Alaina and Brad. Joseph slipped a comforting arm around my shoulders. I turned to see Ashley and Lillian coming around the house with the woman and her son. They were peering down the road, but there was nothing to see but trees.

I spoke to the woman standing there. "Just who are you, anyway?"

"I'm Miriam Perkins. I was married to Johnny Whitlock. We divorced, and I remarried to Darrel Perkins a few years ago," she explained.

"And you're sure that is not Johnny Whitlock?" Lillian broke in.

"That's not the man I was married to, of that I'm sure. Johnny Whitlock had a birthmark on his left hand. It was very noticeable. This guy is similar to him in build and has dark hair and eyes, but this man isn't him. Whoever this is, well, to be honest, he's a whole lot better looking than

Johnny was when I left him. Johnny was an alcoholic. I was shocked to find out he was still living."

Joseph was staring at her. "He practically admitted you were telling the truth when he said, 'Johnny told me you were dead.' He must know Johnny Whitlock."

Lillian was shocked. I could see that. "He certainly knew all about this place and all of my family. The real Johnny Whitlock made this his second home when he was a boy."

Mrs. Perkins was surveying the yard and house. "It's a beautiful place." She turned to face us. "I feel terrible about this. I had no idea what I would be stirring up by coming here."

"Well, thank God you came before my poor daughter married somebody who wasn't who they said they were." My words were fierce, but alongside my fear, there was anger. Anger for the anxiety and hurt Alaina must be feeling. Anger for the deception, for him taking her heart and crushing it like this. Whoever he was, I wanted him captured before he could hurt her anymore.

Joseph was pacing. "I wish I could do something. I don't like this waiting game."

"You're not the police, Joseph," I told him. "We can't do anything else but pray right now."

"I'm doing that, all right," Joseph asserted. "I just want to break the jaw of whoever this guy is."

Miriam Perkins was studying us. "Do you really believe prayer makes any difference?" she questioned.

"Absolutely," I said firmly. "My family and I have been in many tough situations, and prayer is the only thing that got us through them. God has always taken care of us."

"I used to go to church, but I got out of the habit. It's hard to start again. I got busy and had to work a couple of jobs to keep a roof over my head and my son's. Johnny wasn't paying child support. He wouldn't work, so there was no use in having him arrested. He wasn't going to make any money in jail. It's been rough, but I sent Aaron to college. He made good grades in high school, so he got scholarships. That helped." She beamed proudly at her son, and he smiled at her.

I understood her mother's heart. "I'm glad you were able to raise him so well. A good mother makes all the difference."

Miriam was looking toward the white car parked in our driveway.

"I am sorry to ruin your day, but Aaron wanted to meet his father. Johnny has never been part of his life, so naturally, he was curious."

"I just thought it would be nice to see what he was like. I mean, he is my dad. It was mostly curiosity." It was Aaron's first speech, and I felt his disappointment.

I decided to be kind. "I hope you find your father," I told him. My cell phone rang, and I grabbed it out of my pocket. It was Brad.

"Have you found them?"

"Not yet," Brad sounded grim. "They're not going to get far. We've got roadblocks, and we sent out the truck description and Johnny's or whatever his name is description to everybody. Alaina's too. How are you all holding up?"

"We're holding. Mrs. Perkins told us Johnny Whitlock had a large birthmark on his left hand. I haven't seen anything like that on this guy's hands." I told him.

"That's interesting. I had forgotten about that. That might be why this man wanted to get hold of Doc's medical files to keep us from finding that out?" Brad mused aloud.

"Oh, Brad, do you think he killed Doc and Lora?" I was repelled by the thought of my daughter falling in love with a murderer.

"It could be, Jo. I'm not sure. I suppose an old birthmark would be reason enough. Tell you what? When we catch him, we'll ask him. I got to go. Keep your phone handy. I'll call when I know anything." I heard the click of the phone as Brad hung up.

Miriam Perkins and Aaron were leaving, and I waved at them and followed my family up to the front porch.

It was past supper time, but I don't think any of us were thinking of food. Joseph paced, and Ashley watched him anxiously.

Aunt Lillian sat solemnly meditating. "Would you think he had a backup plan if he got found out?" she asked.

I shrugged, and Joseph said. "I don't think he planned on getting caught. I'd like to know what happened to the real Johnny Whitlock."

"I imagine he's dead," Aunt Lillian said sadly.

My entire body felt tense. I just wanted the police to find my daughter.

Joseph stopped pacing long enough to say to me. "I told you there was something not right about this guy. Now, maybe you'll believe me."

"Joseph, I had Brad check him out." He didn't know, but I was kicking myself for not seeing through the imposter. "I don't know what I was supposed to do," I finished lamely. Maybe I was so caught up in my own romance I wasn't viewing things clearly.

"I don't think we should play any blame games," Ashley said. "It's nobody's fault."

"Well, Brad never questioned that he wasn't who he said he was, and Brad knew him," Joseph declared in frustration.

"To be fair, Brad hasn't seen Johnny since he was eight or nine. He's the same height and built as I would suppose Johnny to be," Aunt Lillian said, trying to lower the tension. "Johnny had brown curly hair and brown eyes. He has the same fun-loving temperament that I remember Johnny having."

"I bet he did know Johnny Whitlock and knew him well enough to copy many things," Joseph guessed. "I just can't figure out why he did it."

"Brad said we'll ask him when they catch him," I repeated Brad's words to them.

"Well, at least Mom won't be marrying this guy. Thank God we found out before she said, 'I do,'" Joseph said, trying to think of something positive.

There were three of us who said "Amen" in unison.

Lillian rose to her feet. "I'm going to sit in my chair with my feet up if you all don't mind. Let me know the minute you hear anything." She put her hand on Joseph's shoulder. "Try not to worry, Joseph. Your mother is a clever woman. She'll survive this."

Joseph grimaced. "I just want my mother home and safe,"

"Well, as I understand it, this isn't the first time one or the other of you has faced danger. I think your grandmother was nearly killed last year," Aunt Lillian countered.

"Well, I don't have to like it," Joseph muttered.

"No, you don't have to do that," Aunt Lillian said, stepping inside the front door.

"I just feel so helpless," Ashley said after Lillian had gone inside.

"We all do," I told her. "I want to do something too. We can pray, and I suggest we do that right now."

The three of us bowed our heads, and I prayed to God to protect Alaina and aid the police in finding her and the man who had forced her to go with him. It wasn't a long prayer, but it was a fervent one. I felt just as desperate as Ashley and Joseph, but I was reluctant to allow them to see how terrified I was. If this man had killed Doc and Lora, he could also murder my daughter. I laced my fingers together and stared out into the growing darkness. "Alaina, where are you?" I whispered.

I hadn't heard anything from Brad for an hour, and I prayed he would call soon. I knew he was busy and would do everything he could to find Alaina and bring her safely to me. I didn't dare call him. My stress was not going to make his job any easier. I had already figured out that cops stuck together, and if one had a family member in trouble, they all jumped in to help.

I looked at the kids. "I'm going up to the turret, and I promise not to put any lights on. Are you all staying out here?"

Ashley looked at Joseph. "I'd feel safer in the house, Joseph."

"Okay, and I want every door locked and double-checked," Joseph said sternly. "I don't want him coming in and holding us all hostage. And I'm checking all the rooms just in case he decides to slip back here."

I hadn't thought of that, but surely he wouldn't come near. We all shuffled inside and began going through the house, locking doors and windows. When the downstairs rooms were secure, Joseph checked out the second and third floors; just in case, I climbed the stairs to my turret. It was warm, and the windows were open with the screens. I sank into my rocking chair and began to pray fervently, desperately. Alaina would always be my baby girl. I knew she was an adult, but she would always be that little blonde girl that kicked her legs and grinned up at me in her baby bed. My heart wept for her. She thought she had found happiness, only to discover it was all an illusion. I knew it would break her heart. I prayed to God it would not break her spirit.

I wondered about the mother who had sat up in this turret and watched her garden grow. Would she have sat here and worried about what might happen to her children? Would she be afraid of what her husband might do to them like I was fearful of what this man might do to my daughter? What desperate measures would I be willing to take to protect my child?

I turned my gaze to the back of Doc's house and drew in my breath sharply. The man we knew as Johnny Whitlock and my blonde daughter slipped into the back of the house. I breathed a sigh of relief. Alaina was alive. She was still in danger, but she was alive.

I eased my phone out of my pocket and dialed Brad. He answered on the second ring.

"We haven't sighted them yet, Jo," he said tersely. I could feel his frustration.

"Well, I have. Johnny just broke into the back door of Doc's house. He still has Alaina with him."

I heard him snap his fingers and call out to the other officers. "Jo has just spotted him at Doc Master's old house."

He said, "The sheriff wants to talk to you, Jo. I'm putting him on."

"Jo," Jason Pierce said. "You say you saw them go in the house the back way?"

"Yes, they must have broken in. Aunt Lillian has the keys."

"Well, we're not going to worry about that right now. Did you see your daughter? Is she still with him?"

"She is. She looks okay. I'm sure she's scared."

"No doubt, but she looks unharmed?"

"The best I could tell in the dark, yes."

"Have they turned on any lights in the house?"

"Not that I can see."

"Okay, are you comfortable staying put and watching the house from your location until we can get our people out there?"

"I'm not going anywhere. That's my daughter!"

Brad's voice came back on the phone. "Stay away from the windows, Jo. Don't let him see you. If he's the one who shot at Aunt Lillian, he's probably a perfect shot. Keep praying, and stay safe. Love you." And he was gone.

I leaned back against the wall and dialed Joseph downstairs.

"They're over in Doc's house," I whispered.

"We're coming up," Joseph responded.

"Do it quietly. No lights." I cautioned. "And tell your Aunt Lillian."

"Got you," Joseph said.

I heard light footsteps on the stairs in a few moments, and Joseph and Ashley slipped inside the turret.

"Any movement?" he asked.

I shook my head.

"Why do you suppose he came back here?" Joseph questioned.

"Maybe he still wants to find the treasure." I surmised.

"Well, if Brad's right, he's in the wrong house," Ashley said.

"I know, but he does not know that," I explained.

"Brad and I think that's why he wanted Doc's medical journal because of the birthmark. This guy doesn't have one. He didn't want anybody reading those records and wondering about him."

"Do you and Brad think he killed Doc and Lora too?" Johnny asked.

"We don't know. We can't see what the motive would be?" I answered him.

"It's scary to think how close he came to succeeding in his false identity," Joseph said, shaking his head. "I know Mom must be furious and hurt, but it would be much worse if they had married and she found out all of this."

"True." I stopped and listened.

"What?" Joseph asked.

"I thought I heard something. That's all."

I stared into the darkness and saw something moving in the yard in the shadows. More than one movement and a couple more were maneuvering around the house. I imagined they were surrounding the house.

Joseph was watching intently. "That guy won't have a chance with all that firepower."

"But he's got a bargaining chip. He has Alaina. They can't rush him, or he may kill her." I pointed out,

"He better not even think about it," Joseph growled.

Then I heard Jason Pierce's voice, loud and strong. He had a bullhorn. "We have you surrounded and need you to surrender."

For an answer, I heard glass breaking, and the man stuck a gun out the window and fired. "Nothing doing. I expect I can get whatever deal I want since I have the daughter of Brad Edwards' fiancée. So I want safe passage out of here, and then and only then, you will get Alaina back."

CHAPTER TWENTY

I felt my heart sink. I think I whispered, "God, help us," but I may have said it aloud because I heard Ashley's soft, "Amen!"

I heard slow footsteps on the stairs and turned to see, to my surprise, Aunt Lillian's tall form coming into the turret.

"You shouldn't have tried climbing up here," I scolded her lowering my voice.

"If my family's in trouble, then I'm in trouble," she dismissed me with a wave of her hand.

"We're staying away from the windows," Joseph told her. "But you'd better sit down. Here, sit down at this desk." Joseph gently propelled her to the chair that belonged to my roll-top desk.

"Can you see anything, Mamaw?" Joseph asked me. "It's so dark I can't tell much about anything."

Then I heard Brad's confident voice from the bullhorn. "Is Alaina all right?"

What relief swept over me when I heard my daughter say, "I'm okay. He hasn't hurt me."

"Johnny, what's your real name? I can't keep calling you Johnny if that's not your name." Brad said, and it was spoken conversationally. I wasn't sure how he was staying so calm. Every nerve I had seemed ready to spring.

"It's Johnny," came the short reply.

"Johnny, what?" Brad asked.

"You're not going to like it." I heard a note of sarcasm in his tone.

"Try me," Brad returned.

"Johnny Edwards. Johnny Edwards is my name."

There were four gasps heard in the turret. We all looked at each other in shock.

There was silence for a few moments, and I could hear the murmur of voices from below us.

Then, "Any relation to the Edwards family I'm from?" It was Brad speaking again.

"Yeah, you could say that. My mother was Violet Edwards."

I noticed the past tense and shot a glance at Lillian. She was nodding her head.

"I didn't imagine she was still alive."

"So, do you know where the real Johnny Whitlock is?" It was the Sheriff speaking again.

"You don't need to know that. You need to get me a fast car and let me get out of here. You're just wasting time with all these questions." I heard the defiance in his tone.

"You've got to give us time to put something together," the sheriff said.

"You boys are out of time," Johnny snarled at them. "If you want Alaina back in one piece, you'd better get busy."

"The way we see it," Jason returned, "is that we've got you surrounded...." His voice trailed off when Johnny Edwards fired another shot.

"Quit wasting my time. I've got something you want, and you can provide me with something I want." He sounded hard.

"No deal, Johnny." It was Brad's voice, and he sounded determined.

Joseph and I exchanged glances.

"No deal! They've got to deal. That's my mother in there!" I heard the desperation in Joseph's voice.

A string of curses flew out of Johnny, and then he said. "You don't mean that, Edwards. I'm holding your girlfriend's daughter. You would do anything for Jo. I've seen how you look at her."

The sheriff answered him. "It's not the policy of this sheriff's department to negotiate with criminals."

I covered my face with my hands, praying franticly. Ashley stepped beside me and put her hand on my shoulder.

Then Alaina spoke loud and clear. "But Johnny, you said you loved me. Why would you hurt someone you love?" I could hear the fear in her but also the strength.

"My plan was working out fine until that woman showed up. Of all the bad luck."

I heard the anger in his voice, even rage.

I could see from my pivotal position that the police officers were moving in closer.

Johnny had a view of them, too, for another shot fired into the air.

"I hope they don't have to kill him," I said under my breath. "There are too many questions he needs to answer, and if he's dead, we may never know."

"I wish I could do something instead of standing up here in this turret," Joseph complained. "I feel useless, like I need to be down there doing something."

"You're not a cop, Joseph," Lillian said gently. "Those guys down there are trained for this kind of thing. They know what they're doing. You'd get in the way."

"I guess you're right," Joseph admitted. "But I don't like it."

Then I heard Alaina's voice rise, and her pleading words came clearly to me in the night air.

"Johnny, please. I don't want them to kill you, and I believe they will. Please give up. You wanted me to fall in love with you, and I did. I can't turn my feelings on and off like a light bulb. I want you to be all right."

"It's no use, Alaina. I can't go back now. I've got to finish what I've started."

His tone had gentled in speaking with my daughter. I hoped that was a good sign.

And then I heard another shot, but it was from outside Doc's house this time. One of the cops had repositioned himself where he had a clear view of inside the house. I heard my daughter scream, and then the back door flew open, and she ran across the yard toward the cops. Brad caught her, and the rest of the police moved on in.

I raced down the stairs, Joseph and Ashley directly behind me. Outside, Brad hurried her up the steps and into the house and turned back to join the other guys at Doc's home.

Lillian came cautiously down the main staircase when we poured through the front door. We were all standing with our arms around Alaina, and she was weeping like her heart would break.

"I was so scared, Mom," she said between her tears. "I don't know how you did it last year in Hoover. And it hurts so badly. I loved him, Mom, and he wasn't even who or what I thought he was." A fresh batch of tears started flowing down her face, which was still red from the summer sun.

"I know, Honey. I am so sorry,"

She kept going from me to Joseph, finally realizing that Ashley was there too, and let her daughter-in-law hold her for a few minutes.

Brad popped his head in the doorway a short time later. "We got him. Jason got him in the shoulder. It's not bad. It's a clean shot. He'll live. We'll have to take him to the hospital, and he's in for many questions."

He looked at Alaina's tear-stained face. "Are you okay?"

She nodded and then started crying again. Brad looked at me. "He ought to have an interesting story."

"I hope you can share some of it with us," I responded.

"I'll tell you what I can. I've got to go. We parked down the road and walked in. Catch you later."

I sighed in relief. The terror was over, but I had a lot of questions. Alaina didn't want to be alone, so I had her lie on the sofa. Joseph and Ashley were on the floor beside her holding her hands. I sank onto the love seat, and Lillian took her accustomed chair.

"It's going to be a long night, I'm afraid, Aunt Lillian. If you want to go on to bed, we'll understand." I was studying her drawn face and wondering how much more she could take.

"I wouldn't sleep a wink. I will sit up with the rest of you and wait for Brad to come home. If I need forty winks, I'll catch them right here." She was firm on what she desired to do.

I smiled. "I understand." I looked at my daughter lying on the sofa, attempting to stop herself from weeping. Ashley, who was so kindhearted, also had tears in her big blue eyes.

Joseph was questioning his mother. "Did you ever have any inclination to suspect he wasn't who he said he was?"

She shook her blonde head. "I just took him at his word. I assumed Brad knew who he was. Of course, I knew he hadn't seen him since he was a child."

"I think we all just took his word for it," Aunt Lillian said. "I knew Johnny Whitlock too. People change in looks when they grow up." She reached for the box of photos that we had been looking at and found the picture of Violet before she left home. "He looks like Violet if you look at this picture closely. I wonder if he is her son."

Alaina turned her head as if she couldn't bear to look at it. I hoped this episode would not give her the nightmares mine had given me.

Lillian dropped the picture back in the box. "Violet always wanted things she couldn't have or wanted her own way. The apple didn't fall too far from the tree." She glanced my way. "Do you think he killed Doc?"

I shrugged. "I don't know, Aunt Lillian. Maybe. If he thought there was a chance, Doc might give him away. Doc was looking at his medical records before he died. He may have wondered about that birthmark."

It was a long evening. Lillian did doze off a couple of times. I took off my shoes and swung my legs on the love-seat. Joseph had fallen asleep with his head on the sofa and holding his mother's hand. Ashley was resting her head on her arm, lying on the couch.

Before Brad entered the front door, it was close to four in the morning. Lillian straightened in her chair, and I swung my legs off the seat. Joseph and Ashley sat up, but Alaina never turned her head. Brad stopped by the sofa on his way to me.

"How are you doing, Honey?" he asked Alaina gently.

Her eyes welled up with tears again, and he patted her hand. "It's going to be all right," he promised her. He gave his aunt a weak smile and sat down by me. He pulled me to him and kissed me on the cheek. I could tell he was tired.

"How did it go?" I asked him.

"Well, we got the entire story out of him. At least, I think so. It's hard to tell with him how much is true and what isn't," Brad said.

"So, is he Violet's son?" Aunt Lillian wanted affirmation on that.

"Yes, I think so. The man's actual name is John William Edwards. According to him, he was down on his luck, had no job, and was out on the streets with nothing. I figure he was into drugs too, but he's not going to admit to that. If I had to guess, I'd say he was selling too. That's when he says he met another street person named Johnny Whitlock."

"So, is there a real Johnny Whitlock?" Joseph asked.

"Yes, apparently, Johnny Whitlock and this Johnny got to be good friends, and Johnny Whitlock told this guy the story of his life. That explains why he knew all he did." He paused. "But I'm getting ahead of myself. Johnny Edwards says that Violet Edwards was his mother, but she had always gone by Patricia Asbury, and he only found out the truth about who he really was when she was on her deathbed. Violet had never married his father and had changed her name right after she left here."

I heard a faint "That doesn't surprise me. Sounds just like her," from Aunt Lillian.

Brad looked at her briefly and continued. "The guy she left here with soon dumped her. Violet got herself a job and made it on her own. She had told her son that his father had left them when he found out his mother was pregnant. According to Johnny, Violet never married and never had any more children, although there were a series of men in and out of her life. When Violet (somehow, I can't call her aunt) was dying, she told him the truth about her life. She told him about this house and the hidden money story. Johnny Whitlock made a big mistake trusting Johnny Edwards. Edwards had already decided to come here and try to snow Aunt Lillian into giving or leaving him money. He found out that only Aunt Lillian and I were left in the family. But then, as Johnny Edwards puts it, he got lucky. Johnny Whitlock died in the street one night. This guy won't say whether it was natural or not, but he did admit to hiding and burying the body. He won't tell us where. Johnny Edwards decided on a different plan at that point. He took Johnny Whitlock's identification and essentially became Johnny Whitlock. He knew Whitlock's parents were deceased. Johnny was an only child, so there would be no one to ask awkward questions. And he knew something else. He knew Willis was where the last of the Edwards family resided."

"It sounds like he took after his mother and grandfather," Aunt Lillian said sadly. "Both of them could be schemers."

"He was a schemer, all right," Brad answered her. "His biggest con was pretending to be Johnny Whitlock and going to a Gospel Mission. He counted on one street person looking about like another one. No one would doubt that he was Johnny Whitlock and wonder what had become of Johnny Edwards. Homeless people are here today and somewhere else tomorrow. Then he pretended to become a Christian and change his life. The pastor there is thrilled, thinking this street person has miraculously become a new man. It makes me sick, but I feel that he enjoyed the acting. He probably snickered at the stupid Christian leaders who thought he had really changed. Any difference in appearance could be accounted for when he cleaned himself up."

"It's done all the time, unfortunately," Joseph spoke up. "I mean people who are pretending to be something they're not; even in the church world. Some of them are just deceived, of course."

Brad wasn't relenting. "My relationship with God is too important to me. Mocking God by pretending to be something I'm not is disgusting to me." He looked at me, and I smiled encouragingly to continue.

"At any rate, Johnny wasn't about to come here as an Edwards where we might have started an investigation. He thought he would be safe being a Whitlock. Hometown boy makes good—that sort of thing. This imposter came here, and he is not saying how he got the money to buy the campground. Maybe his mother left him some. I don't know. At any rate, he bought it, and everything seemed to be going well. Nobody would question Johnny Whitlock returning to his hometown, and everybody welcomed him. That's where we all come into the story. I decided that this house might be a place Jo and I could start our married life when I found out Aunt Lillian wanted to sell it. So now, he's not just dealing with a sweet little old lady he might easily sway to leave money or property. He has me-a sheriff's deputy to deal with and my fiancée and her family."

"Did he kill Doc?" Lillian's voice was harsh.

Brad grimaced. "I'm afraid so, Aunt Lillian. He said everything was going fine, but after everybody left on the day of the picnic, he went over to Doc's. When Johnny found him, Doc was lying in his hammock. Doc had been looking up Johnny Whitlock's birth in his medical files and saw the comment about the unusual birthmark. Apparently, Doc questioned him about it. Of course, Johnny might have thought there wouldn't be anybody still living here that remembered it. Doc's inquiry caught Johnny off guard. He didn't have time to think and come up with an answer. He panicked. That's when he smothered him. Doc wasn't well and wasn't strong enough to fight him off. After all, he was nearly ninety-seven."

"I had forgotten about that birthmark," Aunt Lillian mused.

"I had, too," Brad agreed. "I don't think Doc had forgotten. This guy's smart. I'll give him that."

"He would have been better off using his brains for something good," Aunt Lillian said bitterly. "I suppose it was him that first threw suspicion on the Pemberton's,"

Brad nodded. "I think so. There're going to be more questions. He thought he'd gotten by with Doc's death until Lora Hutchins started bragging about knowing so something. He wasn't about to take any chances. He had met Alaina and had fallen in love with her, something he hadn't planned. So Lora had to go too. I think he must have been somewhere around here hearing us talking about Aunt Lillian selling us the property and her needing to get a will made. Johnny figured he'd better move fast, and that's when he took a shot at you," he gestured toward his aunt. "And then he clammed up on us and just muttered about the Perkins woman messing up his plan. I think it's safe to say that he was trying to break into Doc's house to get his medical files and that he covered Joseph up in the cistern. I think he thought that was funny-just a prank. He spent a lot of time snooping around here. All the trees and shrubs made it easy for him. He was furious that Johnny Whitlock had told him his ex-wife was dead, and he had never mentioned a child."

"So the liar was mad because someone had lied to him," Joseph commented. "Interesting!"

"There's a lot of sowing and reaping in this story," I added, thinking of a familiar Biblical verse.

"The Bible has a habit of always being true," Aunt Lillian said softly.

"So it all comes down to money-greed," Joseph said. "Something about the love of money being the root of all evil."

"Legally, I don't know that he could have got anything here since my mother left me everything absolutely," Lillian was thinking aloud. "However, if I had discovered that he was Violet's son, I would have included him, of course. He was right about that."

I heard a soft voice speak up from the sofa. "Did Johnny really say he had fallen in love with me?" Alaina asked.

Brad smiled at her. "Yes, he did. The guy told me he was sorry for what he had put you through. I don't think he would have surrendered if he had not loved you. He still had one good arm. He could have shot you or one of us. I think you brought out some good in him."

Her blue eyes were tearing up again, and she choked out. "Well, at least that was real."

Aunt Lillian was being philosophical. "I don't suppose there's anybody that doesn't have their good and bad points."

I thought about the killers I had known and was forced to agree, although I did think some people had a lot more evil than good.

CHAPTER TWENTY-ONE

The next day was Sunday, and we all attended the Willis Community Church together. We usually always took off the Fourth of July weekend. It made me proud to see my entire family march in and sit beside each other in a pew. Word had quickly spread that the police had captured Doc's killer and that Johnny Whitlock, who was, in reality, Johnny Edwards, had been charged with his murder. Information was still scant, and all of us declined to add to the questioning looks we got from the congregation. A trial would be coming up, and more would come out than we would want anyway.

Pastor Don seemed to realize and respect that we needed our privacy. Brad talked to him about coming over and helping us look behind the mantel one day, which seemed to please him. He told us Monday was his day off, and if we were willing, he would be happy to come. It was vital we didn't damage that beautiful piece of wood. Brad had the day off. The sheriff thought he had been through enough.

Monday was another hot July day, but Pastor Don came over early in the morning to beat the noon-day heat.

I was sitting with Alaina and Ashley, and Aunt Lillian was in a straight-backed chair in the living room.

We watched Pastor Don, Joseph, and Brad gently remove the mantel from the wall. Joseph and Brad were following instructions from the minister and being very careful with the wood. It was a beautifully carved piece.

"Your Dad was right," Joseph exclaimed. "This beauty is heavy. It feels like it weighs a ton."

"Not that much, Joseph," Pastor Don corrected gently. "But it does weigh more than a normal mantel of its age and size."

Brad and Joseph held the massive mantel up while Pastor Don probed along the structure's sides and back.

"Ah," he said suddenly. "There's something here, all right." He walked around to the other side. "It's the same over here." He looked at all of us. "It's very cleverly done, and only a good carpenter could have done it, but it looks like someone slid something inside on both sides to balance it out. You'd probably never notice if you weren't looking for it."

We were all holding our breaths. Joseph was getting more excited by the minute, and some strain had left Lillian's face. Even Alaina was sitting up and displaying some interest.

"Won't it be funny if we find it after all these years, Mamaw?" Ashley whispered to me. "How long has it been?"

"Well, the Civil war was in the 1860s," I reminded her. "So it's been around one hundred and sixty years ago."

"That's what makes history fascinating to me," the pastor commented. "That's not very old when you look at how old things are in Europe or Asia. We're the new kids on the block."

"Well, it seems old to me," Joseph threw in. "It's way before my time."

"It's before all of our times," Lillian mentioned. "I had begun to think it was just a legend, that it wasn't true. My mother believed it, so I suppose I should have."

Very carefully and skillfully, Pastor Don opened the side of the mantel and withdrew a large leather packet. He laid it down on the floor, went to the other side, and removed a second packet. Then with Brad and Joseph's help, he reinserted the wooden piece that had hidden them, and they replaced the mantel against the wall. Looking at it, one would never know anyone had touched it.

Brad and Joseph sat down on the floor, and Brad began opening the leather pouches. Gold and silver coins began to pour out of them; then greenbacks and confederate money. At least, I assumed that's what it was. It was money.

Brad laid the confederate to one side. "This is only valuable to collectors," he said.

Pastor Don viewed it all with a collector's eyes. "I couldn't tell you what this is all worth, but it's quite a lot that I'm certain of."

"Wow!" Joseph's eyes lit up just staring at it. "And to think this has been in that mantel that long. It's amazing."

"We'll have to have it evaluated," Aunt Lillian said thoughtfully. "For now, I think we'd better keep quiet until we can get it in a safety deposit box."

Pastor Don took a deep breath. "Well, as a member of the clergy, my parishioner's secrets are held in confidence. I won't even mention this to my wife. Mrs. Franks is a good woman, and she doesn't mean to expose confidential things, but she hints that she knows something, and sometimes that is worse than if she actually told the story."

Lillian didn't attempt to hide a faint smile.

After the pastor departed, we sat in the den with all the treasures on the coffee table. The coins were cleaner than I expected them to be. I was curious about the confederate money and hoped my country never saw another time where it had been so divided it led to civil war.

"I wonder if Violet knew where this money was hidden," Aunt Lillian wondered.

"I doubt it, or Johnny Edwards would have been breaking in here trying to find it," Brad said. "I think my dad was the only one who heard what Grandpa Ernest had said."

"Violet tended to stay away from Father as much as she could," Aunt Lillian shared. "That man caused this family a lot of grief."

Brad and I exchanged glances. "Do we tell her?" he mouthed at me.

"That's up to you," I said doubtfully.

"Tell me what?" Aunt Lillian asked.

"Well, I don't want to tell you anything that might make you feel differently about your mother," Brad said doubtfully.

Lillian stared at me. "Is it something you read in Mother's journals?"

I nodded reluctantly, and she said. "Well, you may as well tell me. I'm going to find out at some point when I read them. Unless you have destroyed them without my permission, that is."

"No, I wouldn't do that," I assured her.

"Go ahead and tell me. It can't be any worse than knowing my father killed my baby sister or my sister Violet raised a boy, my nephew, who is a murderer, and killed my best friend. If I have survived knowing all that, anything you have to tell me isn't likely to kill me."

Brad raised his eyebrows at me in a question, and I shrugged. Lillian stared from one to the other of us.

"Well?" she demanded.

"Aunt Lillian, your mother confessed in her journal that your father didn't die of a heart attack. She confessed that she killed him." I could barely get the words out.

Joseph and Ashley stared at me, and Alaina's mouth fell open in shock.

Aunt Lillian regarded me silently for a moment. "Well, that explains something I've always wondered about," she said.

"What?" Joseph asked when he found his voice.

"Well, when Mother was lying at the bottom of the stairs the day she died, I called Doc, and he came right over. She knew she was dying, and she looked up at Doc and said, 'Well, I'm going to die just like poor little Rosemary. I guess I call that justice."

"If it's any consolation, your mother was trying to protect her children," I told her, trying to soften the blow.

"How did she do it? Did Mother say?" Lillian questioned me.

I looked down. "She did."

"And how did she do it? Don't make me pull it out of you?"

"She used the Monkshood," Brad came to my aid.

She stared at him. "Monkshood? Well, that would have done it. And then she left it planted there for her to look at every time she went out in the yard." She shook her head, perplexed. "I would have got rid of it."

"I think she wanted to be reminded," I said gently. "Your mother knew it was wrong to kill, and she had to live with what she had done. She did it for you and your siblings. She feared your father would harm one of you after Rosemary died."

"So Doc must have known; Doc Graham, I mean. He signed the death certificate because I have that. I wonder if Doc knew. He never said a word." I could tell Lillian was attempting to put it all together.

"I think Doc Graham loved your mother and knew what kind of man your father was." I was sure about that.

"He could have gotten in trouble if there had been any question, but he loved your mom too much to let her suffer anymore."

"He loved her all right. He would have married her if she had been willing. I think once was enough for her." She frowned. "It's a shame. I think Mother would have been happy with him."

"I think your mother felt she didn't deserve happiness for her actions." I still found it a tragedy. "She knew killing your father was wrong, and I think she wanted to pay the price, but since she couldn't confess and take care of you all simultaneously, she decided to live with it. I think every day of the rest of her life, she lived with it."

I caught Lillian sitting in the backyard in a lawn chair right in front of the Monkshood later in the day. I watched her for a while. I was going to have to see that plant in bloom before I decided whether to destroy it or not. Let Lillian make that decision.

"God's laws were not made to make life difficult but to make life better," I thought.

CHAPTER TWENTY-TWO

It was a beautiful day, the first Saturday in August that year. My friend, Marcella Blessing, had shown up a day early and done all the decorating early on the wedding day. Most of the flowers came out of our garden, and Marcella had purchased enough ribbon and streamers to cover several miles. She brought a white arbor for Brad and me to stand under and decorated it with greenery and floral arrangements. Ashley and Alaina assisted her.

I knew that it was all hard for Alaina. She had hoped to have a happy announcement of her own by this time. This day would be the first time she had returned to Willis since the Fourth of July weekend. I went to her house several times and left Joseph and Ashley to help Lillian. I had talked when she wanted to and just been there when she was silent. She had broken down several times on me. I knew some of her wished to reach out to Johnny Edwards despite everything he had done, but she was wise enough to know she couldn't. I didn't think he expected her to. He had told Brad that she was the best thing that had ever happened to him. I might tell her that someday, but I didn't feel it would be helpful right at the moment. I knew the last thing she needed to hear was that she was young and someone good would come along. I knew she cried a lot when she was alone in her room because I could see her eyes' puffiness and redness in the mornings.

Brad and I talked by phone every night when I was with her. He never complained that he wasn't seeing much of me. He knew she had been there for me after the case in Hoover, and he knew she needed me now.

Lillian made a point of calling Alaina also. Alaina had bonded with her, and that seemed to help. I knew Alaina felt sorry for Lillian discovering that her sister's son was a murderer, had killed her best friend, and wanted to kill her. On top of everything else, she was now aware of the price her mother had paid to protect the family from her father. Brad had informed me that he thought Lillian was dealing with everything with her usual fortitude. Lillian didn't ruffle easily, so I couldn't say I was surprised.

We borrowed tables and chairs from Willis Community Church again. We were having Pastor Don Franks read the love chapter in the Bible-First Corinthians thirteen, at the beginning of the ceremony.

I had ordered a cake from a bakery in Morrisville, and Marcella made the punch and all the hors d'oeuvres. They would all be delicious if Marcella created them. Marcella seemed to know that Alaina needed to stay preoccupied, so she put her to work making some of them. I even heard Marcella coax a laugh out of Alaina a time or two.

I bought a flowing ivory mid-calf-length dress. Alaina presented me with a lovely gold necklace and bracelet. I had a pair of gold heels, and Marcella fixed my hair and make-up. Alaina had a beautiful baby blue dress with diamond earrings and a necklace that Tim had purchased.

Joseph, Brad, and Jason had all gone shopping for black suits so they would be alike. They all wore white shirts and black bowties.

We had taped music, which began when Alaina and I came out of the back door and down the steps. Ashley walked in front of me across the yard to where the guys were standing by the arbor. Alaina went right behind her. Joseph gave me his arm, and I started to follow in my daughter and granddaughter in love's footsteps. Today was the last moment I would be Jo Elliott. When I walked back into this house, I would be Jo Elliott-Edwards. There was something so final about the whole thing.

Joseph looked at me. "Okay, Mamaw? You're not getting cold feet, are you?"

I lifted my chin. "Not a bit," I said firmly and looked ahead to where my bridegroom was standing, with Jason and Pastor Jim watching me make my way across the yard.

To my surprise, the chairs were all filled. Lillian was sitting on the front row on the groom's side, and on my side sat Maude Ashton, dressed in a navy blue dress and looking proud as punch. Marcella was seated beside her, looking more petite than ever. Sue, Pastor Jim's wife, was sitting on the other side of Marcella.

Behind them was a surprise. It was Pearl and Enos Grey and all the grandchildren. Enos was looking great. I guessed Pearl couldn't get him in a suit, but he wore a white shirt and dress slacks. Lillian's church friends and several people from the sheriff's department in Morrisville and Alcott were there. Marcella had told me her friend Renee Kieffer had wanted to come, but there was a conflict with a family wedding. She had sent a gift.

I kept my eyes straight ahead on the man looking at me like his whole world existed in me and only turned my head when I came up to the pew where Pearl was sitting. I smiled brightly at her, which seemed to please her.

Pastor Don read the Biblical text that Brad and I had selected.

"Charity suffereth long, and is kind" Brad had undoubtedly been patient with me. I had seen him be kind to many people like Pearl Grey and her family.

"Charity envieth not, charity vaunteth not itself." Brad was not envious of me. He didn't need to be jealous of anyone. He was comfortable in his own skin.

"Charity is not puffed up." I had seen enough arrogance in other people. I certainly didn't want it in the man I loved.

"Charity seeketh not her own." Brad always considered me, considered my family.

"Charity is not easily provoked" Both of us did our best not to be irritable.

"Charity rejoiceth in the truth." That fit Brad to a T since he was a cop. The truth was always the best thing.

"Charity beareth all things. Charity believeth all things. Charity hopeth all things. Charity endureth all things." Brad had undoubtedly fulfilled that. In the last couple of months, we had borne and endured a lot, but we still believed and had hope despite it all.

"Charity never faileth." And that summed it up nicely. Our love would last the rest of our lives. We were both committed to that.

When my grandson hugged me and put my hand out of his into Brad's, I got a catch in my throat. I smiled and turned to face Pastor Jim, beaming from ear to ear. And then I met Brad's soft gray eyes and saw his love, hopes, and dreams for us.

"It is my privilege to marry this couple today," Pastor Jim said. "They met when a deacon was shot dead in the church I pastor. They fell in love during another murder case while fighting to clear someone innocent of the crime. Now, during their engagement, I understand they have been involved with yet another murder mystery. I think the best thing these two can do is get married and try to keep each other out of trouble."

I could hear laughter across the congregation. Brad grinned at me and squeezed my hand.

Pastor Jim cleared his throat and continued. "On a more serious note, dearly beloved, we are gathered here today to join this man and this woman in holy matrimony."

We had decided on a traditional ceremony, and I duly repeated the vows. Then I listened to my soon-to-be husband promise to love, comfort, honor, and keep me in sickness and health, for richer or poorer, for better or worse, as long as we both should live. And then I promised to do the same thing.

When Pastor Jim said, "I now pronounce you husband and wife, and you may kiss the bride," the congregation stood and clapped. Pastor Jim turned us around to face the audience and said. "May I present to you Mr. and Mrs. Brad Edwards," and I took my first steps as a married woman after ten years of being a widow.

The tables near the gazebo had a lovely view of the river. The bridal party's table was inside the summerhouse, where we could look down and see the rest of our guests. There were the usual pictures, cake cutting, and opening gifts. Maude Ashton sat at our table, as did Aunt Lillian. The two older women immediately took to one another, and I caught them walking around the grounds later in the afternoon, surveying all the different plants. Maude looked to be at the height of her glory.

Pearl Grey and her family were delighted to be there. She had made me a beautiful quilt, and when Brad and I opened it, she was so excited. I knew she had sewn every stitch in love. Enos didn't have much to say except. "It's a beautiful place you've got here, Madam. I'm sure I wish you every happiness." But he was sober and looked healthy. Pearl confided in me that he was now going to church with her and the children. They were all growing and were happy to see me.

Sue and Marcella were discovering a new friendship. Sue hugged me and said. "I feel like we brought you two together."

Marcella said, "Well, she was at my house when they started dating." Then they laughed and said they would share the credit.

Elsie Franks said it was a beautiful wedding, and she hoped we could forget all the bad things that happened there and make it a happy place. I told her I thought we were well on our way.

Alaina went with me to change clothes. Brad had a week off from work, and I had rearranged my schedule so I could be off also.

In my bedroom, Alaina helped me out of my dress and change into street clothes.

I looked at her pale face in the mirror, and I thought my heart would break.

I put my arms around her. "Honey, I wish there were some way I could take your pain and carry it for you."

I could feel her body tremble as the tears started to flow. "You can't, Mom. I know that."

I hold her away from me. "Mothers always want to make everything all right for their children, but we can't always fix everything. It's just a journey you are going to have to walk through. I'm here for you, and so are Joseph and Ashley."

"I know, Mom." She was rubbing her eyes with her hands.

"And most of all, God is with you. He hurts because His child hurts."

"I wonder if Johnny hurts," my daughter said.

"Johnny's going to hurt for a long time," I told her. "People don't get by with doing wrong. Even if they don't get what they deserve now, they will face God one day."

"Grandma Rose got by with it," Alaina argued.

"Did she?" I said. "I think every time she looked at that Monkshood, she remembered. She might not have gone to prison, but she paid every day of her life. She had to live with that. I think it must have haunted her all of her life. What if someone found out? What if her children found out what she had done? And even though she felt she was protecting her family, all her children have paid the price. Lillian never found happiness in marriage, and her mother didn't encourage her to. Violet had a son out of wedlock who was a murderer, just like his grandfather. Eugene, Brad's father, seemed to have done the best, but like his sister, Violet, he avoided coming home. And poor Rosemary and the unborn baby never really got an opportunity at life."

"I loved him, Mom, and I feel guilty about that. How could I fall in love with such a terrible person? What kind of person does that make me?"

"Alaina, you fell in love with what you thought Johnny was. He wasn't what you thought. He was a fake. If he had been what you thought, you would have been happy today." I put my arm around her thin shoulders. "You can't beat yourself up because you fell in love. It's not your fault he wasn't what he projected himself to be."

"You'd better go, Mom. Brad will be waiting."

I searched her face. "Are you going to be all right?"

She nodded. "Joseph and Ashley are coming back home. They'll be close. Joseph told me he was checking on me every day."

"Lillian will stay here until we get off our honeymoon. She needs to get everything settled with Doc's property. She's hurting too, you know."

"She's happy about you and Brad."

"Yes, she handed us the deed to the house this morning." I looked out the window and up at the turret. "That's still my favorite part of the entire house."

"Yeah, Brad said if he didn't know where to find you, he could always find you there."

I laughed, and we walked downstairs together. Everyone gathered on the front porch, and Brad was waiting beside the front door. When we walked out, we got peppered with rice, and Brad took my hand and hurried me down the front steps to his waiting car.

I looked back to the porch before I got in the car and saw my precious Maude Ashton standing beside Lillian, her eyes tearing up. I walked back to the porch and kissed her on the cheek. "Thanks for being my mother today," I whispered.

I felt Brad come beside me and kiss his Aunt Lillian. Then we turned and got inside the car to the sounds of cheering and clapping.

Brad looked at me. "Happy, Mrs. Edwards?" he asked.

"Happy, Mr. Edwards," I answered.

He leaned over and kissed me. "It's a big world. Let's go see what's out there."

ACKNOWLEDGEMENTS

I wish to thank Stan Michaleski for his advice and knowledge on police procedures. Also, I wish to thank Linda Johns for her help with editing.

HOW TO BECOME A FOLLOWER OF JESUS CHRIST

Maybe you have read "The Shadow of a Man", and realized that something is missing in your life. If you do not have a personal relationship with Jesus Christ, I can tell you exactly what you are missing. Without God in your life, there will always be a void. We try to fill that void with many things that we think will bring happiness and satisfaction. The only thing that really works is a relationship with God. It's not just about having a life insurance policy to be certain you go to Heaven when you die. It's about never being alone. It's about always having a friend that stands by you, and goes through everything with you.

You may ask how do I become a follower of Christ. I didn't use the word, Christian; because it has so many negative connotations. I know, and you probably do too, many people who claim to be Christians, but who do not follow the teachings of Christ and the Bible in their lives.

I'm glad you asked. It is as simple as A, B, C. You acknowledge that you have failed to live the kind of life that God wants us to live. In other words, like all of us, you have sinned against God. B: You believe on the Lord Jesus Christ, that He is your Savior, and the only hope you have of having your sins forgiven, and a relationship with God. C. Confess to everyone that you have become a follower of Christ.

The good news is- you don't have to follow Christ in your own ability. The Holy Spirit of God will live inside of you, and give you the ability to please God.

It is my prayer that you will accept Christ as your Savior, and that I will see you in Heaven someday.

ABOUT THE AUTHOR

Joyce Igo is a Southern Gospel artist, having written and recorded over two hundred Gospel songs. She is a lifelong West Virginia native. She was married to a pastor, Denver Igo, for twenty-eight years until his passing in 2000. Besides using her musical talents, she was involved in youth and children ministries in their pastorates. She has spent the last thirty-three years "on the road", carrying the Gospel message through song across the United States and Canada. Since her husband's home going she has expanded her ministry to include several mission trips to the continents of Europe, South and Central America, Africa, and Asia. She is also known for her women's conferences, several of which she has done in other countries.

This is Joyce's third book in the Jo Elliott mystery series. "The Shadow of a Man", and "The Mark of Cain" are the first two books.

9 781662 865411